A

Grafton

Tale

By

Randall Probert

A GRAFTON TALE

Published by
Randall Enterprises
P.O. Box 862
Bethel, Maine 04217

Printed by
Franklin Printing
553 Wilton Rd.
Farmington, Maine 04938

Copyright © 2010 by Randall Probert
ISBN 0-9667308-8-7

The cover and the inside illustrations by
Ed Palmer
Rumford, Maine

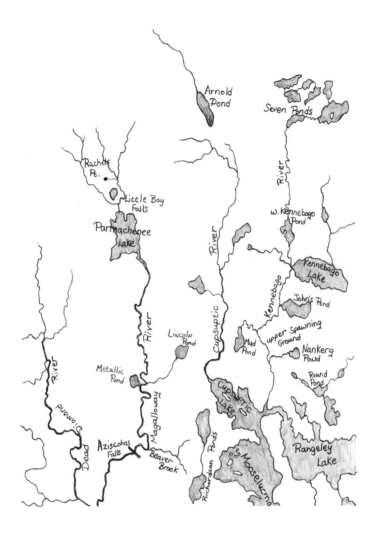

Arnold Pond

Seven Ponds

River

w. Kennebago Pond

Rachof Pt.

Little Boy Falls

Parmachenee Lake

Kennebago Lake

John's Pond

River

Cupsuptic River

Lincoln Pond

Kennebago

upper spawning Ground

Nankeg Pond

Mud Pond

Metallic Pond

Round Pond

River

Cupsuptic Lake

Magalloway River

Diamond

Dead River

Aziscohas Falls

Beaver Brook

Richardson Ponds

Mooselucma

Rangeley Lake

4

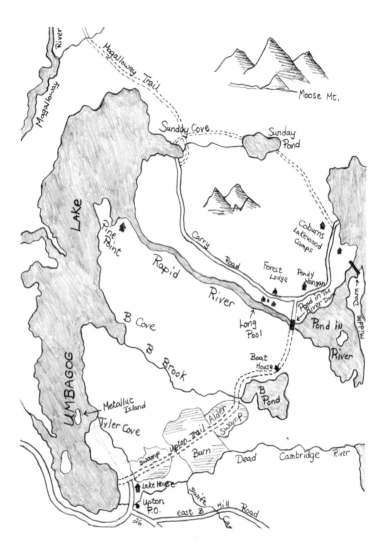

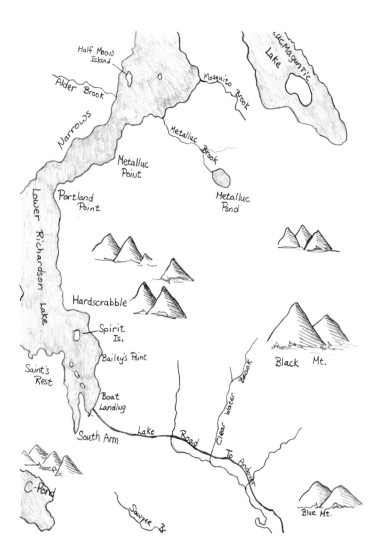

Preface

Joe Chapman stepped through the front door of his house and let the screen door bang against the jams. The sound was pleasing to him. It made him think, if for only a moment, that there was still life there in the little village that he had loved all these years. He had lived his entire life in the village and now he was the only resident who refused to leave, and stubbornly he wanted to die there.

Joe's grandfather had moved the whole family to Grafton shortly after James Brown had sent out word that he would be needing timber cutters for harvesting the tall pine trees there, for masts on sailing ships.

He stopped and while looking up the road to see if anyone would be on it this day, hopeful thinking, he remembered his first trip down through the notch with his grandfather, hauling the extra long pine trees loaded on two sleds and pulled with a team of four oxen. His grandfather was a loving man…..but also unforgiving. As he had said to his grandson Joe, once, "It's a tough love, I have for my family." And Joe had believed every word.

The notch was so steep and abrupt, the pine tree had fetched up on the road when the first sled pitched over the top. They had to unhook the team from the sled and the sled from the tree and drag the tree ahead until they could reconnect the sled and team. They were six hours trying to traverse the notch and it was midnight before they had arrived at the yard in the train station in Bethel. But his grandfather had been paid $210 for that one pine tree. The only good thing about the entire trip, as far as Joe had been concerned, was that they could ride on the sled on the return trip.

Joe laughed to himself then. Remembering his grandfather and their ordeal through the notch. That was some experience for a fourteen year old boy.

He put a pillow on the seat of his favorite chair; a whicker rocker. Set under a large rock maple. Joe sat down and sipped his strong black coffee, while enjoying the fall foliage. The north face of Speck Mountain was brilliant with it's contrast of yellows, orange and reds mixed in with the evergreen trees.

The air was clear and crisp. He could almost see his breath, and there had been a slight frost on the grass before the sun had come over the horizon. He took another sip and simply enjoying being where he was at that particular moment. "I have always said, September weather is the best weather of the year." No heat, humidity or bugs.

He looked up the road again. Wishing and hoping to see someone walking or a horse and wagon. But there was no one left but him. Tears started to fill his eyes as he remembered all of his friends who had moved on, when life in Grafton came to an abrupt end. He thought of his grandfather and how strict he had been all of his life. He thought of the rest of his family and his friends buried in the Grafton Cemetery. Just then, movement across the road caught his attention and he forgot about feeling sad and lonesome for the moment. There was something moving behind some bushes just to the right of the salt lick he had made when his good friend and neighbor had been sworn in as a state game warden. The first of his kind in this country.

There was more movement and eventually a nice plump doe came into view. Instinctively Joe started to get up to get his rifle and then thought better of it. His reaction was more from a sixty year old habit than actually needing the meat. His canning jars were already all full with deer and moose meat. He sat back down and sipped his coffee. Knowing there was a time when he wouldn't have thought twice about shooting that deer. If he didn't need the meat, there was always someone in the village who could use a little fresh meat.

For some unknown reason the doe deer stepped out into the open and started licking the salty ground. Joe coughed and she lifted her head and looked towards Joe with little concern. "This is your lucky day girl. Take all you want."

Joe finished his coffee and went back inside for another cup. He let the screen door bang when he came out and the deer stood her ground. After readjusting his pillow he sat back in his rocker and held the cup in his hands.

There wasn't a sound anywhere. Even most of the song birds had already left. In another two hours the mail truck would stop on its way to Upton. When the town unincorporated in 1919 and most of the buildings burned, the post office went also. Since then the daily mail truck from Bethel had agreed to deliver Joe's mail on its way to Upton.

As Joe sat there in his rocker reminiscing about life in the village, his friend and his neighbor, the game warden, he was filled with happiness. He wouldn't have wanted his life any different. Work and life had been difficult and hazardous at times, but that all goes to building good character. No, there were no regrets.

A cool breeze blew down through the valley and he suddenly felt cold. But neither did he go inside. He would endure. Besides, he had been a hell of a lot colder at times. He finished his coffee and went back inside to fill his cup again.

He had awakened with daylight, but here, the sun would take another hour and a half before it would shine over the top of Baldpate Mountain. Off in the distance he would hear the rumble of a loaded truck coming across the flats. "It should be coming by the cemetery about now," Joe said out loud.

Joe couldn't see the truck yet, but he could see the dust cloud the tires were kicking up. "He must be loaded heavy with hardwood logs."

Eventually the truck came rolling through, dust and all. The driver was carrying rock maple logs and he was loaded with about two and a half thousand feet. Heavy load for a two and a half ton truck. The driver sounded his horn and waved at Joe Chapman as he drove by. Everyone knew Joe Chapman and his story.

Joe started laughing. You would have thought someone had just told a funny joke. But Joe was remembering the time when the game warden had almost caught him with moose blood on his hands in closed season. The warden and his wife had been on one of their safaris up along the Richardson Lake chain. Joe had thought he would be in the clear when a young

cow moose walked into the backyard of his house. Not
wanting to alarm the people in the village, he stood
back in the dining room and shot through the window.
Through the glass. He started laughing again and
almost fell off his rocker.

Joe had had a house keeper then and when she
heard the rifle shot and all the glass flying throughout
the house she started screaming and ran to see what Joe
had done. She stopped in the middle of the room and
looked at the broken window and the bits of glass on
the floor and demanded to know why he had chosen to
scare the living hell out of her.

"I wanted to deaden the noise."

"Well, you almost deaden me!" she screamed.

She only lasted another two weeks before she
quit, and walked home to Newry.

Joe had rushed right out to stick the cow's throat
with this knife, as she was still kicking. He grabbed a
hold of her ear and was just about to stick her throat
when she gave her head a throw trying to get up. Joe
had such a tight grip that she actually threw him over
her and down by her hind legs, where she began to beat
the living hell out of him. He got kicked in the head
once, which kind of dazed him a little, because he never
felt the kick to his ribs. When he finally got
straightened around he crawled away from her. He
didn't want to risk another rifle shot out in the open like
this. It would surely invite trouble. He found his knife
and knew he would have to try again.

The moose was slowly bleeding out, but he still
needed to cut her windpipe. He grabbed her ear again
and at the same time brought his knife down and across
the throat. She slowly stopped kicking. While the
blood was draining, Joe went back inside and stored the

rifle and the housekeeper already had the floor swept clean.

His shirt and pants were torn and covered with dirt. He had brushed off the hair and wiped his hands clean. But he stopped breathing when he looked out the front window and saw the warden walking up his driveway. Joe went outside to greet him. He didn't want the warden to see the broken window or the moose laying dead in his backyard.

Kirby had taken one look at Joe and asked, "What did you fall into this morning Joe?"

Joe couldn't lie to his friend and neither did he want to go to jail. He told him the truth, "A God damned moose just kicked the hell out of me."

"Yeah, sure it did Joe. I just stopped to let you know we're back from Richardson Lake."

"That's good to know Kirby. You want to come in for coffee?" He hoped Kirby would say no and leave. Why he had ever asked him to come in was beyond his understanding.

But he was glad to see Kirby turn and walk away. "See ya, Joe. I'd let that moose alone if I were you."

Joe was laughing so hard now he had to hold on to his sides. His insides were hurting again. And he knew the hurt wasn't from laughing. He finally relaxed and the hurt was vanishing. He sat quietly while looking at the panoramic view of Speck Mountain. Give all this serenity up and move into a noisy town, "I'd rather die." One of those alternatives would come true in the very near future.

"This wouldn't be such a bad place to die," Joe said out loud. "Sitting here in this clear September air and looking at the view of old Speck."

There was another sound now, that of a lighter vehicle coming through the notch from Newry. Who ever it was, was making good time winding through the notch.

In a few minutes Leslie Davis pulled into Joe's driveway and got out and closed the door. "Nice set of wheels Leslie. What is it?"

"It's a 1938 Ford Panel Wagon."

"What are you doing up here so early in the morning?"

"I've come to take you out of here Joe. You can live with me and my wife. The kids are all grown up now and on their own. We both would like you to come live with us."

"You know Leslie, when you were growing up, just up the road here, I always knew you were the pertinent one in the family. Come in and have a cup of coffee, while I fry up some fresh deer steak and eggs."

Chapter 1

Day light was coming early this morning April 1st 1865 at Five Forks, near Petersburg, Virginia and Major Kirby Morgan had not had much sleep during the night. He was going from man to man until midnight, making sure each man was well prepared for the battle that was coming in the morning. Before resting himself, he called all of his officers together to once more go over the battle plans. "More than likely men, this will be the toughest and most important battle of the war for us. The south is rapidly plummeting. They're tired and we have sufficiently weakened their forces. We must take this battle away from them tomorrow. It could mean a quick end to this God damned fighting."

No one said a word. They were as tired as the major and wanted to see an end to the fighting, so they too could return to their families.

Kirby was able to catnap until 3 a.m. Then without starting any fires he made a kettle of cold black coffee and broke out the last of the rations for the men. "This will be the last chance to fill your bellies until this battle is over. All anyone is to take with them is water and ammunitions. I want you to travel light. We have thirty minutes before we start our advance."

Not a word was spoken while the men ate their rations and filled up with cold coffee. Then without a word or signal, each had taken their position. His area of attack at the Five Forks was spread out over a wide area and since he commanded one of the larger companies under General Chamberlain of the 20th Maine, he and his men were chosen for this head on attack.

It wasn't yet daylight and this had been Major Kirby's intention from the get-go. For his men to be in position by daylight. Kirby, two sergeants, two corporals and six line men, proceeded across the meadow on their bellies. The same as every man there. Each of the four captains and their squad were fanned out each following a separate fork in the stream surrounding the embattled Southern soldiers on the low knoll in the center of the forks. The artillery barrage was to start promptly at first light. Everyone was to wait five minutes before starting their assault.

Kirby and his men were in position and he figured they would have a few minutes to rest before the artillery started. There wasn't much to be had for cover. Some men found old stumps or grassy hummocks to hide behind, but most only found low lying bushes.

While he waited for daylight Kirby inspected his rifle one more time. When he was temporarily stationed at an Army outpost on the Big Sioux River on the Iowa and South Dakota border he had been issued one of the new Henry repeating rifles; it was a .44

caliber with a fifteen shot magazine. The only problem with it was the forestock. Instead of being made of wood it was metal and after firing twelve or fifteen shots it became too hot to hold, unless you wore a leather glove. So Kirby had fought through the entire war with a glove only on his left hand. Several of his men had also been issued the Henry .44 and they all agreed it was quite an advantage over the muskets the southern boys had.

Just as daylight could be seen over the tree tops, the artillery barrage started. The exploding shells were landing about one hundred feet in front of them. Right into the Rebs encampment. Kirby could hear men screaming with the first volley.

A quick five minutes passed and Kirby's entire company began shooting. At first the Rebs were slow to return fire, which made Kirby believe they had actually caught them by surprise. And when the Rebs did start to return fire he was mortified by the sound of several Gatling guns. Where had the Rebs gotten those? They could fire one hundred rounds a minute. These men could possibly get shot to pieces. His men were taking hits, but they were still firing back.

Corporal Brown raised up to his knees so he could get a better shot at a Gatling gun, and suddenly let out a blood curdling scream.

"Major! Major! Major Kirby! I've been hit!"

Kirby turned to looked at Brown and saw his stomach covered in blood. He crawled over to Corporal Brown and applied pressure to his wound until it had stopped bleeding. Then he pulled out a clean bandage from his inside pocket and put it over the wound. "Keep your hand on it Corporal. The blood has stopped. Stay right here and when this is over, I'll come back for you."

"Thanks Major. You be careful."

His men were pinned down and could do little else, but keep down for cover. Kirby reloaded his rifle and checked his .45 Colt revolver. "You men keep your heads down!"

"What are you going to do Major?" Sergeant Baker asked.

"Just keep your head down," then in a lower voice, "probably something really stupid."

He waited, listening to the Gatling gun that had them pinned down. He waited until there was a pause and he knew they were reloading which wouldn't take more than a few seconds. He waited. And there it was. Kirby jumped to his feet and began firing as fast as he could at the men around the Gatling gun. He kept shooting until the rifle was empty and then he started running towards the Rebs bunker. He had seen a few men go down, but he didn't know how many, or if they were dead. He had gotten about half way there when he was hit in the left shoulder by a .36 caliber pistol ball. He didn't stop. Hell, he didn't even slow down. His full attention was now directly in front of him at the man who had shot him. He wasn't even aware if his shoulder was hurting or not.

Kirby jumped over the front wall and swung his rifle at the man's head who was trying to reload. The man's head exploded like a pumpkin. He then drew his revolver and finished the wounded who were lying behind the Gatling gun. When his revolver was empty, he turned the Gatling gun on the other Gatling guns in the same bunker.

When those two stations were quiet, Kirby turned his Gatling gun on the next bunker and began firing. He had caught the Rebs there by complete surprise and soon all was quiet there also. Kirby reloaded with a full clip and turned the gun behind him at another bunker. He had a little more difficulty with this one as they were aware of the Yanks having taken control of that bunker and gun. While he was reloading with a new clip, he hollered to his Sergeant, "Sergeant Baker! Get everyone over here and man these other two Gatling guns!"

He turned his attention back to the other bunker and began firing. Another clip and that bunker went quiet. "Sergeant Smith take three men, and take that other bunker!" Kirby shouted over the noise.

There were now more Rebs coming towards them and trying to retake the three bunkers. This went on for several hours. All would be quiet for a while and then suddenly more Rebs would rush them, trying to secure the Gatling guns. Kirby noticed that the noise from far off was slowing down also.

"Sergeant Baker, take two men and secure that third bunker! I'll keep Jones with me."

"Yes sir," Baker replied and turned to leave just as a Reb from somewhere fired a shot and the bullet grazed the left side of Major Kirby's head. Making a burn line the length of his skull and drawing blood. Kirby was knocked unconscious.

"Elliot! You and Ashton secure that last bunker and Gatling gun. I'll stay here with Jones."

*   *   *   *

Major Kirby regained consciousness two days later and he discovered he was in a field hospital bed and in the next bed was Corporal Brown. "Welcome back to the living Major."

Kirby recognized the voice but it took him a few moments to put things together. "Corporal Brown, how are you doing? Oh, my head hurts. What happened?"

"Sergeant Baker said a bullet grazed your head, but only drew a little blood. I'm feeling a little better. But my gut still hurts."

Kirby tried to sit up, but he discovered his left shoulder was bandaged and now hurting. "Guess I forgot about that one."

Sergeant Baker and Smith and Captains Taylor, Albert and Burnard came to visit Kirby. "What happened at Five Forks?" Kirby asked.

"We beat the Rebs and now Lee's Army is so weakened, there's talk that he'll be surrendering soon."

"That is good news. How many men did we lose?"

"You lost two dead sir and you and Brown were wounded. Totally sir, we lost fifteen men and twelve wounded," Captain Taylor said.

"The doc said not to stay long, so we have to go. Sure glad you're feeling better Major, and you also, Corporal Brown," Captain Albert said.

*   *   *   *

Two days later and Corporal Brown took a turn for the worst. "What is it doc? The Corporal was doing so well," Kirby said.

"It's infection. All we can do now is let the body try to heal itself. I wish there was more I could do, but there just isn't. A stomach wound is the worse kind of wound there is."

Kirby knew all too well about stomach wounds. He had lost several men with infections that would happen days afterwards.

Kirby looked at Doctor Yahro, he looked as tired and haggard as any foot soldier. He sure wasn't enviving his job.

"Major," Corporal Brown stammered, "you going back to Maine when this is over, or Iowa?"

"Maine. My Army career is over. I've had enough killing for one lifetime."

"Do me a favor Major?"

"Sure, what is it Corporal?"

"I don't want to be buried here, here in the south. I hate the south. Take me home to be buried."

"Where is home Corporal?"

"Grafton, sir. Between Newry and Upton. Most beautiful spot in the state, sir. And Major, call me by my first name please, not Corporal. I don't think rank means anything from here sir."

"Okay."

"It's Alvin, sir. Alvin Brown."

"Mine's Kirby."

"Major, take me back to my folks, sir. They're good people. You'll like them."

"You better start calling me Kirby, if we're going to be friends."

"No sir, I have to much respect for you sir. Even in civilian life, people will call you Major. I saw what you did at Five Forks. No one else could or would have done what you did, sir."

"Thanks Alvin. Now you'd better get some rest."

Dr. Yahro came over to see Kirby, "Let's take a look at your wounds Major. Any more headaches?"

"Only slightly."

"Good. How's your vision?"

"Everything is clear now."

"Your head wound is fine. You'll always have that scar where the ball traveled along the side of your head. How's the shoulder?" Dr. Yahro removed the dressing. "That's healing good." He replaced the old bandage. "Does it still hurt?"

"Some, but not bad. It's stiff though," Kirby replied.

"That's understandable. Once the wound is completely healed, it'll take a few months before you regain total flexibility. Wet weather as well as the cold will bother you. And as you get older, arthritis will probably set in. But that's years from now.

"I'll discharge you in three days."

"Thanks doc. How's Alvin doing?" Kirby motioned with a tilt of his head.

Dr. Yahro mouthed the words silently, "Not good."

*   *   *   *

Corporal Alvin Brown died peacefully in his sleep during the night and was found by the morning orderly.

"Where are you taking him orderly?" Kirby wanted to know.

"To the morgue sir, with the rest of the casualties. Then he'll be buried here."   Kirby got out of bed and followed the orderlies, carrying Alvin's body outside. "Who's in charge here?" Kirby demanded to know.

"That would be Lieutenant Anders, sir. If you'll wait here, I'll send him over."

"Thank you."

"What can I do for you Major?"

"That body," he pointed, "he's not to be buried here, Lieutenant. I would like him embalmed and put in a box for transport back to Maine."

"That's an unusual request. We don't have the time to respect the final wishes of every dying soldier," Lieutenant Andres said.

"Well, this time you'll make an exception," a deep voice boomed from behind.

"Yes sir, yes General Chamberlain."

"And grant the Major any other wish that he might have. Is that understood?"

"Yes sir, it is."

"You going on a trip Major?"

"I promised to take the Corporal back to his folks in Grafton for burial," Kirby replied.

"Are you well enough to walk with me? I have set up a new field office across the compound."

"Yes sir, I am. Nothing wrong with my legs."

General Chamberlain's headquarters was in the kitchen of an old farm house, across from the infirmary. The exercise and fresh air felt good to Kirby. He took another deep breath before going inside.

"Have a seat Major. I'll fix us a real cup of coffee."

"Thank you, sir. That would be nice."

General Chamberlain handed a cup to Kirby and then sat down behind this makeshift desk. Kirby sipped his coffee. "My, this is good. I had forgotten what real coffee tasted like."

"After reading your report about Five Forks, I did some investigating on my own. I asked each man that was with you in the three bunkers to submit a written report. Captain Taylor, Albert and Burnard, also. I had Sergeant Baker take me back where you were pinned down by the Gatling guns and he walked me through, step by step, of the event. You probably weren't aware of it, but there was one Confederate soldier who survived. He remained conscious throughout the battle. I talked with him also, and he corroborates everything that your men stated in their reports. Major?"

"Yes sir?"

"What made you stand up in all that was going on, to face that Gatling gun, and take it out?"

"I don't think I thought much about what I was doing. It wasn't planned. I just knew that if I didn't, we would all be killed."

"So you reacted without first thinking about what you were about to do?"

"Yes. As I saw it, it was the only course of action there was."

"After reading all the reports and talking to all involved, including the Confederate soldier, and visiting the scene, I quite agree.

"If you had not succeeded in taking out those emplacements and so many of the Confederate soldiers, in all likelihood we probably would have lost Five Forks."

"Yes sir."

"That was a decisive battle and because we were able to secure the Five Forks and so weaken the Confederate forces, the war in all likelihood is over. Lee is expected to surrender tomorrow to General Grant at the Appomattox Court House. I have been requested to be there, so I must leave this afternoon."

"That is good news, sir."

"There is more. And this is for you Major. In light of everything that you did at the battle I am awarding you the highest commendation this country has; the Medal of Honor."

"I don't know what to say, General. I am truly honored and surprised. Thank you, sir."

"There's one more thing. I have also been studying your record Major. Time and again you have served your country exemplarily and I am promoting you to Full Colonel."

"Thank you, sir. But I have to decline the promotion." General Chamberlain was speechless. No one had ever declined a promotion like this.

"I have given this a lot of thought sir. As soon as I am able to travel, I intend to resign my commission. And it would not be appropriate, at least not for me, to accept the promotion and then resign."

"I thank you and appreciate your honesty. You're a good soldier Major. I'll be back in two days. At that time there'll be an official ceremony to award you the Medal of Honor. You can procure a new uniform anytime Major." The General stood and shook hands with Major Kirby Morgan.

*   *   *   *

Two days later General Chamberlain returned, also with Lieutenant Dan from the pay masters office in Washington, carrying thousands of printed U.S. dollars. There were hundreds of soldiers there at Five Forks who had not received any pay since the start of the war.

Kirby Morgan was not the only person to receive an award that day. When his name was announced and the circumstances read around the event, Kirby was proud, but also felt humble. When the ceremony was over General Chamberlain stopped to see Major Kirby, "Before I leave for Washington, Major, I wanted to ask if you had changed your mind about resigning?"

"I have thought a great deal about it, but my mind is made up."

"Well, be that as it may, you are a naturally great leader of men. I wish you well Major, and now I must leave for Washington."

"Goodbye, sir. It has been an experience serving under you."

They shook hands and General Chamberlain left for Washington. Kirby left to find the pay master.

"Major Kirby Morgan, you have back pay coming for the last six years. You moved around so much, we were never able to catch up with you. You have a total of $1,948.00 coming."

Next, Kirby went to see Colonel Webster and submit his resignation. "Hello Major. Congratulations for your award. I can't think of anyone who is more deserving. The General told me you would be resigning."

"Thank you Colonel. I have already written my resignation. If you'll accept it."

"Surely. Here are some papers you'll have to sign. One says you are resigning. One to muster out and the other is a monthly stipend of $18.00 that you'll receive for as long as you live. You're retiring at the rank of Major, plus a disability for your wounds."

"I never expected that Colonel."

"You're a fine soldier Kirby and a good person. I have enjoyed you under my command. I wish you well in your future. Now if you'll excuse me, there is more business requiring my assistance. Good day Major."

"Colonel."

*   *   *   *

The only clothes he had was the newly procured uniform. That would have to do until he got to where ever he was going. Rank has its privileges. There was no problem securing a horse and wagon to haul Alvin Brown's casket to the railway station outside of Washington and a private to help and bring the horse and wagon back.

Much to Kirby's surprise, it wasn't going to cost anything to ship Brown's body all the way to Bethel, Maine. And when he tried to pay for his ticket, "No sah, you don't have to pay any. You a Major," and then the black attendant pointed to Kirby's Medal of Honor ribbon he wore on his uniform. "Yous don't have to pay anything, Major."

"Thank you very much."

"No sah, I thank you." Kirby knew what he was referring to. He smiled and nodded his head in acknowledgement.

Once Kirby found an empty seat in the front car, he relaxed and fell asleep. He slept for most of the trip to Portland, Maine. The only time he would awaken, would be when they had to change trains.

He rested and slept peacefully. Not thinking about the last five years and the war and all the death he had seen. No, this hadn't yet sunk in. It would though, but not yet. For now, all he was conscious of was that he was heading back to his beloved Maine. And he wasn't yet sure what or where he was going once he returned Brown's body to his folks in Grafton.

There was a six hour layover in Portland. Apparently there was extra freight being loaded onto a flatcar that was also going to Bethel. That was okay with Kirby. He was just happy to be back in Maine. Still, he wouldn't let himself think about the war or what he had experienced and seen. He was afraid to bring those memories and images to the forefront of his consciousness. He knew there would be a time when he would have to deal with it, but not now, sometime, though.

Finally the train began to move. Excitement was beginning to stir inside of him and now he couldn't relax. Although the train would not be in Bethel until 6 a.m., Kirby remained awake and for the first time began to wonder what he was going to do with himself now. He had no home to go home to in Bangor. His two younger brothers Bill and Ted had both been killed during their first battle. Afterwords his parents had been notified, they seemed to have given up on life. The farm whiffled away and the bills kept coming. His mother Nancy died first, for no apparent reason than she stopped living. Then his father died two months later of a heart attack, and the farm was auctioned off to pay their debts.

No, there was no sense in going to Bangor. There was nothing there anymore for him. He'd been out west, at least as far as Iowa, and he wasn't interested in seeing anymore. "Maybe I'll buy me some traps and live a quiet life in the wilderness and trap, way up in Northern Maine."

Finally, shortly after 5 a.m. the conductor announced "The next stop is Bethel and we're a little bit ahead of schedule."

That was good news. Kirby was getting hungry and badly needed several cups of strong coffee. When the train stopped at the Bethel Station, Kirby first had to make sure Brown's body was unloaded. Then he could sit down in the small restaurant the Bethel Station provided. Kirby had a plate full of eggs, sausages and washed it all down with a pot of coffee. When he tried to pay for his breakfast, Mr. Yeaton recognized the

Medal of Honor ribbon on Kirby's uniform and said,
"Major, as long as I live, you'll never have to pay for
any meal eaten here. You must be Major Kirby
Morgan."
    "Yes, that is correct. But how did you know?"
    "It was on the front page of yesterday's
newspaper that you were bringing Corporal Brown's
body back."
    "Where can I find a horse wagon? I'll need one
to haul the pine box in."
    Mr. Yeaton walked Kirby outside onto the
station platform and pointed. "There's a livery over
there. Ask for Paul Stokes. We all call him Stokey."
    Kirby thanked him and stepped off the platform
and walked over to the livery. "Hello, is there a Paul
Stokes here?"
    A short barrel-chested man answered, "I'm
Stokey, what can I do for you? Uh….Major."
    "I would like to purchase a horse and wagon. A
Morgan horse preferably. Harness and a comfortable
saddle."
    "The horse, wagon and harness I have. I have
only one saddle and it's new. Might be a little stiff."
    "How much for everything?" Kirby asked.
    Stokey did some figuring out back and then
came back, "$250."
    "$185," Kirby responded.
    "I tell you what Major, you give me $195 and
we'll call it a deal."
    "$190 and you harness the horse and hook him
up to the wagon."
    "You sure drive a hard bargain. Okay. But I
want to see your money first," Stokey demanded.
    Kirby paid him and sat down and waited.
Fifteen minutes later Stokey led the horse out front

where Kirby was waiting. "How far is Grafton, Stokey?"

"About twenty miles from here. You follow the main road here along the river until you come to the T House Trading Post at Newry Corner. That's the easy half. Turn west and Grafton is about another ten miles. You might make it to Kilgore's at Newry flats by evening. Kilgore's is a freight and stage coach way station. Old man Kilgore is kinda gruff at times, but he'll put you and your horse up."

*   *   *   *

The pine box with Alvin Brown's body was put into the back of the wagon and Kirby was finally off on the last leg of his journey.

The horse was young and strong with a good set of lungs. The load was light and easy to haul, also. He had been gelded and didn't have that head strong arrogance. Kirby kept up a smooth easy pace and two hours later he was at the T House. He turned west and headed up the Newry Road.

The sun was overhead now and the day was warm for the last part of May. He stopped often to let his horse drink from the many streams along the way. He hadn't thought about his wounds ever since leaving Washington, but now as he was climbing back on the wagon, his left shoulder was beginning to throb. He was making good time and knew he would reach Kilgore's way station much before evening.

Kirby just thought of a name for his horse, Jake. "Come on Jake you're slowing down."

It was 3 p.m. when Kirby arrived at the Kilgore Station and Mr. Kilgore was out front. Stokey had described him to a 'T'. "Hello Major, I've been expecting you." Kirby guessed that by now everyone knew what he was doing here. "Come, you can put the wagon in the barn. Keep the sun off poor Alvin's body. I'll take care of your horse and you can wash up around the corner of the barn there."

Kirby didn't find Mr. Kilgore's attitude gruff at all. If anything he was going out of his way to accommodate him. "When you finish cleaning up, the coffee pot is on the stove in the house. Just help yourself."

"Thank you, Mr. Kilgore."

"Horace is my first name."

Kirby sat down on the porch with a steaming cup of coffee. Suddenly the trip was catching up with him. He was becoming as tired as he could remember.

Mrs. Kilgore came around the corner of the house carrying a basket of freshly dried laundry. Kirby stood up and opened the door for her, "You must be Mrs. Kilgore."

"Yes I am and I already know who you are Major. You have had a long journey. Would you like to lie down before supper?"

"Yes I would; only though, if you promise to wake me."

Mrs. Kilgore chuckled and said, "Go upstairs and take any one of the rooms. Right now we are empty. The Bethel bound stage is due here at 5 p.m. and I expect there will be some staying the night. So you have the pick of the rooms."

"Thank you Mrs. Kilgore."

Kirby climbed the stairs and took the first open door he found. He stretched out on the bed and was instantly asleep.

*　　*　　*　　*

The Bethel stage arrived and people were milling around and talking excitedly, but Kirby slept on.

At a little before 6 p.m. Mrs. Kilgore sent her young son Ronny up to awaken their guest. "You make sure he is awake and that he comes down stairs."

"Yes Ma."

There were three passengers and the driver at the supper table. "This smells very delicious Mrs. Kilgore."

"It ain't nothing special. Just a beef stew and biscuits."

Kirby took several mouth fulls before speaking again. "Wow, this is the best meal I have had since joining the Army back in '58." He finished that bowl and asked for another. Before he had finished he had eaten three bowls of stew and five biscuits.

"I like to see a grown man eat," Mrs. Kilgore said.

"I'm sorry, all I have for dessert is biscuits and molasses."

"Nothing to be sorry about for that Mrs. Kilgore. That'll be like a treat from heaven."

*   *   *   *

At daylight the next morning everybody was up and Horace was preparing the stage for departure. After breakfast Kirby asked, "How much do I owe you for my horse and me?"

"Nothing. You made the journey to bring Alvin's body back so his folks can bury him proper like. I guess we can take care of you and your horse for a night. We hope to see more of you Major."

Kirby thanked them both very graciously, and left. He was now traveling across Newry flats and some very beautiful farm country. The flats stretched on and on, but there were only four sets of farm buildings. The buildings were well cared for.

After leaving the flats behind, the road started to climb higher up into the mountains. There were still pockets of snow in the mountain tops and there was a cool breeze blowing through the valley. This certainly was beautiful country. Rugged but beautiful. The good farming country was obviously left behind on the flats.

He passed an old grist mill and then he came to another flat expanse with another farm. And beyond that the road really started to incline and narrow. This had to be the notch he thought. He went up over a sharp hill and there were waterfalls on the left; water had cut a course through the ledge rock millions of years ago. He stopped to walk over and have a look see. There was still spring runoff coming off the mountains, and there was a lot of water flowing over the falls. He had a drink and brought some back for Jake.

He continued on and found another grist mill on the right. The scenery was getting better and better. This was really some unique country. No wonder Corporal Brown wanted to have his body brought back for burial. As he traversed up through the notch it was easy to see that there had been some wash outs in the road this spring. The roads having been newly repaired with rock cribbing and gravel.

Kirby felt like he was an explorer as he made his way through the notch. In places the shear mountain sides came down almost to the road he was traveling on. Up ahead he could see a team of horses coming towards him. He pulled over to the right to let

Jake have a break while he waited for the other wagon
to pass. The other wagon was loaded heavy with sawn
lumber. Wide pine boards. "Hello there," the driver
hollered.

"Good morning," Kirby answered.

"You must be Major Morgan. And that must be
Alvin Brown," and he nodded towards Kirby's load.

"Yes sir, it is." It seemed as though everyone
knew he was coming.

"James Brown and Mrs. Brown are expecting
you."

"Thanks. Where are you taking your load?"

"To the Train Station in Bethel. Two more
loads like this one and there'll be enough to load a flat
car. Then it'll go to Portland. This here is some fine
lumber. Parsley dry already. Well, glad you're
bringing Alvin home. I have to get this load to town
and back tonight, maybe."

"See ya," Kirby said. "Come on Jake, let's get
moving."

This was rough and hilly country they were
traveling through, but Jake seemed to be handling his
load well. A large shaggy looking moose stepped into
the road about two hundred feet in front. Jake perked
his ears up, but that was all. When the moose noticed
the intruders he walked across the road and disappeared
behind some bushes. Just then there was a single rifle
shot, up ahead. This startled Kirby and instinctively he
reached for his .45 revolver, but he wasn't wearing it.
It was packed along with his few belongings. As he
drove along, he kept wondering what the one shot was
about. Maybe someone was only getting some fresh
meat.

He could see far enough up ahead to know he
was reaching the top of the hill and almost through the

notch. As he went around the bend in the gravel road, he could see cleared land up ahead. "This must be it Jake. Now where do the Brown's live?"

There was an American flag hanging from a makeshift pole at the first farmhouse and an older man and woman standing near the road. Kirby pulled up to a stop next to the two and asked, "Can you tell me where the Brown's live?"

"Yes sir, Major. At the end of Grafton flats, last place on the right. Right next to the hotel. Maybe two, two and a half miles. We're awfully glad you brought Alvin back here to be buried, yes siree. James and Ruth will be glad, too."

Kirby thanked them and started up again. He knew Jake was eager to get going again. "Me thinks, I got a good deal with you ole boy."

The picturesque setting of Grafton, a large flat valley, nestled with mountains all around was amazingly surreal. "No wonder Corporal Brown wanted to be buried here." This wasn't his home coming, but he was beginning to feel as if it were. Kirby didn't have a home to come home to.

At the next farmhouse there was also an American flag hanging from the gable end of the rooftop and the whole family was standing at the road. "Hello Major. We're the Davis' and we are all glad you have brought Alvin home."

The air was cool and smelled so sweet of pine, spruce and fir. Yeah, he had entered the gates of Heaven when he had passed through the notch. Although he had never even heard of the town of Grafton, let along ever been here before, he was feeling an odd sense of homesickness.

The road was beginning to narrow and tall spruce trees crowded the road edge. He was following a brook on his left and two small boys were near the bridge he would cross over.

He stopped and when he did, the two boys turned and when they saw Kirby in uniform they dropped the alder branch fish pole and saluted. Kirby couldn't resist, he returned their salute and asked, "How's the fishing boys?"

"Real good mister. What you got in the box?"

How in the world was he going to answer that? "Come up here boys." They didn't hesitate at all. They both stood on the bridge next to the wagon. "How old are you boys?"

"I'm Danny and I'm eleven."

"I'm ten and I'm David.

"Do you boys know that we have been fighting a war for four years?"

"Yes sir, we do."

"Do you know who Alvin Brown is?"

"My Pa works for his Pa."

"Do you understand that he died in battle?"

"I'm not sure. Heard Ma and Pa talking about something like that, but they wouldn't let me listen too much."

"Okay. Alvin Brown was a brave soldier. He died fighting for this country."

"Is that him in the box?"

"Yes, he asked me to bring him home to be buried here."

"Okay, can we go back to fishing now?"

"Sure, I hope you catch enough for supper."

"We have already," Danny answered.

Kirby left the boys behind, to their fishing. Oblivious to the day's problems. He could remember being their age and not caring about what was happening outside of his world. "Good luck boys."

During the long train trip from Washington, he
had dreaded making this last part of the journey. But
now that he was here, there were no more worries.
Now he was glad for having made the trip. He hadn't
yet thought about what he was going to do once he had
fulfilled his promise.

Beyond the bridge where the boys were still
fishing, the landscape once again opened up to cleared
farm land. He could see some farms were set back
away from the road but the town seemed to be pretty
much situated around the road. Why waste the farm
land with buildings.

He was coming to another building on the left
and it was flying the flag and there were people
standing out front. This he guessed was the post office.
They all waved and he waved back. "How much
further?" he asked.

"Last house at the end of town. Right next to
the hotel."

"Thank you." He was surprised to find a hotel
here, the Poplar Tavern. No larger than the town
seemed to be. There was a small cemetery across the
road, and only a few headstones.

He wasn't long before he figured he had reached
his destination. The fields and cleared land had turned
back to forest up ahead and he saw the hotel. The
Brown house must be right beside it. He turned off the
road and a man came out of the house and started to
walk toward him. He reined Jake to a stop and waited.

"Hello Major, I'm Jim Brown, Alvin's pa. I
can't thank you enough for bringing his body all the
way from Virginia. If you would help me, we'll set this
box in the barn out of the sun."

Kirby helped with the pine box, but his shoulder
was beginning to hurt. He was relieved when they

finally set it down. He was rubbing his shoulder and Mr. Brown looked up, "I'm sorry Major, I forgot you were wounded in the shoulder." As they were walking back to the wagon another man came out of a shed-like building. "Hey Ronki-Tonk, will you take care of the Major's horse and wagon?"

"Sure thing Captain Jim."

Mr. Brown saw the puzzled look on Kirby's face and knew what he was thinking. "An unusual name isn't it. His real name is Barzelia Hinklgough. He hates that name and prefers Ronki-Tonk. And I have no idea where that comes from. Only that he came wandering in here on foot one day last summer. Looking for work. I figured any man who would walk all the way from Bethel looking for work, had to be made of some fine and tough fiber. And he has proven me right too. He has a room in the barn and he takes care of the barn and animals and some odd jobs around. I've heard he was run out of Bethel because he does drink some. I laid the law down here though; no drinking when you're suppose to be working. Other than that he can drink all he wants. Turns out he's a pretty good man to have around. He just has a problem with the bottle. Or putting it down I guess. Come inside and have some coffee."

Kirby followed Mr. Brown inside and Mrs. Brown was sitting at the table crying. When she saw Kirby she dried her eyes and went over to greet him. "Sorry about the crying Major. It seems that's all I do now. My name is Ruth."

"Hello Ruth, you needn't be sorry for anything. I understand."

"Ruth, won't you fix us some coffee? Are you hungry Major?"

"Please, call me Kirby. I'm no longer in the Army. And yes, a sandwich would be nice."

Kirby sat down at the table with Mr. Brown and Ruth was busy making coffee, when another woman entered the kitchen from another room. Kirby turned to look at her and when she looked at him their eyes locked onto each others. He couldn't stop looking at her and apparently neither could she. Kirby was dumbfounded. He suddenly felt so at ease with this woman. As if he was looking at a friend for the first time. Their eyes still locked onto the other. Kirby began to smile and she did also and her eyes began to glisten like tiny sparks. He stood up, and she took a step closer.

Jim and Ruth Brown looked at each other with surprise. "Rachel.....Rachel, this is Major Kirby Morgan. He has brought our son's body back to be buried here. Kirby this is Rachel. She helps me around the house and at meal times feeding the crews."

Kirby took a step closer and so did Rachel. He extended his hand to shake hers and at first she was hesitant. Almost as if she didn't know what Kirby wanted. Then she gave him her hand and smiled. "Hello Rachel."

"Hello Kirby," and she was still smiling.

"Rachel, will you help me make a sandwich for Kirby?"

Later that night the Browns would discuss how surprised they had been; how Rachel had been so amicable with this stranger. Something the two had never seen before. Other men had tried to get close to her, but she had always made it clear, she wasn't interested.

The coffee was good and the pork sandwiches were delicious. "Will you go home from here Major?"

"Please, call me Kirby. I resigned my commission. I haven't any home to go home to. My two younger brothers were killed in the war and my mother died of a broken heart and my father from a heart attack soon after. I'm not sure where I'll go."

"You don't have to leave soon on our account," Jim replied.

"I plan to stay to see Alvin's body buried. He was beside me when he was hit, and we ended up in the same hospital and when I awoke, Alvin was the first person I recognized."

"You can stay right here with us Kirby, and I won't take no for an answer," Ruth said. "You can have Alvin's room." Rachel looked at Ruth in surprise. She had never let anyone use that room before.

"You know, there were six young men from here, went to that war. So far as we know, there were only three others who didn't make it. Jonathan Winslow. He died in '63. He was a Corporal in the 13th Maine. The second boy was William Brooks. He was killed earlier this year 1865. The last one Barrett Wriston was wounded in '62. He was healed up, the Army doctors thought, so they put him on a train and sent him home. There was no one to pick him up, so he started walking to Grafton from the Bethel train station. His wound must have opened up again, because he died on the road home. Now Alvin makes four. Half the boys made it through.

"I'm familiar with the 13th. They were good fighters," Kirby said.

"There were sixteen boys from Upton who went."

"Where is Upton from here?" Kirby asked.

"It's about an hour's ride by wagon up the road. The town is at the southern tip of Umbagog Lake.

There's probably 400 or so people there, where as there's only about 115 here in Grafton."

"Do you have any clothes with you Kirby? I noticed you were traveling light," Ruth asked.

Kirby looked at his lap and said, "This uniform and the horse and wagon are all I have to my name." He started massaging his shoulder.

"Well, I think some of Alvin's clothes might fit you. Is there something wrong with your shoulder?" Ruth asked.

"It's one of the wounds, why I was in the hospital with your son."

"That line on your scalp another?"

"Yeah, I got both those in the last battle we fought at Five Forks, Virginia. That's where Alvin was wounded, too."

"You know, if you don't mind, I'd really like to get out of this uniform."

"Certainly, Rachel will show you to your room and she can get out some clean clothes for you," Ruth said.

"Maybe we can talk some more after you have cleaned up," Jim said.

"Yes, I'd like that." He followed Rachel upstairs.

Rachel opened a bedroom door and said, "This will be your room and there should be everything you need for clothes. How long will you be staying with us, Kirby?"

"I don't know. I need to figure out what I'm going to do from here."

* * * *

Having her son's body home to bury seem to clear away the grief she had been feeling. This was closure for her. Now she would know where the body would be buried. She wasn't happy by any means. But she stopped her crying and was able to help out with the work around the house.

Kirby came downstairs after changing and Jim said, "Let's you and I go sit out on the porch. The women have work to do and we'll only be in their way."

Before leaving the kitchen Kirby looked at Rachel. She was looking at him. Jim and Ruth both saw them looking at each and then they smiled.

"Sit down Kirby. The crews will be coming in soon. Most of the men are driving last winter's timber down river to the saw mills in Milan, New Hampshire. I have a few men working the fields, getting them ready for planting. On rainy days I start the saw mill up and we saw out a few pine logs. Maybe you saw the wagon load this morning?"

"Yes I did; early this morning."

"We don't saw out much lumber here. I built the saw mill mainly so the new settlers here would have lumber to build framed houses instead of a log house like I had to build when I bought this land and started clearing the meadows in 1834. Actually, I first came into this country from Canton when I was 31, in 1830. Looking for a nice stand of pine and spruce with some available farm land that could be cleared and planted. Back then this was a wilderness territory; Letter A was all it was known by then. Later, as more people bought land here and moved in and cleared the land and started farming, by 1852 we incorporated as a town. My mother Hannah Brown wanted to call this township Grafton because in Massachusetts, Grafton is located next to Upton. Just like here, Upton is the next town to the north. Just up the road a piece."

"What did you do in Canton, Mr. Brown?"

"Lumbering, until the timber started to run out. I didn't want to spend the rest of my life on a farm, so I came up here, as I said in 1830. I was quite impressed with the stands of pine and spruce trees. And this valley looked good for farming and the spring run off here is substantial enough to drive the winter logs down the Cambridge River to Umbagog to the Androscoggin River. Then if there is enough water left here behind my dam, Popple Dam, I keep a few men busy during the summer sawing out pine and spruce. The best pine and spruce logs I keep here and send everything else down river to Milan. I'm very selective with the logs I keep.

"We have been cutting timber here in Grafton since '38, that's what, almost 30 years. Or close to it. There are still some good stands left. Word is coming out of Berlin that the Brown Paper Company, no relations, will soon be wanting spruce and fir pulp."

"Do you have any children besides Alvin, Mr. Brown?"

"A daughter Mary. She was born in 1839. She's married now to George Otis. That's their house across the road. My folks Aaron and Hannah died in the 40's. Mary is up to Upton today, talking to the preacher. I'm hoping he'll come back with her this evening, so we can have Alvin's funeral and bury him tomorrow."

"You didn't have any more children?"

"I wanted more, but Ruth said if she was going to keep house in a house that has 14 rooms and cook meals for 40 men, how was she going to find time to raise any more."

"When I came here in '30, I first built a log house. Then I built the dam. There were some nice poplar trees growing along the river bank where I needed the dam, so that's why it's called Popple Dam and the same with the hotel or Poplar Tavern. By the end of 1842 I finished building this house. There's 14 rooms and five fireplaces. Then larger barns and work sheds. To tell you the truth Kirby, I plain tuckered-out. My son-in-law George helps out immensely."

Kirby knew Captain Jim liked talking about Grafton. He had done a lot of work. He should be proud. He enjoyed listening to him, and he also knew it was a way for Jim to let go of his sadness of Alvin.

"Tell me about Rachel, Jim. Does her family live in Grafton?"

"No, she's not from Grafton. She came here looking for work two years ago from up above Parmachenee Lake somewhere. Maybe even Canada. She's from the Abenaki Indian Tribe. At the start of spring breakup she goes back to her people for a couple of weeks and then returns with a canoe full of fur pelts that she trades for goods, that she takes back in October before freeze up. We don't ask her much about her personal life. She works out real good here and that's important.

"But I have never seen her take to anyone like she was looking at you earlier. For some strange reason most of the young men around here are afraid to talk with her."

"I wonder why?" Kirby mused.

"I don't know unless it has something to do with that wolverine fur she wears. The only time she wears it is when she is traveling. She only got back two days ago from her spring trip."

The door opened then and Rachel stepped out on to the porch and said, "Supper is ready."

"You go ahead in with Rachel Kirby, I'll go get Ronki-Tonk."

*   *   *   *

When supper was over Ronki-Tonk went back out to his room in the barn. Mary was back from Upton with the preacher. Kirby helped Rachel clean the kitchen and the dishes while the others talked in the other room about Alvin's funeral. Ruth and Mary were crying again.

"What was the war about Kirby?" Rachel asked.

"The southern states wanted to secede from the country and form their own country where they could have slaves."

"My people sometimes take slaves. But never so many people die because of it. When I first came to live with my people, I was slave for a while, until others started to accept me as one of them."

"Where did you come from Rachel?"

"Illinois." That's all she would tell him. And Kirby assumed she meant the Illinois Tribe.

"You like it here Mr. Kirby?"

"Yes I do. And it's only Kirby. No mister, please. For some reason I can't explain it, but this seems more like home than where I was raised."

"What you do before the war?"

"I went into the Army when I was 19, almost 20. Three years before the war started. I wanted to go out west and got as far as Iowa."

"What you gonna do now?"

"I don't know honestly."

"Good. Why not you stay here."

Kirby couldn't help but notice at times she would change to using broken English, when mostly she used very correct English. He didn't think any more of it. "I don't know, maybe. I do like it here." Rachel was quiet as she wiped the table and counters clean. Kirby had only a few dishes left to dry. He was watching Rachel as he dried a large pot and he couldn't help but notice how pretty she was. Her hair was brown and matched her eyes which could look right through you or with a look of warmth and kindness. She was slim and a notice figure. She turned and noticed him watching her and she smiled.

"I think I'll go for a walk. Where does the road go across the river?"

"It goes through the fields and eventually up through Dunn's Notch. I guess there once was a road through the Notch that went to Andover. I have never been up to the Notch. I understand that it washed out one spring. Mr. Brown had a crew working out that way somewhere last winter. How long will you be gone?"

"I don't know. I just need to be alone for a while and stretch my legs."

Rachel turned and went upstairs.

*   *   *   *

It was a nice evening for a walk. Although he had enjoyed talking with Rachel and the Browns, he now needed some time for himself. As he walked along he tried to empty his mind of everything. He simply wanted to be alone and enjoy the moment and relax. Not even to consider what he was going to do with his life after tomorrow.

The field on the left was planted to either wheat or oats. Probably oats and the field looked like a carpet of green as the new stalks were about two inches above the ground. At the back end of the same field, it looked like a hay field. The field on his right was planted, but nothing had yet come through the soil and again at the back edge of this was hay. And at the woodline were several deer foraging in the already ankle high clover. There were two bucks; their new antlers in velvet. The others looked to be does and not fawns. Probably they were laying down somewhere.

A redtail hawk was circling over head shrieking a warning to the intruder. Eventually it flew off towards Deer Hill.

The sun was just beginning to drop below the mountains to the west, making a golden glow over the horizon. Kirby found a spruce tree where he could sit with his back against the tree up high enough so he could see the entire field.

He took a deep breath and exhaled slowly, trying to relax. He still refused to let any thoughts enter his mind. The sunset was now turning to a fiery red, mixed with streamers of gold. It looked a lot like the northern lights except the color was wrong. Anyhow it was promising a nice day for tomorrow. "It'll be nice for Alvin's family. To have a nice day to bury their son."

That thought opened the floodgate in Kirbys' mind, and let in all the thoughts and images of all the battles and the screams of the dying, of the past four years. The beautiful sunset was now replaced with blacker images of dead and dying men. Instead of looking at the fiery red sunset, all he could see were images of blood, blood everywhere. How many men had he killed, how many of his friends had died; some screaming until they didn't have any more air to scream with.

He recalled the images of the men he held as they bled out and breathed their last scent of fresh air; Paul, Henry, Jacob, and most of all, he heard his youngest brother Ted, scream out his name as a cannon ball took off both his legs. Ted had died before Kirby could reach him. How had his other brother Bill died? He saw the anguish on his mother's face when she was told about her two youngest sons dying in battle and his father wasting away with a heart attack.

He hated the south for what they did to his family; to him. He hated the country down that way. He was tired of hearing people say potatas, not potatoes, or tomatas, not tomatoes. And the idea of having to enslave people to do your work. He wished he had stayed in Iowa and not volunteered for the 20th Maine.

The sun was gone. It had disappeared hours ago. But Kirby was not aware. He held his head in his hands and cried. Tears running down his arms and soaking his shirts sleeves. He didn't cry for himself. He cried for all those men who died and the mothers and fathers who will never see their sons again. He cried for the human race. For how could a species that is suppose to be so highly civilized and educated, be so cruel, and sadistically feral? So in-human. How could all of this have happened? He cried even more. He looked up into the dark sky and said aloud, "Why! Why did so many have to die?"

His throat and chest were hurting and his eyes were stinging because there were no more tears. He leaned back against the spruce tree and just stared into the darkness.

*   *   *   *

Rachel worried all night when Kirby didn't come back before dark. Had he gotten lost? Hurt? What? So she was up with the sun and after dressing she checked Kirby's room. He wasn't there so she went downstairs. The Browns were already in the kitchen. "Have you seen Kirby? He didn't come home last night. I'm worried something might have happened."

"He probably just fell asleep somewhere. He is still recovering from his wounds and the journey from Virginia probably exhausted him. I'm sure he's ok Rachel," Jim said as he looked at Ruth. They were thinking the same thoughts. Wondering if she had ever been this concerned about another man. And Kirby was a complete stranger.

"I go look for him," as she rushed outside. She had dropped back to using broken English again.

Rachel ran down the road and crossed the bridge and saw Kirby walking back. She kept running. Kirby saw her running towards him and wondered what the matter might be. She ran right up to him and stopped squarely in front of him. "Where have you been? I worry all night, thinking what has happened to you. Why did you stay out under the stars like an Indian without telling me?" She noticed the tear streaks on his face and was afraid she had said too much.

Kirby was so shocked about Rachel's concern for him, he didn't know what to say. For the first time in his life someone was concerned about him. And this made him feel happy. "I'm sorry if you were worried. There were so many thoughts and images about the war going through my head last night, I sort of lost track how late it had gotten. There was so much that I had to think about and get out of my soul. It was a long night." He looked at the warmth in her eyes, as if she could understand what he had experienced. "But I feel better now. I worked it all out last night."

"Good," she said softly. And then an octave louder, "Don't you ever go off like that again!"

Kirby smiled at her and she was smiling back. He stepped closer. She didn't back away. Then he put his arms around her and hugged her, and she hugged him back.

As they crossed the bridge Rachel was close to his side. They stopped when they saw Jim and Ruth standing there watching. Ruth had a twinkle in her eyes and Jim was smiling. Rachel had become like a daughter to them both, although they didn't know much about her. Neither of them said anything about Kirby staying out all night or about the two of them.

While Ruth and Rachel fixed breakfast Kirby went out behind the barn to clean up. He met Ronki-Tonk cleaning out the stalls. He looked to be a gristle old man with a bent back. It was difficult to say how old he was underneath his shaggy hair and whiskers. "Morning Major, sometimes it takes a beautiful sunset and a night under the stars to clear out the cobwebs."

"Good morning Ronki-Tonk. Is everybody up this early every day?"

"Only Captain Jim's wife and Rachel, excepting in the spring like this when most of the men are home. Those two women work longer hours than any man here. Captain Jim is a pious man he is and he won't allow anyone to work on Sunday. Except his wife Ruth and Rachel. They still have meals to cook and dishes to wash. No sir, I wouldn't trade my chores for their's for all the whisky a man could ever drink. And I'm quite comfortable in my room in the barn. Going to sleep each night with the sweet smell of hay is just almost as good, as laying your head on a plump bosom and smell the perfume in her hair."

Kirby splashed water in his face and then stood up drying his face with a towel. Ronki-Tonk noticed the healing wound in his back. "Is that where you were wounded Kirby?"

"One place. This bullet came out my back and didn't tear up any bone, only tissue. I was hit once in my butt also. I could fight all day on my feet, but couldn't ride a horse for two weeks." They both laughed.

"And that line across your scalp?"

"Got that right after the shoulder. Near miss."

"I'd say so," Ronki-Tonk replied.

"Why do you call Mr. Brown, Captain Jim? Was he in the military?" Kirby asked.

"No military. But look at what he has done around here. He organizes everything so meticulously, he deserves to be called Captain Jim."

"Maybe you're correct there Ronki-Tonk." Kirby couldn't help but wonder with his sudden surprises with his vocabulary. Ronki-Tonk certainly wasn't an uneducated oaf. He finished washing and shaving and went back to the kitchen. He could smell bacon frying.

Rachel handed Kirby a cup of hot coffee and Ruth said, "Sit down. Breakfast will be ready in a bit."

Rachel showed Kirby to his place at the table. Next to her. "That bacon sure does smell delicious. I haven't smelled bacon frying since I left Iowa in '60."

"How long were you in Iowa Kirby?" Jim asked.

"I joined in '58 and nine months later I was on my way, supposedly to the Wyoming Territory, but the

Army had set up an out post on the Big Sioux River. That's as far as any of us would go. Some prospectors in the Black Hills had started some trouble with the Dakota Sioux and the Army was there to keep the whites out of the Black Hills and the Sioux out of the white settlements."

"Enough of this army talk. I want no more of it at my table," Ruth said. Everyone was quiet and turned to look at Ruth. The boss had spoken. "Besides breakfast is ready. Rachel would you see that everyone gets bacon. I'll get the pancakes and syrup. This is home-made maple syrup Kirby. Not thinned out molasses. Ronti-Tonk boiled it down this spring. Where is Ronki-Tonk anyhow?"

Kirby stood up, "I'll go get him." Ronki-Tonk met him at the screen door.

"You were almost too late Ronki-Tonk," Jim said good naturedly.

Kirby took one pancake and several slices of bacon and asked, "Ruth do you have any peanut butter?"

Everyone looked at him. "What do you want with peanut butter?"

"I put it on my pancakes."

Ruth just tweaked her head as if saying alright and handed him a jar. Everyone watched as he spread it on the pancake and then poured the syrup. "My family have always eaten pancakes with peanut butter. Mom used to say it was the French in us."

He took a fork full of pancake and sat back in his chair, chewing slowly and savoring the taste. "My word is that good Ruth." Everyone laughed.

*   *   *   *

When breakfast was over Jim and Kirby took a pot of coffee out on the porch, while the women cleaned up the kitchen. They sat there enjoying the crisp spring air and the sweet scent of the Balm of Gilead tree. "I haven't smelled that sweet air since before I left home in '58."

Rachel was standing at the screen door and heard Kirby. Before the day was over she had gone down by the river where many young Balm of Gilead trees were growing. She broke off several branches and put them in a vase and set it on the bureau in Kirby's room, so he could fall asleep enjoying the sweetest perfume on earth.

"My crew will be back from the river drive in a couple of weeks and then I'll shut the gates on this dam and let the reservoir fill and then start the mill and saw out what pine and spruce logs I set aside this winter. That'll keep the men busy until haying. Then it'll soon be harvest time and then back in the woods.

"Have you thought any about staying on here Kirby. Ruth and I sure would like to have you. And I think Rachel would like you to stay also. Have you noticed how pretty she is?" They both laughed.

"I'd have to be blind not to see that Jim. And I think there's more to her beauty than what's on the surface. She has an inner quality about her, an inner charm that has my head spinning."

"You didn't answer my question Kirby."

"Yes, I would like to stay on. But I insist on earning my own way."

"I like that attitude in a man. Until your shoulder is completely healed I'll keep you on light work. How is 75¢ a day plus room and board? As you get stronger and doing heavier work, I'll increase your pay."

"That sounds fine with me as long as I can keep eating Ruth's cooking." They laughed.

"Good, it's all settled then."

"I'll be needing a couple of days to go into town. There are some things that I need."

"Okay, if you'll take a wagon load of pine boards to the depot in Bethel, I'll pay you for the trip. The drivers usually get $2.00 a trip."

The coffee pot was empty, "And now I have a grave to dig. The funeral is at 2 o'clock."

"I'll give you a hand Jim."

"No Kirby. This is something a father has to do alone."

Kirby understood all too well. He nodded his head that he understood and took the pot back inside. "Ruth, is there anything that needs to be done that I could help you with?" Kirby asked.

"Maybe you could bring in some stove wood."

Kirby would normally carry an arm full of wood in his left arm; not yet. He had the wood box full with some kindling also. "If there isn't anything else, I'd like to take my horse for a ride."

"Rachel, why don't you saddle old Brownie and go with Kirby."

"I'll go out to the barn and get the horses ready."

Out at the barn Kirby asked Ronki-Tonk, "Will you saddle old Brownie for Rachel please. We're going horse-back riding. You coming with me Rachel?" Kirby asked as he sat atop Jake.

She swung into the saddle on old Brownie. "You're the guide where shall we go?"

"We'll follow Back Street until we come to the divide in the road. Then we'll turn towards Cedar Brook Meadow. The meadow is a peaceful place." She rode ahead and Kirby caught up and then they rode side by each and turned left towards the meadows.

Rachel pulled her horse to a stop and dismounted and tied the reins to a small cedar tree; Kirby did likewise. "Come, follow me," and she took his hand and led the way along a path following the shoreline of the meadow, to a little knoll with huge pine trees. The ground was a thick carpet of pine needles and the air was scented with the perfume of pine. Kirby understood why she had brought him here. There was a natural depression in the ground at the base of a tree and Rachel said "sit" and pointed. Kirby sat down with his back against the tree and Rachel sat on the ground between his legs. Kirby wrapped his arms around hers and pulled her back against his chest. She felt warm and good in his arms and her hair was scented with Balm of Gilead. The perfume of heaven.

"Look over there Kirby," and she pointed to a cow moose and a real young calf. "That calf can't be more than a day old." It was the color of chocolate milk and not yet sturdy on its legs.

"This is a beautiful place Rachel. I see by this path that you come here often."

"Yes whenever I have free time. It reminds me of my people back home."

"Where is home Rachel?" he asked.

"My people live above the Parmachenee Lake, north of here near a place we call Wells Waters. The water bubbles out of the ground there and is pristine clear."

"Who are your people Rachel?"

Rachel thought for a few moments before answering. "They are a band of the Abenaki Tribe. The chief is Matelok, but white man language has changed it to Metallak. Matelok had a daughter he called Parmachenee that he loved very much. She married a French man with much money and now lives in Canada near St. Francis. The tribe once owned all the land around Umbagog Lake north to St. Francis and west to the Connecticut River. But there was a problem in his tribe and Matelok left and lived along the Magalloway River and Umbagog. He was a great man and well liked by all the white settlements.

"I go back to the village every spring and I bring out fur pelts and trade them for things that will make their lives a bit easier. I go back again in the fall before the water freezes. Maybe you come with me?" She turned to look at Kirby.

He held her face in his hands and kissed her softly and she responded, and squeezed his arm. "I like that. I have never been kissed before. Do it again."

Kirby kissed her again; more passionately this time and he could feel her quivering with anticipation. "I think I like being kissed."

"When were you born Kirby?"

"1838, in February. When were you born?"

"Maybe two years before then in spring."

She felt comfortable in Kirby's arms and she leaned back against him and he held her to him and laid his face in her hair. Wow! He had never felt like this before. Rachel had some kind of control over him, he was thinking. Whatever it was he was enjoying it.

"Tell me more about Matelok."

"He use to come to our village but I was only a young girl then and really didn't get to know him. I remember he had a kind face and was tall. As I understand, listening to Falling Bear our leader, Matelok was a great Indian. Even those in the white settlements considered him great. Falling Bear said that when Matelok was about twelve he and three other boys of the same age were taken and left at a boys farm in Hanover, New Hampshire for four years. They learned to speak English and were taught Christianity. To pay for their education they worked on the farm.

"Matelok's father, Piol, who was the leader then was very proud of his son and told him when he died, 'Matelok will be chief.'

"People in Upton knew him well also. He was a great hunter and guide."

"Who is chief now?" Kirby asked.

"I don't know who is Chief of the Abenaki, but Falling Bear is still the leader of my people. He is old and soon his son will become leader."

"I would like to meet your people some day."

Rachel was so excited she turned and on her knees facing Kirby and smiling radiantly she said, "You make me happy. I feel good in here," and she touched her heart. "You come with me in the fall when I go."

Kirby put his arms around her and pulled her to him; she didn't resist, and he kissed her passionately on the lips, "Yes, I will go with you this fall."

Rachel then kissed him and said, "Good. Now we must go back. Alvin's funeral remember?"

*   *   *   *

Everyone in Grafton attended the funeral service for Corporal Alvin Brown. The service was held in the hotel. Some residents had a long distance to travel in horse and wagon or buggy. Preacher McBride gave a heart thundering sermon. There were a lot of tears and crying, which one would only expect at a funeral. When the Lord's Prayer was said, the sermon was over, except for the burial. Kirby helped to carry the casket outside to an awaiting wagon and everybody followed them to the cemetery.

After the casket had been lowered in the grave Preacher McBride gave the finale committal and said another prayer. Kirby had been standing beside Rachel and now he moved forward to stand next to Ruth and Jim and Rachel stepped up beside him. "I would like to say some things, if I could."

"Please do," Preacher McBride said.

"Alvin was a fine young man Jim and Ruth. He was in my command for several months before the last battle. He was a good soldier, never saying anything hateful about the enemy we were fighting. Like most of us, when he volunteered, he had no idea what to expect, or know just how ugly and gruesome a war can be. We talked often, and he told me all about his family and life in Grafton." He took another step forward and gave a final salute and then he stepped to the temporary marker, a wooden cross until a fitting granite stone could be set in place and removed from his pocket, his Medal of Honor ribbon and pinned it to the cross. "You truly earned this Corporal Brown."

Everyone left except for Jim and Ruth. Kirby and Rachel waited for them at the road side. In a few minutes Ruth joined them, while Jim filled in the grave. Kirby knew enough about Captain Jim to let him have this final duty with his son. He'd wait with Ruth and Rachel.

*　　*　　*　　*

Preacher McBride stayed over that night in the hotel as the following day was Sunday and he would hold church services there, something that he could seldom do for the people of Grafton. The town was simply too few people to support their own minister.

After the services, McBride asked Jim, "How were your potatoes last year Jim?"

"They were okay. We could have used a bit more rain though."

"My brother in Bethel has a big field of potatoes and he was plagued with bugs. I hope they don't find their way up here. Good-bye now."

Ruth came over where Jim and Kirby were talking. "Kirby, if you don't mind, I'm going to send Rachel down with you tomorrow. I need a few things and it'll save me the trip."

"That's no problem at all Ruth," and he turned to look at Rachel.

Jim then had Kirby walk with him over to the mill and showed him the load he was to take in the morning. "Ronki-Tonk will have a double team all harnessed and hooked up for you in the morning. It's doubtful you'll be able to make it all the way back tomorrow, especially considering the shopping you and Rachel both will be doing, so you probably better plan to stay over either at Kilgore's, if you get back that far, or at the T-House at Newry Corner.

"Kirby there's something else I want to talk with you about. Old man Morse Howard spoke to me after the services this morning. Seems like he has bear problems and wanted to know if any of my men could shoot or trap this bugger. I told him you might be interested when you get back from town. Seems as if this bugger has already killed and ate three sheep and Friday night he broke into the pig pen. Morse heard the commotion but by the time he found his shotgun and a lantern the bear was gone. Morse said he'd pay you

$25 when you kill it and you can have the bear. The state is paying a $15 bounty on 'em."

"That's a lot of money for one bear," Kirby replied.

"Maybe, but one of those sheep is worth more than $25. There has always been a number of bear plaguing the farmers and at some of the outlying lumber camps, too. You just might be able to work this into a good side job for yourself.

"I'm a pretty good judge of character and I can see this would be more to your liking than either farming or timbering. You might think about picking up a bear trap or two and a rifle. If you haven't enough money, I can loan it to you."

"That won't be necessary. I have some."

*   *   *   *

The next morning Rachel woke Kirby early and had breakfast ready by the time he came downstairs.

"How long have you been up Rachel?"

"Oh, not that long. I wanted to put up some food for us to take and I wanted to have your breakfast ready."

"I don't know what to say, but thank you." She only smiled and sat beside him while they ate.

Ruth and Jim came downstairs as Rachel and Kirby were drying the last of their dishes. "You didn't have to bother with the dishes. I could have done those few. Why don't you two get out of here and enjoy your trip," Ruth said smiling.

Kirby went outside and Rachel was a couple of minutes before she came out and carrying the basket of food. And she was wearing some kind of a fur pelt over her shoulder. Kirby took the basket and secured it on top of the load and then asked, "What animal is this?" as he brushed the fur with his hand.

"It's a wolverine, Falling Bear gave to me when I left the village to come here. He told me to wear it when I traveled. That it would always protect me."

"It is pretty."

Ronki-Tonk had the team and wagon waiting for them out front. "Thank you Ronki-Tonk. Is there anything we can bring back for you?" Kirby asked.

"By-golly there is." He stepped closer to the wagon so his voice wouldn't carry. He handed Kirby 25¢ and said, "This'll buy five bottles of vanilla extract." Kirby looked at Rachel questioningly. "I'll explain on the way."

*   *   *   *

Ronki-Tonk watched until they were out of sight and then returned to his morning chores in the barn.

Ruth had breakfast ready and was waiting for Jim. "Come on you old fool before everything is cold."

"I'm coming, I'm coming," Jim replied.

After breakfast the two were sitting at the table enjoying their coffee. "What do you make of Rachel and Kirby?"

"The spark kind of kindled a hot fire," Jim said.

"I think they're about the same age and I think it's about time Rachel had a man," Ruth said.

"I think they are well suited for each other," Jim said.

George and Mary were walking across the road towards the Brown home and saw Kirby and Rachel ride out together towards the notch. Jim and Ruth were still at the breakfast table drinking coffee when they walked in. "Good morning, you're just in time to finish the pot of coffee," Jim said.

"Where are Kirby and Rachel going this early?" Mary asked.

"Kirby's taking a load of pine to Bethel and then he has some shopping to do, and Rachel has a list to fill for Ruth. They won't be back tonight," Jim said.

"Don't you think it's a little odd, I mean Rachel has been here for two years and not once has any man gotten close to her, and now a complete stranger to all of us comes into our lives and two days later the two go off on a two day trip together?" George asked.

"I have never believed in coincidences, just maybe these two were meant to meet. Either way, Rachel is like our own daughter and even though we haven't known Kirby for long, I trust him and I like him. There is something special about him that sets him apart from others and I think Rachel can see that, also," Ruth said.

"I hope they both will stay here in Grafton," Jim said.

*   *   *   *

There was a breeze blowing at their back and Rachel felt a chill go through her. She moved closer to Kirby until their shoulders, hips and legs were touching. She could feel the warmth radiating from him. "Two nights ago when you stayed out back all night, you were trying to cleanse your spirit from the memories of the war, no?"

"There were many memories in my head I needed to let go of. Everything from the war was suddenly coming at me at once. All the memories and sadness. The names of all the men I lost in my command. Come daylight though, all those memories were washed away. Now, I can still remember; I suppose I always will, but I'm no longer bothered by them."

"That's good," as she slipped her arm around his and held on.

"How is your shoulder now?"

"It is feeling better with each new day."

"Tonight before we go to bed, I have a special potion that I have mixed up, that I'll use and massage your shoulder. Okay?"

"Okay."

They were making good time. They were now down to the Newry Flats. But then it had been down hill all the way, too. But the two horses were not showing any fatigue. A stage coach was just leaving Kilgore Station. "They must have left Bethel probably around noon. I don't think it's the stage that carries the mail. Maybe it's a special stage bound for Upton," Rachel said.

"How often does the mail come to Grafton?"

"Everyday, except in the winter, or bad weather."

They had been on the road now for most of five hours and the T-House at Newry Corner was coming into sight. "We need to stop here first Kirby. They will have most everything that Ruth has on her list. You might be able to get everything you want, also."

"I'll water the horses first and give them a bit of grain and then I'll be in."

Rachel gave her list of supplies to Mr. Henderson and said, "We'll pick these up on the way back."

"On the Brown account?"

"Yes."

Kirby was over looking at some new rifles that had just come in that morning. "Do you like the feel of that one sir?" Mr. Henderson asked.

"I sure do. Winchester; I have never seen one before."

"Model 1866. It was produced in a hurry because of the war and now that the war is over, Winchester Arms decided to sell those to the public. Takes the .44 Henry cartridge. The same cartridge as the .44 hand gun."

"How much Mr. Henderson?"

"$45."

"I'll take it and two boxes of cartridges. I'll leave this here. I need more. Do you have bear traps?"

"Yes we do. "$8 a piece."

"Two of those." Kirby picked up some clothes; a jacket and a warm winter coat, leather boots and rubber boots, mittens, snowshoes and five bottles of vanilla extract.

"I'll pay for all of this now and pick everything up on our way back, if that's alright?"

"Certainly.....ah, I didn't get your name?"

"Kirby Morgan."

"Oh, I've heard about you, you're Major Morgan, who turned down a full Colonel's promotion." When Kirby looked at Mr. Henderson questioningly, "It's in all the papers sir."

Rachel came over, "Are you done Rachel?"

"Yes. Looks like you bought a little of everything."

"Well when I arrived at the Brown's, I was wearing everything I owned."

"When I find some extra time, I'll make you some traveling clothes," Rachel said.

As they walked over to the wagon Kirby kept thinking what she had meant by traveling clothes. Then he forgot about it when two oafish looking brutes climbed down from their wagon. They were loud and watching Rachel as she climbed aboard their wagon. The two brutes walked over and were about to say something to Rachel when they stopped dead in their tracks. Panic etched across their faces. One of them said, "Carcajou woman." They turned abruptly and hurried off.

"What did he say? I couldn't make it out."

"He said Carcajou woman. Carcajou is French for wolverine."

"They seemed scared of you when they saw the fur you're wearing. I guess it does protect you."

She was unusually quiet during the remainder of the trip to the Bethel depot. And once there, there was no one available to help unload. So the two of them had to unload the pine boards and restack them on a pallet on the ground. When they were finished Kirby's left shoulder was aching. "As soon as we get the delivery slip, we can leave. Where to next?"

"The textile factory on the other edge of town."

This seemed to be a busy place this morning. They had to wait a half hour before they could get their delivery slip. "I'm hungry. Did you by chance pack some sandwiches?"

"Yes, pork and cheese and water." They ate lunch on their way.

"What do you have to pick up here?" Kirby asked.

"Some canvas for Jim and four bolts of cloth for Ruth and thread and needles."

"I think we're going to have a load going back, too. Only not as heavy. I doubt if we get back to

Kilgore's tonight. I assume you have another place in mind?"

"I do. It'll be a surprise."

Before leaving town Kirby wanted to stop at the bank and open an account. He didn't like carrying all of his money around with him and he asked, "I have a monthly military check, can I have it sent directly here?"

"Sure thing Mr. Morgan and here is the form you'll need to fill in. If you wanted to do that now, I could deliver it to the post office for you," Albert Proctor said.

"Thank you." Kirby filled in the correct information and handed the form back to Mr. Proctor.

"Now, how much money would you like to deposit today Mr. Morgan? And will Mrs. Morgan's name be on the account also?"

Both Rachel and Kirby laughed and Mr. Proctor was surprised.

"We're not married."

"Oh, my mistake. I just took it for granted."

After buying what he needed at the T-House he had $1,106.07 left. "What if I need more money than what I have in my pocket. What do I do then Mr. Proctor?"

"We have bank drafts here. I'll give you six and when you make one out, be sure to include your account number. This is it right here," and pointed to the account application.

"Okay, I'll deposit $1,000," and he counted out the correct amount.

"Is there anything else I can do for you today?"

"We're fine now Mr. Proctor. And thank you."

*　　*　　*　　*

"We should have asked what time it was,"
Kirby said.

"Why? As long as we stop before dark, so we
have enough daylight to set up camp and warm our
food." Time didn't mean anything to Rachel.

By the time they had loaded everything into the
wagon at the T-House Trading Post the sun was resting
at the tree tops. "We'd better find a place to make
camp for the night. We'll never make Kilgore's before
dark," Kirby said.

"I know a nice place," Rachel said. "Do you
remember where we crossed Bear River? I saw a nice
spot just below the bridge."

The load was light and the team was not yet
tired, so Kirby picked up the pace. Rachel was still
sitting as close as she could to Kirby with her arm
holding his. They each were feeling the anticipation of
the night together. A chance to relax in each other's
embrace and talk. It didn't take them any time at all to
cover the distance to the Bear River Crossing. "Over
there Kirby," and she pointed to a place where a small
out-cropping of ledge had made a covey close to the
water. The ground was covered with moss and small
spruce and fir trees dotted the area with one tall pine
sitting on top of the ledge with its roots well embedded
in the rocky crevices. The air was cool here which
would mean a bubbling spring somewhere. And the air
was filled with the scent of fir and spruce.

Kirby helped Rachel down off the wagon and
then handed her the basket she had brought along.
"Wow, this is heavy. What did you bring anyhow?"

While Kirby was tending to the horses,
loosening the harness and rubbing them down with a
cloth and giving them each some grain and water,

Rachel was busy setting up camp. She had rocked up a fire pit next to the water and had a fire going already. From the basket she removed an iron kettle filled with the last of the beef stew they had had Friday evening for supper. She hung this over the fire to warm slowly and then she removed two blankets and spread them on the moss near the shelter of the rock covey.

Kirby staked the horses and he walked over to Rachel. He was surprised with her efficiency. Now he understood why the basket was so heavy. Rachel stepped over to Kirby and he took her in his arms and held her close for the longest moment before he kissed her. He wanted to feel the warmth of her body next to his and feel the vibrations of her spirit that so enthralled him. He wanted to immerse himself and drink of the essence of this beautiful and truly magnanimous woman.

"How is your shoulder Kirby? You have maybe overused it today?" She removed his shirt and she saw the wounds on his shoulder and on his back where the bullet had exited. She touched the bullet scar on his head and asked, "Does this one hurt?"

"No, Dr. Yahro said the bullet had damaged the nerves that lie close to the skin and the scar itself will always be without feeling. And that's why hair will not grow there."

She laid her face against his chest and asked, "Are these two wounds the only ones?"

"No, I was shot in the butt once."

"Does that hurt?"

"Not now, but I couldn't sit down for a few weeks or ride a horse."

They both laughed and Rachel undid his pants and let them drop. "Turn around, I want to see." He did and then she pulled his undershorts down and touched the wound. "I'm glad it does not hurt you anymore. Come, we wash up in the river now, before we eat. There is a deep hole on the other side." She was already taking her clothes off.

Kirby had to sit down and take his boots off first. While he was doing this Rachel stood in front of him with her hands on her hips and said, "Well, what's taking you so long?" They laughed and he splashed her with water. Her whole body was a dark tan. Like she had lain in the sun all summer. But he guessed it was her natural beauty. She wasn't the least embarrassed or ill at ease about her nudity. She was happy that Kirby was enjoying looking at her.

Finally, the last of his clothes were off and he stood and took her hand as they walked out into the cold water. "Wow! This is cold!" he said.

"Growing up with my people, we never had hot water," and then she jumped into the pool and splashed Kirby until he too eased into it. She wouldn't deny that it was cold and they didn't stay long, just enough to wash off the day's sweat and dust.

"I only brought one towel. That's all the room there was in the basket." They stood beside the fire warming up and drying and used the towel to dry their hair.

When they were dry and warm, Rachel checked the stew to make sure it wasn't boiling. "Lay down on the blankets and I'll fix your shoulder."

Kirby laid on his back and Rachel straddled him across his stomach and leaned over and removed a tin from the basket and opened it. "This is ground up aspen bark mixed with a little horse liniment to make a salve. The liniment will penetrate the skin and take the aspen powder to the issue that needs healing."

She rubbed some on his shoulder and massaged it until the salve was no longer sticky. "Okay, roll over so I can do your back."

As he laid on his stomach he said, "My shoulder feels hot, but I can feel it penetrating into the muscles."

Rachel did the same to his back and then she wanted to see the wound on his butt. She rubbed the wound with her fingers and then slapped him playfully. He rolled over, back on his back then and grabbed Rachel and pulled her down to him and wrapped his arms around her, holding her to him. They laid there looking into each other's eyes, searching for love, but neither one of them willing to admit. For a long time they laid there, wrapped in each other's embrace. Kirby pulled back just enough so he could cup Rachel's face in his hands and look into her pretty brown eyes. She whispered in his ear, "I have never done this before."

"Me neither," and they both laughed.

Finally he could stand it no more. Slowly he moved down to her perky breast. They were not large, but what did he care about that? He cupped one in his hand, gently massaging and rubbing the tip of the nipple with his tongue. Rachel was moaning and twisting like a little purring kitten. He laid his face on her belly and gently caressed between her legs, creating new excitement and anticipation. He moved and gently spread her legs and laid between them, smelling her natural perfume and tasting her essence. Her scent and taste were sweeter than the nectar of heaven.

It was almost dark now and neither of them knew how long they had been making love. They finally laid on their backs and Rachel put her leg over Kirby's. "Until I met you," Rachel was whispering, "I was beginning to think I would never find anyone who I could experience what we had together.   Falling Bear told me many years ago, that because who I was, I may never find someone like you." She kissed him and laid her head on his arm.

"Rachel, I don't know what happened when we first met, but since that moment I have not wanted to be apart from you and you are all I can think about. And now you know what?"

She picked her head up to look at him and resting on an elbow she said, "No, what?"

"I'm hungry."

She leaned down and bit his nose.

"Ouch!"

"You deserve that. 'I'm hungry.'" They both laughed and got up and put their clothes on. While Rachel was dishing up the stew, Kirby went after more wood. He didn't have far to go.

When everything had been picked up and cleaned, they both went after enough wood to last the night. Then they undressed, crawled in between the blankets and Kirby put his arm around Rachel and they lay talking and watching the stars and enjoying the warmth and love that was incubating.

The next morning at first light they awoke still wrapped in each other's embrace. "I think there is enough stew left for breakfast. That and some coffee. I'll let you make the coffee."

$$*\quad *\quad *\quad *$$

They arrived back at the Brown farm late morning. Rachel and Kirby both took an arm load of the things that Ruth had wanted inside and had to make another trip. "The canvas can go in the barn. Ronki-

Tonk will know what to do with it," Jim said. The rest, Kirby took up to his room.

"When do you think you can do something about Morse's bear? He was here early this morning. I told him you'd be back today."

"I'll harness up Jake to the wagon and I'll go upstairs and get my rifle."

"Bring the bear back here Kirby, Ruth wants the fat to make lard."

He met Rachel in the kitchen, "I have to go up to the Howard farm and take care of a nuisance bear. I'll probably be gone all night."

Rachel kissed him and said, "Be careful. I'll see you, when you get back." Others were watching, Rachel and Kirby didn't care.

Kirby took a jacket and hat and walked out to the barn. Ronki-Tonk had the team already harnessed to his wagon. Kirby made sure no one was watching and slipped the vanilla extract from his jacket pocket and handed it to Ronki-Tonk.

"Thank you Kirby."

"Thank you for harnessing old Jake for me." As he rode out of the yard Rachel stood on the porch waving goodbye.

It wasn't a long ride to the Howard farm. In a way he was glad to be working alone, but on the other hand he was already missing Rachel. "Oh, ...what has she done to me?"

Mr. Howard was coming out of the barn when Kirby reined Jake to a stop. "Mr. Howard, I'm Kirby Morgan and Captain Jim says you have a bear problem."

"I'll say I do young fella. That son of a bitch carried off another lamb last night! Just a younger'n too. Won't be more than a lunch for him. He'll be back tonight I can guarantee you. You get him tonight and I'll give you $30. Each sheep he gets from here on will cost you $5. Is that understood Mr. Morgan?"

"Clear as day sir. I only have one question. Why haven't you shot the bugger?"

"Not like I haven't tried. But by the time I get dressed and load my rifle and light a lantern the son of a bitch is gone. He's a big one too. Last night he had that little lamb tucked under a front paw and he reared up when he saw me and stepped over the fencing like a man. I pulled my rifle up but I had forgotten to put in a firing cap, I was in such a hurry. I'd go out after him, but then chores here wouldn't get done and besides, after farming this hillside for twenty years my knees are hurting."

"Why do you farm so high up?"

"Frost don't hit so early up here as it does down on the flats. My garden, wheat and oats have a longer growing season. Captain Jim always buys what wheat and oats I don't use."

"I'd like to unhook Jake and keep him in the barn if that's okay. I'm going to do some scouting first. Where is the sheep pen that he has been raiding?"

"It's out behind the barn." Morse left Kirby to his work.

After taking care of Jake, Kirby loaded his new rifle and went out back to the sheep pen. He found a gob of hair on the barbed-wire fencing and huge tracks inside the pen. Kirby couldn't understand why Morse didn't lock the sheep up in the barn at night since he was having bear trouble.

There was a clear trail the bear had been using coming and going from the pen. He walked about five feet beside it, so not to leave his scent in the bear's trail. He had only gone a short way from the pen, maybe two hundred feet or so, when he found the remains of the small lamb from last night. There wasn't much, some lumps of hair and one little hoof. As brazen as this bear seemed to be, he would probably be back again tonight. He had seen enough for now. He went to find Morse.

He was inside sitting at the kitchen table drinking coffee. "Come in young fella. What did you find?"

"The bear is using the same trail each time he comes and goes. What time does he come in?"

"Once between nine and ten at night and the others after midnight."

"I'll need some small twine, maybe fish line if you have any."

"I have a fly rod, but I don't get much time to go fishing anymore. You're welcome to use it. But why?"

"I want to set up an alarm clock. Where is the fly rod?"

"In the barn. Why don't you plan to take supper with the Mrs. and me."

"I was counting on it. I haven't eaten since early this morning. I'll get the fly line and I'll be back in an hour or so."

Kirby found the bamboo fly rod and stripped the line out. This is just what he needed. He needed a tin can and that was easy to find.

He went back where the bear had eaten the lamb and dropped down the trail another 100 feet. He tied a stick to the fish line and threw the stick across the trail and through the notch in a small beech sapling about two feet off the ground and then threaded the line through more branches on his side of the trail about a foot off the ground and walked back up the trail until he came to the end of the line. Then he tied that end to the can and set the can up right on the ground and put a couple of stones inside. Hoping the stones would rattle around only briefly, enough to alert him, and fall out, so not to make too much noise and scare the bear. He would have to wait until later before deciding where he was going to wait. It would depend on wind direction.

Everything was all set now, so he went back to the house and had coffee with Morse until supper was ready. "What time will you take up your position along the trail Kirby?" Morse asked.

"Just before dark. This seems like some hard country to farm."

"The hard part was making a suitable road up here. The ground is fertile and crops do well. I lumber some, because what crops I grow and sell isn't enough to live on. There were a few nice pine but mostly I cut spruce. I built a loading ramp down on the level and it's an easy twitch for the horse from up here. On a good day I can usually work up two spruce trees and get them down to the ramp. When there's too much snow, I have to stop for the season."

With supper over, Morse and Kirby sat outside with coffee. "I'll need to drink more of this, so I don't fall asleep."

Morse wanted to ask Kirby to tell him about the war. But he had a feeling Kirby didn't want to talk about it. He guessed he could accept that.

The sun was disappearing fast, even at this high elevation. Kirby said goodnight and hiked down to the trail with this rifle loaded and ready. Before leaving the clearing he checked the wind direction. It was coming from the west and only a slight breeze. He would have to position on the east or right side of the trail. He found a spot where he had a clear view of the trail ahead and where he could lean up against a maple tree.

The moon was almost full last night, as he and Rachel laid on their backs watching the stars. But as he remembered, the moon didn't come out until a couple of hours after dark. He hoped tonight the ole bugger wouldn't come hunting until the moon was out.

He knew from experience on his father's farm, once a bear developed a taste for sheep or pig, there was no way to discourage him without having to kill it. Kirby settled down for a long wait. The night air was cool but not cold. At least there were no bugs. He wanted to dream about Rachel, but if he allowed his mind to wander there, he knew he wouldn't be paying attention to the task at hand. And a bear this big wouldn't hesitate about killing and eating a man, especially one who was trying to kill it.

His heart was beating fast with the anticipation. If the bear were to come up the trail now, he would never see it. It was so dark, he couldn't make out the trail. He hoped to God that the bear would wait until the moon was out.

A fox was barking off in the distance down over the height of land and a screech owl was making an awful racket. A mouse scurried up to Kirby and started squeaking.

Then all of a sudden everything went silent. There wasn't a sound anywhere, even the slight breeze had stopped. It was eerily quiet. But he could now see shadows, so the moon must be coming out. The mouse was still sitting by Kirby's left leg, looking up at him.

All of a sudden there was a noise, coming far down over the hill. It was loud, whatever it was. Maybe the bear had broken a dead fall, or perhaps a dead tree had fallen. But it sharpened Kirby's senses. His heart was once again beating faster. He looked down and the mouse was still there.

There was another noise and the mouse turned in the direction from where it came. To Kirby it sounded similar to a yawn. He waited and so did the mouse, nervously. A half hour passed and another sound, much like the first noise. Almost like a tree had fallen. Kirby knew it must be the bear, coming towards him.

He could hear more sounds, steady sounds, like something walking. The mouse was paying attention also. Kirby checked his rifle; the yawning type noise, only closer this time. The mouse burrowed under Kirby's leg. He wanted to laugh, but he knew the bear was close. He could hear him blowing air out through his nose. He knew bear do this to clear olfactory sensors of old scents, and then the bear breathes in again through the nose to detect any new scents.

The bear was clicking his teeth together. He knew there was danger up ahead. Kirby remained motionless, rifle to his shoulder. The noises were coming closer and Kirby could see movement, but no profile. The last thing he wanted was to only wound the bear.

He listened, the bear had stopped. Probably sniffing the air. Then the bear made a deep throated roar. Not loud, but Kirby knew the bear knew where he was. The bear started scuffing the ground with its front paws. The bear wasn't happy. He started coming up the trail again, head low to the ground, smelling Kirby's scent as he moved along silently.

Kirby could see him now. The bear was looking right at him, no more than twelve feet away. He pulled the hammer back, taking the rifle off safety. The bear heard the click and made a blood curdling roar while looking directly at Kirby. He pulled the trigger and the rifle roared louder than the bear, and the flame momentarily illuminated the bear. In that moment, Kirby could see how enormous the bear was. He was sure he had hit it, but the bear roared again and stood up on its hind legs, still roaring and walking towards Kirby. He fired again at the bear's chest and he didn't even flinch. He fired again and the bear roared louder, in anguish this time. But it kept coming. Kirby fired again and then again.

The bear finally fell to the ground. He was clawing at the ground trying to stand. He was only six feet away from his target, but he couldn't stand and he gave up and drifted off into that eternal sleep. Kirby didn't move. He stayed where he was for half an hour. The rifle to his shoulder and ready to fire.

In the moonlight, he could see a misty vapor rising from the bear into the cooler air. Finally he decided it was safe to approach the bear. He stood up and taking one step at a time, rifle ready to shoot again. The bugger's head was resting flat on the ground and the eyes were closed. It was a huge brute. To save the fat for Ruth he would have to dress it here and prop the rib cage open. He couldn't do it in the moon light so he hiked back to the barn for a lantern.

Morse was standing in the walkway from the house with a lantern. "Heard you shoot. Did you get that son of a bitch?"

"Yes, I need your help to roll it over on its back while I clean out the innards. He's too big for me to handle it alone in the dark," Kirby said.

"Sure thing. You're sure he's dead?"

"He's dead alright."

It took all that the two men could do to roll the bear over on its back. Morse held onto the front legs and held them apart while Kirby slit the hide and pulled out all of the viscera. It was a bloody job. Once he was done he found a dead stick to prop open the ribcage.

"You sure seem to know what you're doing young fella. This will be worth the $20."

"$30 Mr. Howard."

"Oh, yeah. I did say $30 didn't I. What are you going to do now?"

"I'm going to sleep in your barn after I wash up. Then in the morning I'll bring Jake down here and drag it back up where I can load it into my wagon. Mrs. Brown wants the fat for lard."

They walked up to the walkway and Morse handed Kirby the lantern.

*   *   *   *

Jake wasn't liking this ordeal at all. He could smell blood and worst of all he could smell bear. Kirby was finally able to get him to stand long enough so he could tie him to a tree while he tied a rope around the bear's neck and then to Jake's harness.

He had backed the wagon up to a loading ramp at the barn and in no time the bear was in the wagon and he was on his way home. Morse handed him $30 when the bear was in the wagon. "Thank you Mr. Howard."

The sky was looking like rain so he made Jake move right along. That was alright with Jake, too, because he could still smell the bear and to him he must have thought it was following.

When Kirby pulled to a stop in the Brown's yard, Rachel came running out. Not to see the bear; she ran by without looking. She ran right up to Kirby and hugged him, "I missed you Kirby," she whispered in his ear.

Everyone else was at the wagon looking at the bear. "That is a big brute," George said. "Jim, do you still have that set of scales? We should weight it."

"It would be interesting to know. The scales are in the tack room."

Kirby drove the wagon into the barn and Jim and Ronki-Tonk hooked up the scaffolding scales. When the scales were hooked up, Kirby took Jake by the halter and led him forward enough so the bear was free of the wagon.

George was watching the scales as Jim and Ronki-Tonk hoisted the bear up. "631 pounds." Jim tied the rope off, so he could see.

"That's the biggest bear I have ever heard of being taken. Well Kirby, Ruth wants that fat soon so she can start rendering it to lard."

After Kirby had taken care of Jake he skun the bear and put the hide aside while he stripped off the fat. Rachel had a big kettle for the fat. "This hide will make a nice rug for the floor." They worked together nailing it onto the back of the barn. They stretched it tight as it was nailed to the barn.

Rachel reached into a pouch and brought out two flint scrapers. "Now I'll show you how to clean all the sinew off."

"How has your shoulder been, since I used my ointment on it?"

"It is much better. I just need to tone up the muscle tissue."

Kirby looked at one piece of flint. It had an edge sharper than his knife. He watched Rachel and did the same. The fatty sinew came off surprisingly easy. "Once it is clean of fat, we'll stretch again and then every day until it won't stretch anymore. And every day we rub the hide with hemlock bark. The oil in the bark will soften the ride and help to preserve it. Once it is done, it'll make a nice rug for a floor."

"You need travel clothes Kirby. Like mine. You shoot me two nice big bucks and I'll make you clothes." That evening he and Rachel went for a walk out back and he took his new Winchester.

"Where are you two off to?" Jim asked.

"Rachel said she would make me some traveling clothes, if I would get her two bucks."

"Good idea. We are getting low on meat. And we need to start canning for the lumber camps this winter, too."

The wheat and oats were growing good in spite of the dry weather this summer and there were already deer feeding on the clover that was growing between the rows. The deer didn't seem to be at all alarmed. Kirby and Rachel went into the trees at the edge of the field and started to sneak along, to close the range. There was one larger deer standing off by itself. This had to be a buck, so Kirby took a fine bead just behind the head and squeezed the trigger. The deer fell and the others ran off, but didn't leave the field.

That night before going to bed they removed the hide and nailed it to the side of the barn and scraped it clean of sinew and meat. The next day Ruth and Rachel canned all but enough for supper. Some fresh venison steak with eggs in the morning would be a good breakfast.

Kirby was busy during the day in the hay fields. Half of the fields were already cut and in the barn. The next evening Rachel and Kirby went out after the second deer and just like before they found one lone deer and shot it.

*   *   *   *

When the deer hides were finally cured Rachel started making Kirby his traveling clothes. When she had finished he tried them on and was surprised how comfortable they were.

They didn't have much time to be alone. There was always so much work that had to be done. And now other farmers were complaining about bear raiding their sheep and pig pens. The summer was dry and the berries were few and those few were poor, so the bear made up for the lack of natural foods with lamb and pork.

That first summer at Grafton, Kirby shot six nuisance bears and trapped two others. The money he earned from the bear and their bounty he set aside in a little box in one of his burrow drawers. Rachel also was setting aside as much money as she could.

"The town of Upton has invited everyone from Grafton to the 4th of July celebration this weekend at the Lake House. We'll take the big carriage up, that way we can all ride together. Ronki-Tonk and I will sit up front and that'll give everyone enough room."

They left right after breakfast and Rachel and Kirby both were dressed in what she called their deer skin traveling clothes. They were a pretty couple and everyone wanted to meet Major Morgan. They had heard so much about him. Rachel stayed by his side even when others would try to lure him away for some reason or other.

Not everyone in Grafton was there, but there were many and most of the local people were there, as well as a few fishermen from New York. Toward late morning Rachel excused herself from Jim and Kirby who were talking with Enoch Abbott, she had to go to the bathroom.

On her way back, three of the New York fishermen accosted Rachel and were making a nuisance of themselves and upsetting her.

Kirby saw what was happening and left Jim and Enoch and went to Rachel's aid. Enoch started to follow Kirby. He felt a little responsible since the fishermen were his guests. Jim stopped him and said, "No Enoch, wait. Kirby has to do this himself. I have a good feeling about him." The two stayed where they were and watched.

The three fishermen saw Kirby coming towards them and the fact that he was dressed as Rachel was attired, didn't seem to register with any of them.

"Are these three bothering you Rachel?" More of a statement than a question and he never stopped looking at them.

The tall one said, "This your woman mister?"

"Yes, Rachel is my woman. And you three need to apologize to her."

"The hell we will mister." They obviously had been drinking.

The same guy pulled his right fist back to strike Kirby in the face. When he threw his punch, Kirby caught his fist in his hand and began to squeeze. "This isn't the place for a fight. Now you need to apologize." And he started to squeeze the man's hand harder and harder.

The man was on his knees before he apologized and then Kirby released his grip. "Now you two apologize also." They did. They didn't want to ruffle Kirby or his woman any further. "Now, you three leave this celebration and don't come back." They left and didn't look back.

"Those jackasses, I really wanted to hurt them."
Rachel put her arm around Kirby's and all was
forgotten.

Enoch and Jim walked over then, "I'm sorry
about that Rachel. I hope you were not embarrassed."

"I'm fine really," she said.

Jim left to find Ruth. "They were fishing the
other day near Metallak Point and had been drinking so
much they capsized their boat. I should have kicked
them out of here then."

"Why is that Metallak Point?" Kirby asked.

"Walk with me, both of you." They walked
down to the shoreline of Umbagog Lake. "Metallak or
Matelok was probably the greatest Indian that has ever
lived. He was an enigma certainly. You must have told
Kirby about him haven't you?"

"Some, yes."

"He, or his tribe, owned all the land to the north
and west of here. He was ahead of his time and saw the
importance of staying on friendly terms with the white
settlers. He deeded off huge parcels of land, but always
with the understanding that the portion in and around
Indian Stream to Parmachenee would always be land
for his people. He was educated and learned to survey.
Once he made a trip out to Andover for a doctor for one
of our residents, in the winter. When anyone was low
on food, he would kill a moose and divvy up the meat.
He built a cabin on that island," and Enoch pointed to
the island. "He saved three men in a snowstorm once
who were coming down the lake in a blizzard and he
went out after them and brought them to his cabin."

"He was a friend to everyone here. And one in
particular. Daniel Bean. Daniel moved here after
selling his farm in Bethel. Daniel and his wife
Margaret lived up the shore that way. Any time

Matelok was passing through, he would stop and visit Daniel and no matter how cold it was, they would sit out on the porch looking up the lake and sip whiskey.

"When Daniel died in 1833, Matelok took his death real hard. He was never the same after that. He always believed that Daniel's death foretold his own death coming soon.

"Daniel was a cabinet maker and he made a lot of the cabinets here abouts.

"Matelok was tall with broad shoulders and the kindest person I have ever met. It was s terrible shame to lose your eyesight like he did."

"How did it happen?" Rachel asked.

"He went out back of his cabin and tripped on a stub and fell on another, putting his eye out. Soon after, he lost the other eye also. He tried to stay in his cabin, but when his daughter Parmachenee who was living near St. Francis, Canada, learned about her father's accident, she came down and took him to Steward's Town, New Hampshire, where he died later in 1847.

"I can hear Mrs. Abbott calling for me. Maybe I should go back. You two can stay here and enjoy the view."

They sat on the shore under a tall pine tree. He put his arm around Rachel and she snuggled as close as she could. They were never lacking for something to talk about. It seemed they were always talking and laughing about something.

Jim and Ruth stood back and watched Kirby and Rachel next to the water. A smile crossed Jim's face, "What was that all about Jim?"

"I was just thinking about the two of them," and he nodded his head towards Kirby and Rachel. "As sad as it sounds, it took the death of our son to bring these two people together, from two completely different worlds. Maybe Ruth, Alvin didn't die in vain after all. He completed his task in the war; whatever that was and in his dying he brought these two people together."

"I don't believe in coincidences either Jim. Kirby will never replace the loss I feel about Alvin, but he has certainly brought a new sense of life to our family."

"Come, we should get everybody together and start back. I want to be home before dark."

Enoch and his wife walked with the Browns back to their carriage. "Where is Ronki-Tonk anyhow?" Ruth asked.

"The last I saw of him he was talking with some men by the mill. I'll go look for him."

"Thank you both for inviting us. This was a nice turn out," Ruth said.

"We don't get to see much of the people in Grafton. It was good you could join us today," Mrs. Abbott said.

After a while Kirby came back with Ronki-Tonk. "He was drinking with some friends of his and I think I'd better drive the team home." Rachel, of course, sat next to him and Jim rode in comfort next to Ruth. Ronki-Tonk was already asleep.

Chapter 2

The end of August was nearing and the hay,
wheat and oats crops were all in. The wheat was being
ground in the grist mill and the oats were in storage.
The potato bugs had not found the crops in Grafton yet
and the tops would have to be killed soon before the
potatoes could be harvested.

Both Rachel and Kirby, along with everyone
else, had been working from sun up to sunset every day.
Jim had to count on enough feed for about one hundred
horses, once all the winter crews arrived in October.
He had butchered a cow and pig. Some of the beef was
smoked along with the hams and bacon and the rest of
the beef was canned.

Kirby had thinned out the bear problems and it
was looking like everyone could have a break from
work for a week or so. It was late Saturday afternoon
and Rachel asked, "Kirby, lets put some food together
and eat out in the meadow and spend the night."

Kirby grinned and then Rachel did, too. "That sounds like a wonderful idea. And we'll have tomorrow for ourselves, also."

There were never as many people around for supper on Saturday as weekdays, as most of the crews would be on their way to their own homes, since no one worked in Grafton on Sunday.

While Rachel was packing the food and blankets, Kirby harnessed Jake to the wagon. Ronki-Tonk came over to help Kirby, "Where you and the 'Wolverine Lady' off to so late?" He'd been at the vanilla extract, by the sweet odor of his breath.

Kirby let the remark slide and said instead, "Thanks for your help Ronki-Tonk."

Rachel was waiting on the porch when Kirby drove around to the front, "You ready?" he asked.

"I've been ready all week." Kirby knew what she meant and they laughed.

Kirby built a small fire where it was wet while Rachel unpacked the basket. "What did you bring? I'm hungry."

"Sandwiches."

"What?"

"And for dessert, more sandwiches."

Kirby wasn't laughing. While he was stewing over sandwiches, Rachel went and cut two sapling bushes with a fork or 'Y' at the top of the branch. "Here," she handed one to Kirby. She then buttered both sides of his sandwich. "Put this on the forked branch and roast it over the coals." She did the same with her sandwich.

The sandwich was made up of scraps of beef from canning and laced with strips of smoke cured bacon. "This is really good. I have to apologize for ever doubting you."

For dessert she did the same except now the inside was filled with sweetened venison mincemeat. Cooked between two buttered pieces of bread, it became a poor man's pie. And washed down with fresh squeezed apple cider.

When they had finished eating Rachel took care of the basket and what was left for food, Kirby spread the blankets over a thick carpet of moss. The summer had been so dry the mosquitoes had not been a problem.

Kirby sat down on the blankets and brought his knees up so Rachel could sit between his legs. He wrapped his arms around her, burying his face in her hair. "You know Rachel, it seems like we have known each other all of our lives. I never dreamed I could be this happy or love someone this much." There, it was said before he knew what he was saying.

She turned around to face him and interlocked her legs around his waist. "It took you longer enough to say so." They were both smiling and laughing at the same time while trying to kiss.

"I knew I was in love with you that night you stayed out all night thinking."

"I think I realized I was in love with you Rachel on the trip to Bethel. Before that night, when we made love together. Sitting on the wagon seat beside me, I could feel your warmth and goodness and I didn't ever want to be without that feeling."

He took her face in his hands and looking in each other's eyes, he winked and she broke out laughing. When she had composed herself he asked, "Will you marry me Rachel?"

Tears went streaming down her face and she tried to say yes, but nothing would come out. She hugged him and kissed him so ardently, they both had to stop and surface for air. Finally her voice came back and she said, "I love you Kirby and I want to be your wife."

"I don't know how this is said in English. There is no word for it in my people's language. How do you say --- ah --- when you have this want, or desire to make love, like I have felt all week about you. I was --- what? I don't know the words."

Kirby laughed softly, not wanting to hurt her feelings. "Well when I feel like I really want to make love to you really bad, it's because I'm horny."

"Horny? I don't know this word. But it means when I have this desire really bad, to jump your bone? Is that what horny means?"

Kirby cupped her face with his hands and smiling he said, "Yes that's what horny means."

Rachel was laughing now as she pushed him on his back and said, "I'm horny."

$$* \quad * \quad * \quad *$$

"We didn't expect you two back until later today. What's up?"

Kirby and Rachel walked arm in arm up to the porch and she went inside to find Ruth. She was in the kitchen and the two women came out to the porch. Ruth sat down beside Jim.

"We have something we would like to tell you." Everyone remained quiet.

"We are going to get marry."

Ruth was all tears as she jumped up to hug them both. "Well when is this going to happen?" she asked.

"If it is alright, two weeks from today," Kirby said. "Work has slowed some and we would like to leave early this year --- Rachel wants to take me back to her people. Then we'll be back after however long it takes us. And for this winter we would really like to continue living here."

"I don't see any problem do you Ruth?" Jim asked.

They missed church services at the tavern. There were too many plans to be made. "Kirby, Ruth and I, hell everyone in Grafton hopes you'll stay in Grafton. I know you're not the farmer type and I think you'd get board with lumbering, although you'd work as hard as anyone else. But I believe a man should always work at whatever he chooses because, one, he is good at what he is doing, and two, he is happy doing it. I don't think either one of you is destined to be only a farmer, lumbering, or cook. You both are destined for, probably more than Ruth and I can imagine. But wherever your destinies take you, we hope you'll stay in Grafton. And that's why we have decided to make you this offer."

Kirby and Rachel looked at each in complete surprise.

"A year ago I purchased forty acres of land south of the Chapman homestead. The land is no good for farming. I bought it because of the few pine trees that are on the side hill there. There is a very nice spot to build a house at the base of a thousand foot waterfalls. Ruth and I have talked this over days ago, -- we were going to make you the offer then. Well, now it is a wedding gift to you both. The forty acres.

"And here is the rest of the deal. You both can continue living here until you have your own house built and finished. This winter Kirby, you work here on the farm and the mill, sorting out the best pine and spruce logs. You'll be in charge of receiving the logs from the crews and piling them down for the spring drive. When there is sufficient water behind the dam, I run the sawmill. We'll saw out enough lumber for you this winter to build you a house come spring. I already have some pine and spruce that have dried for a year at the back of the log yard. You mark the ends of those for yourself and we'll set those aside. When you devise a way to cut those few tall pines on your land and get the logs to roadside and then the mill, this wood will pay for the lumber you use to build your house. And when you get ready to build, the whole town will pitch in. Instead of a barn raising, we'll have a house raising.

"Now, how does that sound?"

Kirby was dumbstruck, speechless. And Rachel began crying as she hugged first Ruth and then Jim. "I don't know what to say. You and Ruth have been so good to both of us."

"You're family damit," Ruth said in between tears.

"This seems too good to be true." Kirby was holding Rachel now. "You two are the only family we have."

Rachel wiped the tears from her eyes and asked, "Jim, will you give me away at the wedding?"

Jim stood up and walked over to Rachel and hugged her. "I would be honored to do so."

*   *   *   *

While Ruth was busy with the wedding plans and making sure every person in Grafton was invited, Kirby and Rachel were busy planning their trip to visit her people north of Parmachenee Lake, next to the Canadian border.

As a wedding gift for Kirby, Rachel had asked Ronki-Tonk to make her a double-end paddle, "like the one Falling Bear had made for me. Only a little longer

Ronki-Tonk, because Kirby's arms are longer than mine."

Ronki-Tonk turned her paddle over and over examining it. "I never see a paddle like this. I can make you."

"Can you have it finished in time for the wedding?"

"Yes ma'am, you can count on Ronki-Tonk."

"This will be your gift to us Ronki-Tonk," and she kissed his cheek. "No one must know."

One evening Kirby saddled Jake and took a quick ride to Upton to the canoe factory there near the saw mill. Rachel had a short birch bark canoe that was fine for one person, but they both decided they would need a larger canoe for two people and all the supplies they would be carrying.

"Hello Mr. Abbott," Kirby said.

"Call me Enoch please."

"Enoch, I need a canoe in eight days. Do you have anything already made?"

Everything Enoch showed him was too short and too narrow. "Tell me what you need for a canoe and I'll have the crew build it and I promise it'll be ready by September 2nd."

"Okay, twenty feet long, gundle forty inches in the middle. A seat in the bow and stern. I hate kneeling on my knees."

"Do you want a keel?"

"Yes. And are you sure you can have this ready by the second?"

"I can guarantee, it'll be done."

"How much? I'll pay you now."

"This is a special order you understand. How's $40 sound?"

Kirby counted out $40 and handed it to Enoch. "Rachel and I will be here to collect the canoe on September 2nd."

*   *   *   *

Saturday night before the wedding, a thunder storm rolled through the valley and dumped over an inch of rain. But the dry ground had absorbed the rain and the sun was clear in an indigo blue sky.

People were arriving early; they just wanted to socialize for a few minutes with each other. Kirby was not the least nervous, as he talked with friends of Grafton. He had not seen Rachel at all that morning --- due to Ruth's insistence. Rachel was as calm and collected as Kirby, only wanting the day over with, so they could be on their way to visit her people. Ruth on the other hand was all tears. She was so happy for both Kirby and Rachel.

No one wore fancy clothes. Probably no one had any since Grafton was a pioneering lumbering town. Kirby and Rachel wore their deer skin traveling clothes Rachel had made and as they stood in front of Preacher McBride, they were a splendid looking couple. They looked like they belonged to each other. Rachel had attended weddings in her people's village and this white settler's ceremony was surprisingly new to her.

Finally the preacher announced, "I pronounce you man and wife. Kirby, now you may kiss your bride." They kissed for a long few moments.

The reception was short. There were sandwiches, coffee, and apple cider to eat. For wedding gifts most people brought canned goods or something that they had knitted or sewn. Everything was appreciated and Ruth said, "Don't worry about all the gifts. We'll put them in your room. I assume you will be sharing Kirby's room after you return."

Rachel hugged Ruth and said, "Thank you Ruth for everything. And you too Captain Jim," and she smiled as she kissed him also.

*   *   *   *

They waved goodbye to everyone as they left the Poplar Tavern and instead of turning to the right onto the main road, Rachel said, "Let's take the Back Street." When they came to the fork in the road, she pointed to the left and then Kirby knew what she had in mind. "I wanted to spend the first night as Mrs. Kirby Morgan alone with my husband under the stars."

Rachel gave the blankets to Kirby and said, "You make the bed. I'll be right there." She had hidden the double-ended paddle in the bottom of the wagon.

Kirby was laying on the blanket with his clothes already off. "A little eager aren't you?" she said smiling and holding out the paddle. "This gift is from me. Ronki-Tonk did most of the work."

"I have never seen one like it before. It must work really well."

"It does. I have one, too, stored with my canoe at Upton. Falling Bear gave it to me when I left. Do you like it?"

"Yes, of course. I can't wait to try it out."

He set the paddle against the tree and said, "I have something for you, too. I found this beautiful green stone (green tourmaline) back in June when I was working in one of the back fields. I've been trying to make a hole through one end to make a necklace for you. I didn't finish it until last night. Whatever the stone is, it sure is hard. I didn't think I'd ever get a hole through it. I put it on this piece of rawhide."

"Oh Kirby, it's so beautiful. How did you put the two ends of the rawhide together? There is no knot."

"I split both ends and made three thin strands and braided the ends together."

She put it on over her head and it was just the right shade to go with her attire. "I'll never take this off. My people --- when they become coupled they don't wear gold rings like this," and she held out her hand. "It's beautiful, too, but where --- how did you get them?"

"A month ago Jim sent me to Warren Douglas' store in Upton for a few things and Mr. Douglas was showing me these rings he had sent up from Portland. He said that with all the unmarried folks around, the young folks would be needing some rings."

"And you were planning this way back then and you didn't say anything?"

"Well, everyone was so busy with summer's end work, we couldn't very well expect everyone to stop for us," he explained.

"Oh, Kirby I'm just so happy."

Kirby kindled a fire and Rachel prepared something to eat. Afterwards they lay on the blanket, talking about the future and then the conversation changed to the trip they would start tomorrow. Kirby was as excited about the trip as Rachel.

"Falling Bear told me once that his real Indian name was Ogawinno, which means bear. But as a small boy he kept falling down a lot, so everyone started calling him Falling Bear."

They were quiet, as they laid on the blankets and watching the stars in the sky. Rachel pointed to the Milky Way and said, "We call that band of stars there 'Ketaguswawt.'"

"We call it the Milky Way."

The northern lights were beginning to dance in the northern sky, making beautiful swirling shades of greens, yellows and a pale blue. "Wababan," Rachel said.

"What?"

She pointed to the lights in the sky and said, "Wababan."

"Northern Lights."

"Northern Lights," Rachel repeated. "Who makes such pretty lights."

"I really don't know Rachel. And I don't know if any one does."

"My people always said that the lights were caused when Kchi Niwaskw was playing with the stars." Rachel saw the puzzled look on Kirby's face and explained. Kchi Niwaskw is the Great Creator. The Christian teachings say God. I prefer Great Creator. The name sounds more befitting for one who created everything." Kirby laughed and understood her point of view.

A shooting star made a long trail across the sky. "What is that husband. My people have no words for that."

Kirby tried to explain that it was the last remnants of a dying star. "A shooting star." That sometimes small chunks of star strike the earth and look like any other rock. Rachel wasn't understanding any of this. "If you say so husband."

Eventually they drifted off to sleep wrapped in the glory, warmth, and security of each other.

*   *   *   *

They were up at first light and soon on their way to Upton. From there the Back Street route would be shorter. Rachel had pulled on the wolverine pelt over her shoulders. Her entire outfit was quite striking. "Can we stop at Douglas' store first? He will have everything that I need to take."

"Good morning Mr. Douglas. My wife has a list we need to pick up." As Mr. Douglas was helping Rachel with her list, Kirby wandered around the store. He was surprised to see that Warren had such a variety. He bought a green felt wide brimmed hat for himself and one for Rachel. It certainly fit her attire.

"I hope we can put everything in your new canoe. I hope it is big enough."

"So do I," Kirby said.

They drove off the hill down Mill Street to the canoe shop. "Good morning Mr. and Mrs. Morgan. Your canoe is ready, just like I promised." It was on racks sitting in front of the shop.

Kirby and Rachel both walked around it and admiring the workmanship. "Do you need paddles?" Enoch asked.

"No, we're all set there. But we do need an anchor. I forgot to bring one."

"Sure thing we sell those also. I'll throw it in for a wedding gift."

"Thank you," Rachel said.

"Where are you going to put in this time Rachel?" Enoch asked.

"Right here I suppose. If we could leave the horse and wagon."

"With all that gear you are carrying, there is a shorter and better way. You follow this road out to the Lower Dam. It's the outlet of Pond in the River. After crossing the bridge, you go a short distance and you come to a split in the road. Take the left, that's the Carry Road. This will take you to the Magalloway Trail which will take you to Magalloway, right to the Magalloway River. That route will save you a day's paddling, especially if Umbagog is rough."

"Where would we leave the horse and wagon?" Kirby asked.

"When you get there ask for Captain Wilson. Captain is a nice fellow and he'll let you pasture your horse and leave your wagon there. He might charge a small fee ---course that's his road you'd be using."

Kirby and Rachel loaded the canoe in the wagon and tied it off.

*   *   *   *

It was about 11 a.m. when they arrived at Wilson's landing in Magalloway. Captain Wilson was there. "No charge for the wagon, and you can leave your harness in the shed. For the horse I get 50¢ a week."

Kirby paid for two weeks up front and by noon they had the canoe loaded and were on their way up the Magalloway River. "We should be able to reach Aziscohos Falls before dark. If not we'll make camp on the Magalloway."

"I can't believe how well this new paddle works. When we are in sync, look how fast we can travel, even loaded as we are," Kirby marveled.

"I thought you'd like it."

"Where did Falling Bear get the idea for this?"

"He said he watched my father make one when he was on the Ohio River." There was a long silence. Rachel had been expecting this. She wanted to say something earlier, but the timing never seemed to be right.

"I had assumed that Falling Bear was your father."

"No Kirby, Falling Bear was not my father. My father's name was Emile La Montagne. And Kirby," he stopped paddling, "Kirby --- I'm not an Indian either. I'm French Canadian by birth. But due to some circumstances, I was brought up by Falling Bear's tribe since I was about six years old."

"Why haven't you said anything before now?"

"I wanted to, but there never seemed to be the right time. Are you upset Kirby?"

"No, surprised yes."

"Does it make any difference between us?"

"Certainly not. You are my wife and I love you."

"Good. Then we won't speak of this again until we make camp tonight. There is much to tell you."

They paddled along in silence for a while. "I have never seen such beautiful country. This Magalloway River is fantastic. The only problem is, it's like ribbon candy. There are so many bends and bows. Sometimes it seems as if we double back on our own backwater."

They saw huge numbers of beaver, otter, mink, sable and one lone huge bear. When he saw the canoe, the bear turned around and ran off. Kirby was hoping to see deer or moose. Preferably a small deer, that they could roast for supper and take some with them for the next day.

Rachel must have been reading his thoughts as she said, "I never see any moose until we get up near the falls and there are few deer along here. Even fewer above the outlet at Parmachenee Lake. There are a few but not like Grafton. I think maybe there are more caribou than deer."

"What did you bring for supplies for your people? I never looked in any of the packages."

"Blankets, mittens, two heavy winter jackets, coffee, sugar and salt. I'd like to bring more, but that's all I could get with the money that I got for the pelts I brought back on the spring trip."

The nice thing about this trip, they had the river to themselves. There was no evidence that there was another soul around. That is until they would canoe through Wilson Mills. Before they reached the Mills, the river was winding through marshy wet land. The shoreline was covered with lily pads.

Rachel stopped paddling. "Take us in close to those lily pads."

"Okay, why?" Kirby asked.

"You see all of those huge frogs?"

"Yeah."

"That's supper tonight." As they came along close to a frog, she would hit it with the end of her paddle and then retrieve it and put t in the bottom of the canoe. She had about 24 before she said, "I think that's enough."

"You're sure about his, huh?"

She grinned back at Kirby and said, "You'll see."

"I don't like to stop at the Mills, so we'll go through and make camp before we reach the Falls."

"Sounds okay to me. I'm hungry and getting tired."

*   *   *   *

Rachel found the campsite she had used on previous trips. Again it was nestled under a canopy of tall spruce and fir trees, with thick moss to sleep on. After the canoe was secured and they had what they would need of the supplies, Rachel said, "I'm going to go find some food to go with the frog legs. You can clean the frogs."

When Rachel returned from foraging in the forest, Kirby had a fire going and the frog legs were cleaned. "What did you find for edibles?"

"I found a large bear's head tooth mushroom on a rotting beechnut tree, and some others I don't know the names of."

"How do you know they aren't poisonous?"

"You can eat any mushroom that grows on wood. Some may not taste so good, but they won't hurt you. I've been picking wild mushrooms since I came to live with Falling Bear's people." Kirby noticed this was the first time she had not said 'my people'. Instead she had said 'Falling Bear's people'.

"I found some wild onions, also."

Rachel put the frog legs in a fry pan along with the mushrooms and onions and set the pan on the fire to simmer. While supper was cooking she sat between Kirby's legs watching the river. They sat there like that for several minutes before speaking. They were simply enjoying being there with each other.

"I must tend to the cooking," Rachel got up and checked the frog legs and mushrooms.

"Hey, these are all cooked. Sorry, all we have to drink is coffee or water," she said laughing.

"Well, maybe I'll have water."

Everything was smelling delicious, but he was still skeptical about eating frogs, even if the meat was so pure white. "Go on, try the frog," Rachel said. She had already eaten two.

Kirby nibbled on one and then another, "My God!" he said. "I never imagined these could be this good." Rachel only smiled at her husband; happy that she had pleased him.

The mushrooms and wild onions were almost as good. When they had finished there was nothing left in the fry pan. While Rachel cleaned up the (kitchen), Kirby went after more wood. There was a chill in the air and he didn't want to have to get up during the night to look for more. When she had finished, she helped with the wood.

"That should be plenty." Rachel was heating some water so they could wash up before going to sleep. Afterwards Kirby sat down and leaned back against a spruce tree and Rachel laid between his legs and rested her head against his chest. "You said earlier that you were not Indian. But --- but you look so much like you were. I mean the tan of your skin."

Rachel began laughing then and she was sometime before she could stop. "I came to live with Falling Bear's people when I was about six. I was a little white girl. All the other children use to tease me because I was so pale. I wanted to be accepted because I had no family. I was tired of being teased and picked on. I tried to gain Falling Bear's favor. I remember back home near Cincinnati, the same tree that you call Balm of Gilead, how sweet it smelled in the spring. So I would pick a bouquet of branches and put them in our hut. This tree smelled so nice I tried to make the perfume from the sticky stuff on the leaves. I boiled the leaves in water until I had an oily substance. It really smelled good. Well, being a little girl, I put some on my arm, so I would smell good." She began laughing again. Finally she was able to continue. "My skin turned brown where I had put the perfume. It wouldn't wash off either. So I decided to become like everyone. I covered my skin, everywhere, with this and soon I was as brown as everyone. From then on when we girls went swimming and I removed my clothes I no longer had any pale skin. Everyone stopped teasing me.

"I spread this on my skin several times that summer and some how I think it really changed the color of my skin. Now I am always brown. I have been brown like this all of my life, or most of it."

She turned to face Kirby and he was smiling so radiantly she knew that no matter what she told him about her and her life, would not matter to him.

"I am amazed," he said, "at you. A young girl wanting so badly to belong. I love you Rachel."

"You said earlier that you were French Canadian, how did your family end up near Cincinnati, Ohio?"

"When my father left mother, (her name was Celest), we used to sit on the porch of the house for hours at a time and she would tell me all about my father. Because I don't think she ever really expected him to return. Before my mother and father met in Montreal, my father had gone north to winter out and trap. He had a friend with him. I don't remember his name. They stayed for two winters and had many animal pelts of all kinds and they found gold. And I guess a lot of it. This is where Val d'Ore is today.

"My father survived to return to his family but his friend did not. My father was a rich man. When he left mother and me, he knew there was enough money he had left behind to always take care of us.

"My mother said that my father Emile was a great man and it was this greatness that made him leave us behind while he went exploring out west. Mother said that he had promised to return in two years. But he never did. I still don't know what ever happened to him. I don't want to believe that he abandoned mother and me. She knew there was something inside of him," and Rachel put her hand flat on her chest, "that was stirring, keeping him from being happy. Mother said she had to let him go, so he could find his answers."

Rachel turned to look at Kirby. Her eyes full of tears. "I don't want you ever to leave me, like that my husband," and she cried against his chest.

"I will never leave you Rachel. I promise that where I go, you will always go with me. I promise."

He knew that was an ordeal for Rachel to tell him about her life. But somehow he knew it was good for her, and him too, to talk about it.

But maybe this was enough for now. They were both tired and tomorrow might be another long day.

*   *   *   *

When they crawled under the blankets that night Kirby held her in his arms and tenderly caressed her scalp and face with his fingers, as she snuggled close to him. This was enough. There was no need for either of them to have sex tonight. He was making love to her as she drifted off to sleep with his caresses.

They awoke with the sun and to a loon out front in the river, calling to them to get up. It was a lonely and lovely call. "This is good."

"What is?" Kirby asked.

"This loon. If a loon visits your camp, especially in the morning to greet you, it is a good omen." She kissed him and got up and put her clothes on.

There were enough coals in the fire so she put on a few sticks; they were soon blazing. "Are you going to get up?" she asked jokingly.

"I'm enjoying watching you work." He did get up though when Rachel didn't reply.

"Breakfast is coffee and before we left home, I made biscuits of corn meal, jam, and pork fat. This will stick to your ribs until we stop tonight at my special place. No one knows about this place, but me. I have built a small wickitup there."

"How far do we travel to this place?"

"It lies a short distance north of Parmachenee Lake. Today we travel mostly on open water; Azischohos and then the length of Parmachenee Lake. I hope the wind doesn't blow today."

"What did the loon tell you?" he asked.

"That this will be a good day."

As they were pushing off from shore Rachel asked, "How is your shoulder? I meant to ask last night but I forgot."

"It was a little stiff and sore last night, but it's okay now."

"Remind me tonight and I'll rub on some more of the ointment."

The September air was cool this morning, and mist was lifting from the water.

"I can hear water up ahead. Is that the falls?"

"Yes, it is still a few minutes away. We'll put ashore just before the falls and portage up to the dam. Fred Cyr provides a carry service back and forth from the dam. He does charge for his services though."

"That's fine with me. It'll be better than making several trips back and forth carrying all these supplies up hill."

The water current was stronger now and they both had to lean into their paddles. Up ahead Kirby could see a landing, with a crude looking dock jutting out into the river.

Kirby guided the canoe along side of the dock and Rachel climbed out and then held the canoe while Kirby got out. "No one is here. Is that his cabin there?" pointing to a small log cabin on a knoll.

"Yes, he must be at the dam end." Rachel walked over to a rope tied to a tree and pulled it twice and then she waited. She saw the puzzled look on Kirby's face and explained. "There is a bell attached to the other end of this rope at the dam end. I rang the bell twice to let Fred know someone wants to go up." Just then the bell on their end rang. "That means Fred heard the bell and will be here shortly."

"That's some system he has."

While they waited for Mr. Cyr, they unloaded the canoe and pulled that ashore. "I'm sure glad we didn't have to haul this up to the dam. It is heavy," Rachel exclaimed. "You could throw my little birch bark canoe over your shoulder and hike up without stopping."

They sat down waiting for Fred and they could hear the wagon creaking along the gravel path. "Hello," Fred hollered. "You're early this year. And who have you brought with you, you have always traveled alone."

"Well not any more Fred," she said, "this is my husband, Kirby Morgan."

"Hello Fred," they shook hands.

"Going up are you? There'll be 75¢ for both of you and all your gear. Up front, of course."

Kirby handed him a dollar, "I don't have change."

"Well, I'll apply it to your return trip."

"Done, now let's get all this stuff on board the wagon." Rachel rode on the seat with Fred and Kirby with the canoe.

*   *   *   *

The wind was blowing more now that they were above the dam and Kirby kept close to the western shore line where there was warm sunshine. It was a pleasant trip up the Mallagoway River. Rachel said, "Swing the canoe around and look at the scenery looking down the river."

With one strong back stroke, Kirby had the canoe pointing southerly downstream in the deadwater. Rachel was right. The view was extraordinary.

They picked their way in and around the many islands at the head of the deadwater and found the inlet from Parmachenee Lake. This stretch of the river was like the lower end of the Magalloway River, deep and calm water and in no time they emerged on to Parmachenee. The wind was blowing strong here also, so Kirby kept to the west shore and calmer water.

"That's a large island up ahead Kirby. We need to skirt around it on the right. There's better water there," Rachel said.

This meant crossing the tip of the lake with the west wind blowing at their side. The canoe was long and wide with two strong paddlers and they didn't have any trouble. They found the east inlet and started up that. The going was slower. "In the fall before the ice freezes hunters from the tribe will come down this river and canoe up the other branch. There they hunt moose and caribou. We are not far away now from my campsite. Watch for a dark narrow stream on the left. It'll almost be hidden with alder bushes."

A little further up the river and Kirby asked, "Is that it there?" and he pointed with his paddle.

"Yes."

"I see why no one has ever found your campsite before now. Not many people would think this was a stream. How did you find it?"

"It was storming and I needed shelter away from the lake. I discovered this little hidey-hole by accident. But just wait until we break clear of these bushes."

Ahead they could see spans of open calm water. There was no wind here. The little stream opened up into a small deep pond of crystal-like water. "You brought some fishing line I hope," Rachel said. "Or we do not eat tonight."

'I did."

"Do you see that little point of land over there? Behind it is a sand bar where we can drag the canoe up out of the water."

Kirby swung the canoe around the point and there was Rachel's wikitup. Set in amongst tall spruce trees and backed with cedar.

Rachel stepped out of the canoe and then Kirby. He inhaled deeply and smelled the fresh scent of spruce and cedar trees. "This is a beautiful spot Rachel."

"And the trout here are this big," and she held up her hands. They unloaded only what they would need. "We probably will need a fire inside tonight, so while you make one, I'll take the hide cap off the top, so the smoke will go up. Maybe leave the front flap open to air the inside out."

Kirby started a fire and put everything inside. "I need to wash up," and he removed his clothes and waded out into the water. Rachel took her clothes off also and joined him.

"God, this is cold."

Rachel sat down in the shallow water, scrubbing her skin with the fine sand that was on the bottom. Kirby wasn't interested in going any farther either, so he sat down beside her. His teeth were already beginning to chatter. They were not long cleaning themselves and then running for the fire inside of the wikitup. They stood inside and beside the fire, letting the warmth dry them.

When they were dry and clothes back on Rachel said, "We can catch all the fish we need right off this point."

Kirby dug out his line and hooks and made two alder fish poles. While Rachel looked for fat grubs in a rotten log. She found four.

They baited the hooks and threw the line out and sat on the bank to wait. Kirby had no more than sat down and he felt something take his bait and the tip of the alder branch dipped and almost hit the water. He jerked the pole to set the hook and the trout fought for its life. He stood up and back up slowly pulling the huge trout in over the bank. "Wow, this alone should feed both of us tonight."

Rachel's alder pole dipped and she set the hook like Kirby had done and she backed up pulling her trout in over the bank. Hers was about the same size. "We'll cook both of them tonight and eat one tonight and the other one in the morning."

Kirby cleaned both fish and threw the visceral into the water and a school of trout came up out of the depths to feed on it. He then filleted both fish.

Rachel put the fillets on a rack over the fire, to cook slowly.

"Are you warm now?"

"Yeah, I feel pretty good."

"Good. I'm horny," and then she laughed and Kirby did also.

Kirby started to guide her to the blankets spread on the ground, when Rachel said, "Wait a minute I forgot something. You wait here. I'll be right back." She went outside. She returned in a few minutes with one of the packages from the canoe.

"What have you there Rachel?"

She undid the paper and unfolded a bear rug. "This was one of the smaller bear you shot his summer. Ronki-Tonk helped me to nail it up and stretch it. I had to clean the hide myself. I didn't tell you because I wanted to surprise you."

Kirby pulled back the blankets and Rachel laid the rug down for a sleeping mate. "You're a remarkable woman Rachel Morgan. I love you," and then he took her in his arms and held her close and kissed her.

They laid down on the new bedding. "This bear rug sure makes it a lot softer. You're always thinking ahead Rachel." He held her face in his hands looking into her eyes, and literally seeing that special sparkle of life she had. He smiled and said, "I love you Rachel."

They kissed and his hand moved slowly down her back and between the cheeks of her butt. She squirmed and moaned with desire and anticipation.

With their love making finished and Rachel was no longer horny, they dressed and ate their supper of broiled trout on a stick.

The sun had set and the air was cool, much cooler than what it would have been back in Grafton.

Kirby went after more wood. "Husband, I need to talk some more. To tell you things about my life." They sat down on their bedding with their supplies as back rests. Rachel picked up the wolverine pelt and held it in her lap for a few moments before speaking. Kirby waited patiently.

"Falling Bear can not read the words he knows in English. When he gave me this fur, he said that it would always protect me in my travels. But he didn't explain why and I didn't think to ask. Neither did he explain where he had come by it, because you see this animal does not live around here. While on my travels away from the village one night I was looking this fur over and over. It is very beautiful and the fur is soft and like new. It doesn't change." She looked into Kirby's eyes and said, "My husband, I think this fur had belonged to my father, Emile La Montagne." She turned the fur over and showed Kirby something burned on the hide.

Kirby took the fur and held it closer to the firelight and then said, "This is your father's name?"

"Yes. Falling Bear must have seen this also, but not knowing the English words, it probably never meant anything to him."

"What do you think this means Rachel? Do you think Falling Bear may have killed your father and then taken his pelt?"

"I thought about that too. But it doesn't make any sense. You see, my father left us near Cincinnati to travel west. Falling Bear's people have always been in this corridor of the northeast. How could the two of them have ever met?"

"I don't know. But there has to be more of the story that Falling Bear could tell you."

"Maybe he is ready to talk," Rachel said.

"Rachel?" Kirby said questioningly.

"Yes."

"What about your mother Rachel? Celeste. You have said nothing about her."

There was a long silence then, as Rachel stared at the fire. Kirby thought that he might have hit upon some hurting memories. He waited for her to say something. If there was some hurt there, she needed to talk with him and let it out.

"I can only remember memories of my mother until I was about six. There are no memories after I came to live with The People." She was silent again and again staring at the fire.

Kirby was wondering if Falling Bear had killed her parents and Rachel had witnessed it and then had blocked the images from her memories. But if Emile had traveled west and did not return ---. He decided he didn't know any more than Rachel did. Only Falling Bear could give her answers.

He put his arm around her and said, "Come, it is time we were asleep. Before we start back we will talk with Falling Bear and get some answers."

She looked at him and kissed him and then they removed their clothes and crawled in between the blankets.

Chapter 3

Rachel had dreams all night about her mother, but when she awoke, they all seemed like a jumbled mess and she could not see any clear meaning. Kirby had lain awake most of the night with his arm around his wife, holding her close and wondering what had happened to her family and how she came to live with Falling Bear's people.

Sometimes during the night Rachel would stir and her skin would start to be clammy and she would moan unintelligible guttural sounds. Then he would tenderly caress her, to let her know she was not alone and that she would never be left behind again. He didn't care if he slept or not. His only concern was his wife and to comfort her.

He did finally fall asleep about two hours before dawn. And he awoke in the same position with his arm around Rachel at first light, to the lonely cry of a loon just off the point. He wished the loon would stop or move on so Rachel could sleep a little longer. But she had heard the call also and stirred and looked up at Kirby. "The loon says another good day."

"Would you give the loon a message for me? Ask him not to awaken us so early."

She laughed and said, "Come we must get up."

"We both forgot my shoulder last night."

"How is it this morning?"

"Okay, no stiffness or soreness. Maybe all I needed was some exercise to tighten the muscles."

After a breakfast of leftover broiled trout, they loaded the canoe. The bear rug was left there in the wikitup. Rachel put the top back on to keep the rain out and closed the flap.

"This is the most pristine spot of the whole trip Rachel."

They canoed out through the alder strewn stream channel back to the river and headed north. As they continued north, the river kept getting smaller and smaller until they were once again in alder bushes on both sides. "When we clear those alders the river widens again."

An eagle suddenly dove into the water just ahead of them and then flew up in a spiked top of a pine tree and carrying with it a huge brook trout.

The river was narrowing again but this time there were no alder bushes. "We are almost there Kirby." They had been a little less than two hours on the river. They could have made the village yesterday. But Kirby was glad they had had the night to themselves.

Kirby could see birch bark canoes up ahead that had been pulled ashore. He swung the canoe hard to the right and planted his paddle firm on the river bottom steadying the canoe while Rachel climbed out.

There were kids playing that noticed Rachel first and they started screeching out her name and soon the entire village was coming to the river to greet them. An older man and woman stood out on top of the slight rise, that formed back away from the river, they were older than anyone else, and Kirby decided this must be Falling Bear and his woman. Rachel had never spoken much about her or her name. They were helping each other down the incline. Falling Bear had a broad smile. The woman looked stern.

Rachel was just as excited about seeing everyone as the kids were about seeing her. Falling Bear was looking directly at Kirby, not with concern, but more with interest, who was traveling with Rachel?

Rachel came and took Kirby by the hand and led him up to meet Falling Bear. They stopped directly in front and Rachel said, "Hello Falling Bear and Pollinoke. This is my husband Kirby."

Polllinoke didn't say anything. Falling Bear looked at Kirby and smiled and said, "To be husband of Rachel, you must be strong in character. It has taken long time for Rachel to find a mate." He signaled for some of the young men to unload the canoe and bring everything to the lodge.

"What did you get us with the pelts this time Rachel."

"We will show you everything when we have eaten. We are hungry."

Kirby was a curiosity entity. The only other white man that most of them had seen would have been an occasional missionary from around St. Francis, Canada. And certainly they found his clothing a puzzlement. He was dressed like Rachel, but he was not one of The People.

Rachel unpacked the coffee supply and while Pollinoke prepared food, Rachel made some rather strong coffee. Kirby figured to drink his without sugar, seeing how Rachel had brought the sugar for the village.

"You come early this time," Falling Bear said.

"Yes, we were just married and I wanted my husband to meet Falling Bear's people."

"Tomorrow you marry him according to our tradition."

Rachel stood behind Kirby while he was seated and replied, "We will be happy to marry according to tradition, tomorrow." She whispered in Kirby's ear then. "This means we can not sleep together tonight."

"Where will I sleep?"

"Everyone sleeps in the one long lodge, but it is divided up according to families. You will have to sleep with one of the other families. Falling Bear will decide who, later."

Everybody in the village was gathered around them as Rachel unwrapped the supplies and handed each one to Falling Bear. He and he alone would decide who was to get what. The pipe tobacco, "I keep this." Everyone laughed, even Kirby. The two heavy winter coats were given to two older men who Falling Bear said did a lot of traveling in the winter scouting for moose and caribou. The food supplies were divided amongst the families equally.

Falling Bear stood up holding the tobacco he said, "Come," indicating Kirby and two of the older men to follow him. "We smoke and talk."

Kirby looked at Rachel and she nodded her head and then smiled. Kirby stood and followed the other three inside the long lodge to what Kirby assumed was Falling Bear's living quarters. The floor was carpeted with bear hide. That didn't surprise him. There was a rocked up fireplace in the center and a warming fire. He was surprised that there was no smoke inside. It was all going out the vent hole at the top. Falling Bear indicated that everybody should sit.

While the four men talked, and Rachel thought she knew what about. Every time Rachel had returned to the village Falling Bear wanted to know about the white settlements, how close were they coming. Rachel very happily visited with her old friends. All the other women, even younger than her years, had children. Some had three and four.

She and a friend walked to the river and her friend Wiona, helped her pull the heavy canoe out of the water. Wiona had never seen such a large canoe before and one not made of birch bark. "You have husband now Rachel. This is good. But will you not come back to the village anymore?"

Rachel hugged Wiona and said, "My husband and I will still come in spring and early fall. He likes traveling, too."

"You and husband stay this time," Wiona said.

Rachel shook her head, "We can't Wiona. Don't ask me to explain, because I can't. No more than we can stay."

"Have you seen a lot of the white settlements? Are there as many white people as Inidians?"

Rachel supposed this was on everyone's mind. "I have seen a few white settlements. The people are friendly and they grow in numbers every day. They are fascinating people Wiona. They know how to build machines that help makes their work easier. They live in big warm houses with windows and doors. They ride in wagons, which have wheels, and pulled with horses."

Most of the people here had never seen a horse. They traveled by canoe or on foot.

"This all sounds so strange Rachel. Do you like living like that?"

"Yes, more now than ever, now that I have Kirby by my side always. He is a good man.

*   *   *   *

Falling Bear was in no hurry and no one spoke until he was ready. He pulled out a long stem pipe with a large bowl and filled it with the tobacco Rachel had brought. He lit the tobacco and handed it to Kirby. Kirby did not smoke but here he was afraid of offending his host. He took the pipe and drew a long breath and held it and then passed the pipe back to Falling Bear. Kirby exhaled and blew the smoke out. When Falling Bear had taken a pull, he passed it on to the other two. "This is my eldest son Wonnocka. He will be leader of this village when I go. This is Noison my youngest son."

"Tell me about this war with your own people. Missionary who comes here says war is over. Why did you fight your own brothers?"

"Many farmers to the south of here had slaves to work in the field and the people in the north did not like this. The leader of our people said slaves no more. He set them free. The people in the south then started a war against the rest of the country. The war is over and the country is whole again."

"You fight in this war?"

"Yes."

"You kill many of your own people?"

"Yes."

Falling Bear was silent then thinking about what Kirby had said.

"I fight no more with my brothers."

Falling Bear touch the scar on Kirby's temple and said, "You were injured here. But enemy could not kill you. This is a good sign. I think maybe you good for Rachel. She lived too long without a man. Most young braves are afraid of her. You are not. This is good. She needs a strong man with good character."

Noison passed the pipe to Kirby again and he took a long drag and passed it to Falling Bear.

"I know about you." Falling Bear took another drag before passing it to Wonnocka. "You Major Kirby Morgan, who quit army to bring body of friend back to family to bury. This is good sign of man with character." Falling Bear winked at Kirby and then he said. "Missionary brings paper with words on it, and tells me what it says. The paper told me about you. You hero amongst your people.

"Tell me Major, white settlements coming north this far?"

"No, I don't think so. There may be white people who come to see the beauty in Falling Bear's country and to fish. But I don't think they will build any settlements here," Kirby said.

"This is good. Because --- you know Matelok? He very important man amongst the Abenaki people. All this land all way to Kwini-tegub (Connecticut River) to Straford to Umbagog was all land belonging to Abenaki people. Matelok deeded over some of the land to whites, so they could build their settlements, but he made the white man understand that his people could forever hunt and fish," he spread his arms, "in all this land. No white man is to trap north of Parmachenee.

Matelok was a good man. He understand it was good for his people to be friendly with the whites.

"But you say whites not come north into our land?"

"I don't think so, not for a long time."

"This makes me happy. Come, we smoke some more."

It was clear to Kirby that Falling Bear was concerned about the future of his people. He was old and he was afraid for them. It was also obvious to Kirby that Falling Bear had been a very courageous individual in his younger years and a valiant leader now. He wished he could tell him something that would put his mind to ease.

Kirby was handed the pipe again and he took a long drag from it and slowly exhaled the smoke. "This country of yours, Falling Bear, is beautiful and so peaceful," and he put his hand on his chest to indicate an inner peace. "It would be wrong for the white settlements to come here. I will tell you this Falling Bear, Wonnocko and Noison that when Rachel and I leave here, I will never tell any of my brothers where I have been. I will keep you and your people a secret."

"The whites are no all bad. We have learned plenty from them. Rachel has taught many of The People how to talk her language, so when we travel north to St. Francis, we can talk and understand the white man's tongue. When Rachel came to live with us, it was her job to teach all the children her words.

"We learn about your God and Christianity, but do not know church. We still talk to Pamolo and the Great Creator. The missionaries that come here some, show how to plant vegetables. We already know how to corn, but they show us vegetables we not ever see before. We now store for winter, squash, turnip and cabbage."

Kirby wanted to ask him about Rachel, before she came to live with his people, but not in front of his sons and Rachel should be here. That decision will have to wait.

"Too bad our way of life and that of the white man could not come together," and he intertwined his fingers as an analogy.

Just then there was a lot of excitement outside. People were running and hollering about something. Falling Bear looked at Noison and indicated the entrance with a tilt of his head. Noison went outside and returned only moments later. "A lone caribou has been spotted in the wetland behind camp. But it is too far for our arrows and too much open ground to sneak up closer."

"Falling Bear," Kirby interrupted. "Maybe I can help you. I have a rifle that will reach out and can kill this caribou."

"You show me this rifle," Falling Bear said.

All four left the lodge and Kirby went to find Rachel. She was just coming back from seeing the caribou. "Rachel, where is our gear. I offered to shoot it with the rifle, but Falling Bear wants to see the rifle."

Rachel walked over to the other side of the long lodge where everything was put. Kirby had rolled the rifle and ammunition up in a piece of canvas to keep it dry. "If Falling Bear agrees to let you shoot the caribou, then you will be accepted as one of The People, because you provided food. This is a good thing my husband," and she was smiling radiantly.

Kirby handed the rifle to Falling Bear to inspect. "I have seen something like this, but not like it."

Wonnocka and Noison handled the rifle and then gave it back to Kirby.

They nodded to their father and Falling Bear said, "It is agreed, you should do this."

Rachel walked with Kirby and their entourage of the entire village followed. There was no need to tell them to be quiet. This was more natural to them than to Kirby. At the edge of the marshy clearing Kirby stopped and indicated for all to wait there while he and Rachel worked their way through the forest to get a little closer and a clean shot.

Kirby found a leaning cedar tree that he could rest the rifle on and he aimed high on the neck to allow for the bullet to drop. The distance he figured between one and two hundred years. He took his time and sighted a fine bead and calmly squeezed the trigger. The roar from the rifle filled the valley and sky and roared back and forth against the mountains. Each echo getting quieter. The caribou stood for a few minutes after the roar and everyone, included Rachel thought he had missed. But then the caribou suddenly dropped to the ground.

"You must teach me Kirby how to shoot."

"Yes I should. I don't know why I didn't think of it before now."

Falling Bear and his two sons walked up behind Kirby and Rachel. "Today we take care of the caribou meat. Tomorrow at the celebration of Rachel joining this man, we will feast on roasted caribou meat. Come, now we take care of the caribou."

Whether it was tradition or courtesy, Kirby wasn't sure, but no one walked ahead of he and Rachel as they hiked out to view the caribou. Once there, Wonnocka and Noison cleaned the viscera out; all except the heart and liver. The women, Rachel included were now beginning to clean the stomach and intestines as these were used by The People.

When Kirby tried to help he was rebutted by Noison. Rachel saw what was happening and came to Kirby's side. "You are not expected to help from here my husband. It is enough that you killed this caribou, now let the others do their part. This is the way of The People," she smiled at him. Her smile could always make things better and reduce him to melted butter.

"Okay, I'll watch. But I feel like I should help."

*   *   *   *

The rest of that day the entire village worked together taking care of the meat. Nothing was wasted. Not a scrap; except for the visceral. The intestines Falling Bear explain would be stretched and dried and then separated into fine threads for the women to sew clothes with and for bow strings and braided for rope. The marrow was cleaned from the bones and would be cooked in a stew. Even the eye balls and tongue would be eaten.

By the time everything had been taken care of everyone was tired and sleep came easy. Rachel slept with Falling Bear and Pollinoke, while Kirby slept with Wonnoka and his family. He was tired.

At sunrise the women were up already preparing breakfast and preparing for the feast later on. The men, while it was usually women's work to set up the smaller wikitup, the men now were busy making one for Kirby and Rachel for their celebration tonight after they were joined and the feast. And this is where they would stay whenever they came to visit.

Again Kirby was not allowed to help. He was really feeling useless. The meat was being roasted over an outdoor cooking fire. Some women were putting together other food, some were cleaning the ground of sand and twigs and Rachel had disappeared.

The joining and feast wouldn't be until the afternoon, so Kirby decided he would take a hike back out to the marsh where the caribou had been and do some exploring. The People kept a cleaned trail from the village to the marsh. Probably they had killed a lot of caribou and moose there in the past. But he discovered the trail continued on, beyond the marsh and he was walking along this when he heard voices hollering. He stopped and looked around, but he didn't see anyone. But the voices were still screaming. And they were coming from where the caribou was shot the day before. He worked his way out across the marsh, stepping over and around the grassy hummocks. The screaming was getting louder, but he still could see nothing. He stopped and hollered and someone answered. He followed the direction of the reply and found Wonnocka's two sons buried up to their chins in blackmuck.

There wasn't time to go back and get a long pole or stick. The boys would be gone by then. He took off his shirt and waded out as close as he could get, the ground was spongy, but he wasn't breaking through. He threw his shirt to the boys and the movement caused him to sink to his knees in the muck. He laid flat trying to disperse his weight more evenly. It was working.

One of the boys grabbed on to the shirt and Kirby began to pull him out. Kirby was all covered with muck except for his back. He told the other boy to grab the foot of his brother and he would drag them both out.

When the second boy was free he told them both, "Try crawling on your stomach, like you were swimming." This seemed to be working okay. Now Kirby had to free his legs so he could crawl-swim out. He had no alternative but to roll over on his back, to free his legs. Once that was done he had to roll over again and crawl out.

By the time all three were out, Kirby was as black with the muck as the two boys. "Come on boys, let's go home."

Falling Bear was the first to see the three blackened figures stroll back into the village and then it seemed as if all at once, everyone was yelling and coming towards them wanting to know what had happened. Falling Bear stood back watching. He was smiling and laughing, while he tried to explain to Pollinoke, as she stuck her head out of the lodge opening, what the excitement was all about. Falling Bear knew without any doubts that Rachel had chosen well in Kirby. He had as strong a totem (character trait) as did Rachel. He would no longer have to worry about her. Tears came to his eyes as he thought and then understood that he was finally finished with his lasting ordeal with Carajou.

He motioned for Kirby to come over. "Time is almost. It is time you bathed for the joining. Follow me." Falling Bear led Kirby to the river upstream a short distance from the village. There was an enclosure there with smoke coming out of the top. "Take your clothes off and give them to Kikas."

Kirby turned around and saw a young girl standing there. "Take clothes off and bathe in river." This was more a command than a suggestion, so Kirby did and handed the muddy clothes to Kikas. As soon as she had them, she ran back to the village.

Kirby stepped reluctantly into the cold water and sat down. He was cold and his extremities started going numb, he had been in the water long enough. He stood up and turned and Falling Bear had also disrobed. "Come, now we sit in sweat lodge and heat and smoke will cleanse spirit."

The hot steamy lodge felt good to Kirby. Until the cold had left him he was not aware of the heat. But now he found it excruciatingly hot. Falling Bear put water on the hot rocks and the steam filled the lodge. Kirby thought he was going to suffocate. But he would accept it as long as Falling Bear could.

"My daughter," (this is the first time Kirby had heard him refer to Rachel as his daughter), has chosen well with you. She will not be broken hearted in her years to come. For a long time I afraid she would never find a man that was as strong as she is. There was no young brave here, that is why I asked her to go into white man's settlements. Maybe she would find a strong man there.

"I like you Kirby Morgan. Everyone in the village likes you, there will be no opposition to you joining with Rachel." Then on a lighter note, "Let the smoke and steam cleanse the spirit. And maybe you need to push out the cold." They both laughed.

"Tomorrow after you and Rachel have celebrated the night together, we will talk again, with Rachel.

"Come now, we have sweated long enough. Now we stand in the cold air and dry our skin."

Outside lying on a log was clean clothes for Kirby. Falling Bear put his old ones back on.

"Rachel and friends have made you these new clothes for your joining."

Once back in the village Kirby decided he wanted to shave off his whiskers. So he found his personals; put the small mirror on a makeshift table and poured some water into a clay bowl and began to lather his face. When the children saw him with soap on his face they all gathered around to watch him shave. This was totally new to them. When he opened his straight razor they thought he was going to cut his face, until they saw him scrapping off the soap. When he had finished and dried his face, he said, "See," and he rubbed his face, "no more beard. Smooth." Two of the children stepped forward and wanted to touch his face. Then they all ran off laughing.

*   *   *   *

The ceremony was held on a small knoll a short distance from camp. Everyone was there. Then Pollinoke escorted Rachel to Kirby's side. She was dressed elegantly in white deer skins, and she was wearing the stone necklace Kirby had given her. She was so very beautiful. He smiled and started to tell her and she put her hand over his lips and shook her head no.

They were now standing in front of the entire village and Falling Bear was about to speak. It was so quiet, there wasn't a sound anywhere. "Kirby and Rachel you are here to be joined today. I speak for everyone here, when I say no one has any objections. Rachel, you have chosen well with Kirby. He is as strong as you. You each will be good for the other. Kirby from this day, you are part of this village and my family. That you are joined, we now can feast."

*   *   *   *

Everybody ate until they couldn't eat anymore. There was only a little of the caribou left, and little of the other dishes. Three young men played drums while other young men and women danced around the fire. There was story telling and here Kirby was doing most of that. He told of strange and mysterious things that The People could not ever imagine. He told them about trains and how you could ride in rail cars that traveled on two iron rails. But no one knew what an iron rail was. When he tried to sketch a train, everyone thought it was a long snake. But all were having a joyous time. And most of all Rachel. Because she was so happy that her husband had been so readily accepted by The People.

Falling Bear finally announced that the time of celebration was over and Kirby should take his new partner into their new lodge and that everyone else retire to their own lodge.

Someone had kindled a small fire inside and covered the interior with many fur pelts. "This wikitup and these pelts are ours, given to us by all The People," Rachel said.

Kirby held Rachel in his arms and said, "I have been wanting to do this all day. And to tell you how beautiful you are. I can't imagine anything any more beautiful. Even this country you have shared with me. Your clothes are beautiful. Where did you get them?"

"Pollinoke has been working on them for the past year. It takes time to do all this fancy work."

"But how did she turn the skins white?"

"With pee. She collects a lot of it and when it turns…..I'm not sure what it changes to, but it has a strong smell and burns the eyes. Well when the pee becomes this then she soaked the clothes in the pee until they turn white. The only time a woman makes white clothes is for the joining of man and woman."

"Falling Bear told me you made my clothes this morning?"

"Yes, and four other girls. It didn't take long. Do you like?"

"Yes very much. I'm afraid I might have ruined the others in the black muck."

"No. When muck dries, it'll brush off."

"Enough talk," Rachel said as she removed Kirby's clothes. "You lay down and watch me."

Kirby laid on his back and bunched the pelts up under his head for a pillow. As Rachel began to remove her clothes in the firelight she was taking her time about doing it and being very seductive, with enticing movements with hands and body. Kirby was excited. She sat straddling him, not letting him inside of her yet, as she caressed his body.

Finally even she could stand it no longer and she moved just right to allow him to enter her. Her whole body began quivering with sensual ecstasy and excitement.

Kirby too was exploding with excitement.

Chapter 4

Kirby and Rachel awoke in the dawning of early light the next day. Still wrapped in each others arms. A loon called from the river. "Does that loon follow us everywhere we go?"

Rachel laughed and said, "Well he is promising another good day."

There were still a few embers in the fire and Rachel threw some dry kindling on and then some heavy wood. Soon it was ablaze and she busied herself with pouring some water into a clay pot and making some of their special tea.

While it was brewing, she crawled back under the blankets with Kirby. They lay in each others embrace listening to the stillness of the forest and the loon of course and the snapping of the fire. Neither of them wanted to talk. They were so totally engulfed with each other. They thought of nothing else. They lay there looking into each other eyes, not searching for anything in particular, simply looking.

The water was boiling in the clay pot and Rachel finally had to crawl out and make the tea. When Kirby tasted it, he was really surprised how good it was. "What is the tea made from?"

"There's a little plant that grows close to the ground in the shady wet places. In late summer there are red berries. I don't know how you call it."

"It sounds like the Teaberry plant and there is the slightest taste of teaberry. But that's not all."

"There's tyne," Kirby knew what that was. "There's roasted beechnuts for body." They sat drinking tea in the warmth of the firelight. They still had not put on their clothes.

After they had drank all of the tea, others were beginning to stir in the village.

*　　*　　*　　*

After all the people had eaten, Rachel changed back into her other clothes. She stored the white ones and would take them home with her. The entire camp was busy, going about their usual chores. Wonnocka, Noison and two other young men were going hunting for moose. Wonnocka asked, "Kirby, would you like to come with us?"

As he started to say yes, Falling Bear interrupted and said, "No, not today. We must talk." So the four left the village on the trail that went to the marsh.

"Rachel, you and your husband follow me." They followed Falling Bear into Kirby and Rachel's lodge. He put wood on the fire and said, "Get comfortable. We have much to talk about." They all fixed a place to sit with something to lean back against.

Falling Bear filled his pipe with tobacco, lit it and handed it first to Rachel. She was more surprised than anyone. Women just did not smoke the pipe. She took it reluctantly, until Falling Bear nodded his head, to take it. "Today my daughter," there he goes again with my daughter, what is going on, Rachel noticed also, "You must smoke first."

"There is much that I must say." Rachel took a long drag and almost choked on the smoke; no one noticed. Kirby took a long drag and let the smoke exhale through his nose. Falling Bear did the same. Then he passed the pipe around again. And this continued until the tobacco had turned to ash. Then Falling Bear sat there with his eyes closed and hardly breathing. Kirby and Rachel looked at each in wonder. What was going on? Rachel had never been part of a talk or discussion before and she had no idea what to expect.

When Falling Bear opened his eyes there were tears, but he spoke in an even tone. "There is much Rachel that I have wanted to tell you for many years. But never thought you ready to hear my words until now.

"Many years ago when I was a young brave, my father Bright Owl was chief of the Attignawantan People of the Wyandot Tribe." He paused to let them digest that and then continued. "My father was preparing to go to the spirit world and I would soon be chief. But there was a problem. I had never done anything with fortitude to show my people I could lead. The Shaman talked to me and convinced me that I should go on a quest to find or do something that would show my people, I could lead.

"I packed a few things and left. I traveled to the north for a long time. Always wondering if I would recognize what I was supposed to see or do. Then one day in spring I happened onto this trapper who had a canoe full of different animal hides. He had pulled ashore and was talking to someone, but I never saw another man. He was talking to himself and carrying on so, it looked like he was dancing to wild things.

"I moved on thinking there was nothing here for me. I travel one more day and came across another white man lying on the ground and about to be attacked by a wolverine." Rachel gasped and Kirby turned his attention to look at his wife. Color was draining from her face.

Falling Bear continued. "When the wolverine did attack, this man reared up on his knees and met the attack and killed the wolverine. He cut out the wolverines heart and ate it. This gave him his strength back. He took the hide off and made a hole for his head and wore it over his shoulders. He ate more of the fresh meat and eventually he moved south." Rachel had her hands over her mouth. She knew Falling Bear was telling her about her father.

"In one day he met up with this strange acting trapper. The strange one tried to kill the man wearing the wolverine hide and was killed."

Falling Bear looked directly at Rachel and said, "This man who had killed the wolverine was your father. Before you were born."

"I followed this man every day, every where he went. Sometimes there would be much distance between us. I was on foot and he was in a canoe.

"I followed him down the Ottawa River and saw him attacked by three other men and they were all killed. He was still wearing the wolverine hide and I started calling him 'Carajou.'" Memories were coming back to Rachel. Things her mother had told her about her father. And one of these memories was that all the Indian tribes held him in high esteem and called him 'Carajou'.

"My father's name Falling Bear was Emile La Montagne."

Falling Bear was surprised that Rachel would know her father's name. "May I leave Falling Bear? There is something I want to get to show you." He nodded his head.

Kirby knew what she was after.

Rachel returned with the wolverine fur and showed Falling Bear her father's name burned into the flesh side of the fur.

"I can not read. I saw this but did not know what it was."

"What happened to my father Falling Bear?"

"I will tell you but there is much to say before I do."

"I followed him up the wide river that you can not see across."

"The St. Lawrence River," Kirby interrupted.

"Yes, to his home on a farm. I waited until he left. It was cold and water was freezing in the river. But he traveled by canoe. He met your mother Rachel in a town on an island. I can't say the name. I can not get my tongue around the word."

"Is it Montreal, Falling Bear?" Kirby asked.

"Yes that sounds right. He and your mother traveled south for many days to the Cincinnati River. There he made a house and farm. You were born Rachel. Then one day he left and went down river in canoe. Your mother and you stayed at the farm."

Rachel and Kirby both found it difficult to believe that Falling Bear continued following Emile to the Cincinnati River and now was continuing to follow him further.

"I followed your father for many months, along wide rivers. Always I had to swim across to follow. I had little to eat, but my spirit was being drawn to follow this man.

"All the people in all the tribes were now calling him Carajou and no one dared to stop him. They were all afraid of the man who wore the skin of a wolverine.

"One day he turned north on another river. I followed for days and the air was getting colder.

"I followed him to the Dakota Tribe in what I now know as the Black Hills. He stayed there with the Dakotas during that winter. He was telling the tribe leader, I learned later his name was Tall Feather, that the white man would soon be coming to his land. He told Tall Feather all about the white men that would be coming and about his world. Things Tall Feather couldn't understand and wouldn't believe. But there was one thing that he was certain of, that if his people didn't change and try to accept the ways of these new people, they would have to surrender and leave their land.

"In the spring your father left the Dakotas. I think he was coming home. He headed south toward the land of the Wyoming and Cheyenne to tell them about the white settlers who were coming.

"But he never saw either the Wyoming or the Cheyenne. He rested one day on a beautiful knoll that overlooked a water. He sat down with his back against a tree. There was a rattle snake that he didn't see and it bit him and slowly he died Rachel.

"I have always believed he was coming home."

"It's difficult to understand why you followed him for so long, thousands of miles from your home," Rachel said.

"Many generations have past since, there is a legend; a true one. There was an Indian baby born among the Algonquin People, his name was Dekanawida. His mother unable to care for it was convinced by her mother that she must kill the baby. The mother did try and the baby could not be killed. So she told her mother that she was going to keep the baby, because since he could not be killed he must have been sent by the Great Creator for a purpose. Dekanawida became the Great Peacemaker between the Iraquois and the Algonquin Nations.

"I believe Dekanawida's spirit came back in your father, as The Great Peacemaker to tell the Indian about the whites and that they had to change if they were to survive. When your father was bitten by the snake, his job had ended, and he could go back to the spirit world.

"I buried your father and piled rocks over the dirt. I took his wolverine skin and wore it. Tears were in my eyes as I left. I came back to tell you and your mother about your father."

Rachel was in tears and crying. Kirby got up and knelt in front of her trying to comfort her. After a few minutes, she dried her eyes and said, "I'll be alright."

Falling Bear continued.

"I wore Carajou's wolverine fur because I thought Dekanawida's spirit, your father, would protect me on my travels back to Carajou's farm. I call him Carajou because that is the only name that any of the people knew him by. Because he had given his life to help the Indian people I thought I owed it to his family to tell them what had happened and why.

"Months went by before I returned to your home on the Cincinnati River. Along the way I talk with many runners between different tribes and told them about Dekanawida's spirit that had return to help the Indian People."

"As I walked up to your house Rachel, I saw three dirty men that had been drinking the whisky and they had just raped your mother."

Rachel almost fainted with this revelation. And again Kirby was kneeling in front of her trying to comfort her. He wanted to tell Falling Bear to stop, but he knew there was more she must hear.

"The three men killed your mother when they were through with her. I was enraged and I ran towards the three of them and I killed all three."

"And you buried my mother," Rachel's face was red from crying so much.

"Yes, I buried your mother and left the three for the worms to eat. Then I heard you crying. I didn't know what to do, but to take you with me."

Kirby saw Falling Bear was crying also. This had to be as difficult for him to tell as it was for Rachel to hear.

He continued, "I took you with me back to my village. I could not leave you there.

"I had been gone from my people too long and they thought me dead and my cousin became chief instead. At this time the English were trying to influence all of the tribes to raid and kill the white settlers, that they would be paid well for this. I tried to tell them that we had to learn to live beside the whites and not raid their settlements. I was laughed at. Nothing I said made any difference. There were others who thought like I did; a few. We banded together and moved into the Abenaki land. For days I counseled with their leader Matelok. He finally agreed we could stay, as long as we promised not to raid the white settlements. And he said we could have the land north of Parmachenee."

Falling Bear looked directly at Rachel with kindness filling his eyes and heart. Kirby could see this bond between them. "You Rachel, you adapted so well into the ways of The People here I didn't know how to tell you. I knew you were strong, but I was afraid, this knowledge might destroy you. Now you have found a man that is as strong as you and I think you will be okay now. Your father was a great man Rachel and when you wear this wolverine skin over your shoulders when you travel, you will always be protected by your father's spirit and Dekanawida's spirit.

Falling Bear was silent then. He was exhausted. It took a lot of strength to go back in his memories and tell Rachel about her father.

"That is quite a story Falling Bear," Kirby said. "Maybe Dekanawida's spirit was there with you on this journey, guiding and protecting you, so you could bring this news back to Emile's daughter and other tribes so there could be peace."

Falling Bear rose and without saying anything else, he left Kirby and Rachel to tell Pollinoke he had told Rachel about her father.

Rachel looked at Kirby. She was still crying and drained of emotions. "I need to go for a walk my husband. I need to be alone, like you needed to be alone when you first came to Grafton. I need to, as you said, roll this around in my head and let go of it." She kissed him and then left to walk along the river.

* * * *

Kirby wasn't sure how long they had been talking with Falling Bear, but he was hungry and the sun was in the afternoon sky. So he went for another walk along the trail that goes to the marsh and then beyond. He wondered if he would ever learn where the trail would go. There certainly wasn't enough daylight left today to explore beyond the marsh. He found a dry dogwood branch and broke a piece and sat down to whittle a flute; like his grandfather had done for him.

When he had finished he blew through it and working his fingers over the notches on top, he was able to make different tones.

It was getting late so he started back for the village. He was worried about Rachel. Not that she might get lost, because she had grown up here. But he was worried about her mental state. Could she accept what Falling Bear had said and more importantly, let go of it and not let it weigh her down.

When he was back in the village he saw a group of small children playing to one side. He walked over and began playing the flute. This fascinated the children and they gathered around him. There was one shy little girl standing off to the side, just watching. Kirby motioned for her to come over. When she did, Kirby asked, "Would you like to play this?"

He showed her how it was done and gave it to the little girl. When she made the flute make sounds she was all smiles and giggling. "What is your name?"

"Niboiwi," she said and then ran off with the other children, laughing.

Kirby looked up to find Rachel had been watching him with the children. Kirby was relieved that she was back and she was the same old Rachel.

The worries now gone. She walked slowly over to Kirby as he stood, watching her and smiling. Yes, she was back.

* * * *

The hunting party returned the next day and everyone went to help. On their way home, empty handed, they had found two moose in the marsh and had called it in close enough to bring it down with arrows. This was the moose's mating season and they very readily respond to calls like that of a moose.

On the hike out, Kirby said to Rachel, "This marsh seems to be a favorite place for moose and caribou."

"There is much feed here for them. We call this marsh, slologan."

The two animals were so heavy they had to be quartered and carried back. Many trips had to be made to bring back everything. The hides would be stretched, dried and cleaned and would make warm rugs for a floor. There was much meat to take care of and this would take several days.

"Falling Bear, Kirby and I must leave here in the morning. We must prepare for winter also."

Falling Bear didn't argue or try to persuade them to stay. He knew their destinies were outside this land. "Like to see rifle again."

Kirby dug it out of their gear and handed to Falling Bear. "How many beaver for one rifle?"

"Rachel how much are you getting for one beaver?"

"A large about $10. A super blanket $15 to $18."

"It would take five beaver to trade for one rifle."

"You come next spring I have enough beaver for two rifles and blankets. Okay?"

"Okay," Kirby replied.

Wonnocka came over to speak and said, "Next spring you bring me hat like yours?"

"Yes, we'll bring hats."

As Kirby and Rachel lay awake that night in the comfort of each other, Rachel said, "Everyone likes you my husband."

"I like everyone here. They have treated me as family. As much as I would like to stay longer, I know we can not. We have responsibilities with the Browns. I will look forward to each trip here. I have a feeling Falling Bear would have liked us to stay permanently. But deep down I think he understood you and I have to make a life of our own."

"I am happy to hear you think so much goodness of The People. I too know you and I must make our own life. And I am happy to be leaving in the morning."

"While you were walking today Rachel, I had a chance to do some thinking also. I know I don't want to farm for the rest of my life and I'm not so sure about lumbering either. I made more money this summer taking care of nuisance bears than I did working for Captain Jim. What would you say that after we have the house all built and everything, that we come up here about the first of September and stay until the ice starts to freeze and trap beaver. We could stay at your wikitup and trap away from The People so we wouldn't encroach on them."

"What does this word encroach mean?"

"To impose, to trespass."

"Do we have enough money to do all this about the house?"

"I have a $1,000 in the bank. I have my monthly money from the Army and I have everything I have earned this summer on account with Jim."

"I have my money too. That is also on account with Jim. I need very little money. I have saved most of everything since I started work at the Browns."

"I think we can do it Rachel. And once we cut those pine trees Jim showed us, that'll pay for the lumber to build the house."

Rachel was getting as excited by the idea as Kirby was, and they laid awake long into the night talking about their future.

*   *   *   *

They were up before anyone else in the village. It was the anticipation of going home. Kirby put kindling on the outside cooking fire and then some dry wood. He would miss this place and the people, but he was anxious to start building a home, a life for him and Rachel. They loaded the canoe and then waited for the others to awaken. A loon called and Kirby said, "This time we were up before the loon."

The loon's cry was like a natural alarm for the village as they started to appear from inside the long lodge.

Kirby and Rachel drank the hot tea and ate only a little. She announced to everyone, "It is time. We must leave."

Everyone walked with them to their canoe. The goodbyes were short. Falling Bear looked at Kirby approvingly, smiled and nodded his head. Wonnocka had tears in his eyes.

Kirby climbed in first and got seated and then he steadied the canoe while Rachel climbed in. Then

Wonnocka push them out into the river. The current caught the bow and swung it downstream. Everyone was hollering goodbye and waving. Rachel turned once as her family disappeared behind a bend in the river.

"Going with the current and the wind at our back we will be below Aziscoshos Falls in daylight," Rachel said. She wiped tears from her eyes.

Chapter 5

The air was getting cooler each day. They had a steady breeze to their back during the two days of travel and made it back to Grafton a little after dark. There was plenty of moonlight and they wanted to push on and make Grafton that night.

Ruth and Jim were surprised to see them back so soon. "We wanted to come back early so we could start tomorrow, clearing trees and bushes from our land. Tomorrow is Sunday isn't it? We lost all track of time."

"Yes tomorrow is Sunday. Will you be needing any help?"

"If you're offering, then yes, we could."

"James, tomorrow is Sunday." He has always said, "No work, no working on Sunday," Ruth reminded him.

"Well this is different."

They were all up early the next morning and after a hearty breakfast of bacon, eggs and beans, they loaded the wagon with tools and chains and ropes and headed towards Kirby and Rachel's new home site.

There were very few large trees that had to be cut down. The forest was spacious enough so they could make a driveway without much difficulty. There were quite a few low growing bushes that had to be cut. Everything was thrown into a pile to burn later on. The hard wood was blocked up for firewood and stacked off to the side of the drive. There was a natural berm of gravel on the right side just as you left the road and this was used to fill in low and wet spots.

There was already a natural clearing at the base of the falls where they would build their house. And there was a natural covey against the steep ridge which could be made into a root cellar. Things were looking promising.

By the end of that day they had cleared and made a driveway up to the clearing at the falls. "This has been a good day's work."

*   *   *   *

Whenever there was a chance, and every Sunday, Kirby and Rachel were hauling building supplies for their new home. By the end of October, Kirby and Rachel had built a deck, the bottom floor, and had it nailed off and square and plumb. There wouldn't be any need of digging a cellar, since he had found a perfect place for a root cellar. Besides there was too much ledge in the ground to be digging.

There were a few days of slack time and during those few days, Kirby and the mill crew would saw out pine for the house. Then on Sunday, he and Rachel would load the wagon and haul them down. His goal was to get all of the lumber there this fall before the snow got deep. Then in the spring they could start pounding nails and putting the house up.

*   *   *   *

There was a big Thanksgiving celebration at the Poplar Tavern. Every family brought something and afterwards there was still plenty of food left. The timber crews were all back in the woods now and since there wasn't much snow yet, the crews were getting a good start on the winter's quota.

Kirby stayed in the yard recording and scaling the logs as they were hauled in from the different crews. The best of the pine and spruce logs he diverted to the saw mill yard. The others were piled par-buckle style next to the Cambridge River. Jim was pleased with production so far this year. As much as he would have liked to have been more in the woods ramrodding the crews, he was slowing down with his age and his son-in-law George Otis was handling things away from the farm.

One day Kirby and Rachel sat down to see how much money they had. "I have $1,000 in the bank. I have $175 upstairs, $108 from the Army, Jim is holding my wages about $22.25. That's just over $1,300."

"I figured up last night and Jim is holding $450 for me," Rachel said.

"That's $1,750 we have together. And by spring that'll be close to $2,000. I think we'll be able to finish the house and the inside and buy what we need, especially since we don't have to pay Jim for the lumber until we cut the pine trees. I think we are in pretty good standing Mrs. Morgan." They laughed.

"That's a good feel Mr. Morgan."

There still wasn't much snow yet and Jim was worrying that there might not be enough for spring runoff to float the logs down to Umbagog. "Jim you know we always get a lot of rain before you start driving the logs. Why are you worrying so much about it now?" Ruth asked.

She was right of course. Better to cut as much as he could while the going was easy. The horses didn't have to wade the deep snow, and the mail was still being delivered daily from Bethel.

By Christmas, the crews had already cut half the year's quota of logs. But the weather changed abruptly with the new year. It was cold and a lot of snow. The cold kept the snow soft and fluffy so the horses could still travel through it and break open new trails. And the main road to Newry was still being rolled, packed, so horses and sleighs could travel. The mail was once a week now.

Kirby and Rachel were looking forward to spring so they could start building their house. Kirby was doing the work of two men. Jim had never seen the yards so orderly and so much sawn lumber sitting on pallets ready to be shipped to Bethel. Jim knew of Kirby's and Rachel's plans after this season was over and he wasn't begrudging them at all. In fact, if he was young again he would do the same thing.

Rachel's work load was more also, as Ruth was getting on in years and was not able to do as much around the house. But neither did she ever feel sorry for herself for getting older and a bit slower.

March came in with a thaw and this gave everyone a little reprieve from the cold. Some were working in shirt sleeves and sweating. The snow settled and when it would freeze again during the night, the men and horses were no longer wallowing in snow up to their chest. One thing about living in a crew camp, there was always plenty of good food, and Jim had planned well, the previous summer and had stocked the camps with more supplies than he had in the past. He believed in keeping good living quarters for the men, sparse as they may have been, and good food.

The sawn lumber Kirby had in the yard was a bonus this year and Jim pulled some men out of the woods to start daily trips to Bethel while the roads were still snow and ice covered. It was easier for the teams to pull a loaded sled on snow and ice than a wagon over a gravel road.

Kirby had volunteered to take one team and Jim said, "Not this time Kirby. I like what you have done here in the yard and the mill and I'm going to keep you here. At least this season."

*   *   *   *

The weather was warming and Jim pulled all of the crews out of the lumber camps, except for skeleton crews to make sure everything was hauled to the yard and the camps were closed up.

Some of the men left who lived the furthest away. Those who lived in Grafton, some of them had a few days off until the ice broke in the river, so Jim could start the log drive. Jim also had the mill shut down to save the water for the drive. Kirby and Rachel stayed busy though. The time and waiting actually went by faster that way.

Kirby and Rachel had talked it over with Jim and Ruth and as soon as all the logs were in the river and most of the men now on the river, Kirby and Rachel would leave early this year for the spring trip to Falling Bear's village. "I don't want Rachel having to make the trip alone this spring with a bigger and heavier canoe and we'll be loaded heavier with beaver pelts this year than she has carried before. This will have to be a quick trip, as we have a house to build."

Kirby was full of nervous energy. He wanted to get started on their house but he would have to wait for the snow to melt and the ground to dry before he could start hauling in lumber and other supplies. He cleared all of the saw dust from the mill, sharpened all the saw blades, repaired the broken carriage, recounted every log in the yard ready to float downriver, to make sure the tally book was correct. Jim was slowing down still and George had to take on more responsibilities.

The day finally came when word was brought back from Upton that the Cambridge River was free of ice and Jim could start his log drive. He filled the river with logs before he opened the sluice on the dam. And when the men had those logs over the dam, the sluice was closed until the river was full of logs again. This went on for a week before all of the winter logs were in the river and now on their way to Umbagog Lake.

The next day Kirby and Rachel said their goodbyes and were on their way. They stopped first at Douglas's store for a few supplies they couldn't get at the farm. Kirby spotted a new bucksaw hanging from a peg on the back wall and said to Rachel, "I think I'll give this bucksaw to Falling Bear as a gift."

"How much is it Kirby?"

"$5.00."

"That's more than either of us makes in a week. Are you sure you want to do this?"

"Yes. It'll help make life for his people a little easier."

Douglas didn't have any more felt hats, but Rachel told him, "When we make trip in fall I want six green hats and six yellow hats."

Kirby asked, "What about the kids? Shouldn't we bring something back for them to play with?"

Rachel looked around the store and saw a big ball. "They'll have fun with this."

"You bringing back more beaver this year Rachel?"

"Yes, maybe more than last time."

"Mr. Douglas, would you have a map of this area?"

"Yes I do. A Lapman-Faltar Company updated an 1859 map in 1864."

"That's exactly what I need. How much?"

"25 cents."

"Why do you need a map?" Rachel asked.

"To show Falling Bear. We can show him on the map where his village is, where Grafton is and where our house will be."

Kirby paid for the items and stored them in the wagon.

As they rode through Upton they could see that the end of Unbagog Lake was full of wood. They rode by and on to Captain Wilson's depot on the Mallagoway River. Wanting to make a quick trip, they canoed until dark before stopping at the same campsite below Aziscohos Falls.

They found ice above the dam in the deadwater the next morning and had to stay close to the western shoreline, and even though they could have made it to the village that day, Rachel wanted to stay that night in her wikitup at her special place. This was alright with Kirby. They were both tired after two days of strenuous paddling. "We would not have made it this far today if we did not have these paddles."

While Kirby unloaded the canoe, Rachel opened up the wikitup to air it out and then she kindled a fire inside. There was still some patches of snow in the shaded spots under the trees. But inside the wikitup, it was warm and after drinking some of Rachel's special tea they took off some of their traveling clothes so not to sweat in them.

After eating they laid back on the bear rug and Rachel sat up looking at Kirby and grinning, then she said, "I am horny."

*   *   *   *

Everyone in the village was really surprised to see them this early. "Ice not leave big lake yet, and you come?"

Rachel explained that there was an open channel along the shore and they were early because they needed to get back to build their house. Kirby pulled the canoe ashore and Rachel threw the ball to the kids that had gathered around her. They knew what to do with it and they went off yelling and throwing the ball at each other. Kirby handed the bucksaw to Falling Bear and he held it and looked it over and turned it over, not really understanding what it was.

Kirby went to work and lashed two short poles together, making a crude looking sawhorse. He then said to Wonnocka, "Bring me a long piece of fire wood," and he held out his arms to show how long.

Wonnocka was not long coming back with just what Kirby wanted. "Put it on the sawhorse."

Wonnocka did, but he looked real doubtful at Kirby, as if Kirby had lost his mind.

Kirby placed his left foot on the pole, to hold it in place and began sawing. He was through the wood in a short few strokes. It was clear to everyone then how useful this would be. "What you call this Kirby?"

"Bucksaw." Falling Bear and Wonnocka repeating the word several times, so they would remember it. The word was strange to them.

Pollinoke brought Kirby and Rachel some tea and offered them something to eat. They were hungry and ate ravishingly. Afterwards Kirby spread out the map on the makeshift table and explained to Falling Bear and Wonnocka where the village was located in reference to Cananda, Parmachenee Lake and where Grafton was. No one from the village had traveled beyond Parmachenee. Kirby showed where there were white settlements, fishing camps on Parmachenee and Umbagog and the Richardson Lakes. He showed them where the train ran from Portland, but this didn't mean much, as no one understood what a train was or where Portland was. They had never heard the word Portland before. But Falling Bear was intrigued, and saddened. He could see and understood how close the whites were coming to his land. He probably wouldn't live long enough to see it, but his sons, surely would. And this worried him, because he knew there was nothing he nor anyone could do, to stop it. But he was glad Kirby had showed him the map, and he wanted to keep it.

Rachel explained that they couldn't stay but one night, because they had to build a house before cold weather this fall. Not many understood why it would take so long to build a lodge. "How many beaver do you have for us to take back?"

"Come, see." Falling Bear led them to a storage place in the long lodge.

Rachel counted out 26 hides. "This good Falling Bear. Next trip we bring you two rifles and more supplies."

For the rest of that day the women prepared a feast to honor the arrival of Kirby and Rachel. Other than the moose meat, Kirby had no idea what he was eating. Only that it was very good.

*   *   *   *

They stayed only the one night. They both would have stayed longer, but finishing the new house on time was worrying them. And Rachel, if truth be known was excited about having her own house. "How will we do the inside?" she asked.

"Well, the walls and ceilings will be plastered. The ceilings will be painted and the walls will be covered with wallpaper. Like the Brown's house."

Rachel laid awake most of that night thinking about how she would like the inside of the house to look.

When morning came Rachel had had very little sleep. While she prepared tea and something to eat, Kirby loaded the canoe. They said their goodbyes and settled in the canoe for another quick trip home.

During the night the wind had shifted and blew out of the east, pushing the ice in Parmachenee Lake onto the west shoreline, so they had to follow the east side and hoped that the wind wouldn't shift directions again until they were off the lake.

Fred Cyr met them at the landing at Azischos Dam. "My, you didn't visit very long."

"No, Mr. Cyr, we have a house to build this summer. But we'll be back in the fall." Even without much sleep the night before, Rachel was still an excited bundle of energy. She couldn't wait to start down the Magalloway River.

They made camp on the head of the oxbow in the river just below Diamond Peaks. By now Rachel's sleepless night had caught up with her. They were close to Wilson's landing but they chose to stay on the river that night. The temperature was dropping and it would be cold again before morning. Besides, Kirby had been a good student and now knew how to build a quick shelter in the woods. And after eating, Rachel was soon asleep. Kirby sat up a while watching the stars.

Rachel slept soundly all night and the next morning they were on their way at first light. They had no more food. They reached Captain Wilson's landing an hour later and harnessed up the horse and wagon and loaded the beaver pelts into the wagon.

They stopped at the Lakeside Hotel in Upton for breakfast. Douglas's store wouldn't be open this early. It seemed good to them both to sit down and relax at a table. They had been pushing themselves on this trip.

After a hearty breakfast of bacon and eggs and a whole pot of coffee, they proceeded up the hill to Douglas's store. Warren was just opening the door. "My, you're early this morning. Have you been all the way to the village and back already?"

"Yes, this had to be a quick trip." Kirby and Rachel unloaded the wagon and carried the pelts inside.

Warren ran his fingers through the hair and said, "These are sure some nice looking pieces of fur. I don't know how they get the flesh side so white."

Rachel was about to tell him, but decided against it. Twenty-four extra large and two large. "I'll give you $13 each for the extra large and $8 each for the large."

Kirby was about to accept when Rachel, who knew more about the fur business, said, "No, not good enough. Make it $15 and $10."

Warren Douglas scratched his head with his pencil. He always had to pay more for her beaver than anyone else. "Okay. That's $380 total. Do you want cash, on account or trade?"

Kirby said, "We'll trade some now, and leave the rest on account for the fall trip."

Warren looked at Rachel and she nodded her head in agreement.

"How much for two .44 Winchesters, and two boxes of bullets?"

"$81 total."

That was settled. "Now Mr. Douglas, we want to do some buying. We'll need some traps. If you have them now we'll pay for them and pick those up in the fall also. If not, you can get 'em any time before September and we'll pay for them when we pick them up."

"What are you wanting for traps?"

"One dozen of #2 Blake & Lamb, one dozen of #4 Blake & Lamb, and six #3 Blake & Lamb."

"That comes to another $45."

"Remember Mr. Douglas, no hurry on the traps, but we will expect to pick them up in the fall when we stop on our way up country."

On their ride to Grafton, they were both jubilant about the money they had gotten for the beaver. "I think this is going to work out good for us Rachel. A few more beaver and it would be more than we both would make all year for the Browns." Rachel was also glad that there would be plenty of money left over, after paying for the two rifles to purchase much more for The People.

*　*　*　*

That evening after supper Kirby and Rachel told Jim and Ruth about their plans to trap beaver for a living instead of farming or timbering. "We really hate to disappoint you both, but we would be happier this way," Kirby said.

"We still will be here in Grafton all summer and winter and most of the spring. We'll take the fall months to trap," Rachel assured them.

"And you won't have to worry about us paying you for the building materials. We will still cut those pine trees."

"Well, can't say that I blame you much. You're one of the best working men on the crew Kirby and you sure made the mill productive this last winter. But, hell, you'll still be around," Jim said.

"And I'll miss you also Rachel. But the Tenny girl is going to be looking for work at the end of the summer and that'll work in fine."

The ground was still soft in places from the winter freeze and Kirby, would not be able to get a loaded wagon of supplies up to the house site, so he worked around the mill yard and farm, helping Jim. Rachel still had work to do. There were crews to feed. At night she and Kirby would make lists of things they would need from town.

One day Jim asked if he and Rachel would take a load of lumber to the depot. The next day they left at sunrise with a lunch; they could eat along the way. Water from the spring run off had washed across the road in several places through the notch. Other travelers had partially repaired some of the wash outs, but there were two that Kirby and Rachel had to fix before they could get the wagon through. But this gave their team a breather and once they were through the notch they went faster, making up time. They would like to be back at the farm by evening, but that probably wouldn't happen.

At the depot in Bethel, they unloaded the lumber and picked up a delivery slip and went over to the local hardware and mercantile store to buy windows for their house and some wall paper and paste. By the time they had all of the windows loaded there was little room for anything else. The trip home was slower because of the glass and that night they stayed at Kilgore's Station.

The next day before going directly to the Brown farm they decided to try the driveway to their house. It was soft in places, but the road held. The snow was all gone and the deck boards were dry. The first thing he decided to do would be to nail down another course of boards to insulate against the cold, since there wouldn't be a cellar under the house.

The following Saturday Rachel helped Kirby nail down another course of flooring, and they were finished before supper.

*   *   *   *

There was more water in the river this year and the men returned from the river drive a week earlier this year. Jim had everyone gather in the mill yard; the mud had dried by now. Ruth was standing by his side when he announced, "Since we had such a prosperous season we are giving everybody a bonus." The bonuses were not all the same, so he handed each one of them an envelope containing anywhere from $30 to $100. Kirby and Rachel received one envelope with a combined sum of $150.

"Jim and Ruth," Kirby said, "you have already done so much for us, we can't accept this much."

"Nonsense," Ruth said, "you both have earned it. It should have been more," and she looked at her husband, 'Captain Jim.'

The men who had families away from Grafton left and the local men returned to their farms. Kirby hired two men to help him and Rachel with the new house, Leslie Davis and Mos Tenny. The ground was finally dry and Rachel helped Kirby haul the rest of the supplies for the house.

The next morning the four of them started sawing lumber and pounding nails and by the end of the first day they had stood up two studded walls. The next day they stood two more and on the third, the walls for the entryway and shed. Things were coming along faster than Kirby had imagined.

On the fourth, Saturday, a dozen more people showed up to help. The women all brought food to feed the hungry men. While some men boarded up the walls, others cut out the roof rafters and others nailed them in place. By the end of Sunday, the roof was all boarded over and so too were the walls.

"What have you decided to do about the roof?"

"Cedar shakes I guess," Kirby said.

"It would be a waste of time and good money up here Kirby. If I were you I would take a trip to Bethel and buy some steel roofing. It'll last your life time, and you won't have to worry about it leaking."

Monday morning Kirby and Rachel set out for Bethel with another load of lumber for the depot, and a load of roofing on the way back. The roofing was almost as heavy as the pine boards and the trip back was slower. They camped out near Bear Brook where they did almost a year ago.

Kirby had never worked with steel roofing before, but Leslie Davis had and he was boss on this job. The work was slow and it took a week to finish. The next day they hung the exterior doors and nailed in the windows. It was beginning to look like a house.

"What about the outside Kirby? Are you going to leave it like that?" Rachel asked.

"No, I found a pallet of clapboards in Jim's barn and he said we could have them." Two days later the siding was on.

Everyone took a break and Kirby and Rachel were cleaning up around the house. Putting the board shortends in the shed and throwing everything else into a pile to be burned later.

Rachel was sweeping the inside and Kirby was cutting bushes when a young boy walked up the driveway. "Gee mister," Kirby stopped cutting bushes and turned to see who was speaking. "It sure didn't take ya long to build this house. Anything I can do to help? I'd like to earn some spending money, too."

"How old are you?" Kirby asked.

"Almost eight. My name is Joe Chapman. I live in the last house before this one."

"Well, I tell you what Joe, you can pick these bushes up as I cut them and throw them into that pile of garbage."

When they were finished with the bushes Joe said, "What's next mister. I'd like to earn some more spending money."

Kirby took Joe in the wagon and they went down to the road and loaded all the hardwood that had been cut down for the driveway. They brought the load back to the shed and unloaded the wagon.

It took a full week to nail the lathes to all the walls and ceilings and another two weeks to trowel on the plaster. When that was finished Kirby, Rachel and young Joe Chapman hauled sawdust down from the mill in old grain sacks and filled the walls with the sawdust. "I don't understand why you're putting sawdust in the walls Kirby?"

"Back home on the farm we didn't have a root cellar for cold storage, so my father built an ice house. He lined the walls and ceiling with sawdust and cut ice in the winter and stored it inside and the ice would keep all summer. My mom could keep meat, eggs, vegetables and milk in it much longer than a root cellar. So I figure it'll keep the cold out in the winter also."

When the walls and ceilings were full with sawdust and the upside of the ceilings, boarded over also, Kirby and Rachel made another trip to town. They bought a wood heating stove for the living room, a polished ram-down. And for the kitchen they bought an Atlantic wood cook stove with a water tank on back to heat water.

"How is that going to work Kirby? I don't understand."

"We have to pick up some steel piping also. We pipe in the water from high up on the falls to the kitchen sink and the cook stove. The fire in the stove will heat the water in the tank and we'll always have hot water and running water in the sink. But we'll have to let the water run at all times in the winter so the water won't freeze in the pipes."

"That's wonderful Kirby. But can you do it?"

"No problem." They stopped at the mercantile store and bought the piping and Rachel picked out what she wanted for wallpaper.

During the ride back Rachel asked, "How much money do we have left? We have used an awful lot of it haven't we?"

"We should have just over a $1,000 left in the bank. I'm sure glad for that government check each month."

While Joe helped Kirby with plumbing water from the falls to the kitchen sink and cook stove, Joe's mother Abby helped Rachel with the wallpapering. They were having better luck with the paper than Kirby was with the water pipes. But after three days Kirby had running water to the sink and the water tank was full.

"Joe, I have another job for you. I have to build a chimney to pipe the smoke from both stoves outside. I'm going to need a lot of rocks. I need all the rocks you can find about this big," and he held up his hands.

This kept Joe busy for three days, finding enough rocks for Kirby to finish the chimney. When he had finished the chimney and water pipes and Rachel and Joe's mother had finished papering the walls, they stopped and looked at each other. "I'm tired," Kirby said.

"Me too. If we had a bed we could lay down."

"We still need to build the root cellar, get in enough firewood for the winter, stock up on food, build cupboards, a table and a bed. And all before we leave in September to trap. What month is this Rachel? I haven't any idea."

"Third week in July."

"There's enough lumber left to build a bed, but we'll need a mattress. There's enough for a table also. I'll build those tomorrow. The cupboards may have to wait until after we get back from trapping because we need to concentrate on firewood."

*   *   *   *

Young Joe Chapman helped with the firewood. He was actually a lot of help. After a full week, Kirby figured they had more than enough wood. The only thing left now was a mattress and house finishings. "Joe," Kirby said, "I don't believe there'll be any more work for you. We are about done. You have been a lot of help. Do you have any idea how much I owe you for your help?"

Joe sat on the edge of the wagon thinking. "Probably more than you want to give me," was his answer.

Kirby laughed so hard he had to sit down to keep from falling over.

"How does $5 sound to you?"

Joe's eyes got as big as silver dollars. "You mean five whole dollars?"

"I sure do."

"Silver or paper?" Joe asked. "My papa says paper money ain't no good."

"Well, how's five silver dollars?"

"Holy cow Mr. Morgan! I have never seen this much in my whole life."

*   *   *   *

They moved into their new house in the middle of August. There was still work to do, but that could be done as Kirby found the time. The root cellar was done even. There had been no time for Rachel to can any vegetables, so they had to buy those and other food stuffs at Douglas' store. "All in good time," Kirby said one evening.

"Come with me, I want to show you something," and she led the way up the steep ridge behind the house to a spot about 200 feet up. The brook made a natural flateau there, where they could look out across the valley and mountains below. There was one huge old cedar tree, and there was a natural rock bench to sit on.

Later that evening they lay wrapped in each other's goodness and warmth, listening to the water falls just outside their window.

They were both exhausted and they soon fell asleep.

Kirby had an idea about how to get those tall pine trees to the roadside. He'd build a slide of ice and snow and slide them down the steep ridge. He saw where he needed to fall the first tall pine tree and he cleared a path of all bushes, sticks and rocks and leveled out any bumps. As soon as there was snow on the ground, he'd make an ice flume. It would take a lot of work. But he didn't see any other way to get those giants off the ridge. At the butt end they were only about three feet across but held their symmetry well. He would top them off over a hundred feet long.

One day Jim had ridden down to ask Kirby for his help. "Kirby, I sent Oliver down the river this week to inspect it for problems driving logs next spring. He says he found two beaver dams not far below the dam that will have to be removed and the beaver killed. Can you do this before you leave?"

Kirby looked at Jim and said, "I think so."

"Good, I'll pay you daily wages and you keep the beaver. I have some new explosives. It's called dynamite. Do you know how to use it?"

"Yes, we were using it in the war."

"Good, when can you leave?"

Again Kirby looked at Rachel and she nodded her head and Kirby said, "We can get started on it today."

Somehow Jim had missed the communication between them. They had not said anything to each other, only a look and a silent nod. On his ride back to the mill, Jim couldn't help but think how in-tune Kirby and Rachel were with each other.

*   *   *   *

"What is dynamite my husband?" Rachel asked.

"It's a chemical that is very explosive. You can use it to break away ledge or rock; on the farm back home we used black powder to blow stumps. In the war we used dynamite to blow up fortifications. Today we'll use it to remove beaver dams from the river." They put some traps in a bucket and the dynamite in another and Kirby put the fuses in his pocket. Rachel carried an axe and his rifle.

The first dam was only a ten minute walk from the mill. Kirby made a trough in the top of the dam to sluice some water. Knowing the beaver would soon come to repair it, then he set a leg hold trap at the mouth of the trough. While Rachel made another trough and set a trap like Kirby's. Then they left to find the next dam which was within sight of the first beaver dam. "This will be full of beaver. The first dam was probably a couple of two years olds striking out on their own." They set two traps in troughs here also, then hiked back to the first dam to wait.

When they got there, there was already one beaver in the trap Rachel had set and it had drowned already. This was a large beaver. As Kirby skun and fleshed the hide, Rachel reset the trap. "When will we blow the dams?"

"As soon as we think we have all the beaver."
Just then another beaver had snapped Rachel's set again
and gone out in deeper water and was now drowning.

"When it stops thrashing you can pull it in."

Rachel was having fun and Kirby was having as
much fun watching her. "We need some pack baskets.
Do you know how to make one?"

"As a young girl I had to make all kinds of
baskets. There are some nice ash trees at home. You
bring one down and I'll show you how to make strips
from the wood."

When Kirby had the second beaver skun and
fleshed he said, "We'll leave these two hides here and
go check the other dam." There they had an otter in
one trap and an extra large beaver in the other. The
traps were reset and the two were skun. Rachel built a
fire and roasted some of the beaver meat while Kirby
finished the otter.

Before they had finished eating, both traps
snapped again. There were two more awfully large
beaver. "I don't know how much an otter is worth but
we have about $100 in beaver so far," Rachel said.

By the time they figured they had all of the
beaver, they had a total of eight. Some of those were
kits and Kirby didn't waste his time sinking 'em.

He put three sticks of dynamite, spaced out
across the dam and ran for shelter after he lit the fuses.
When it went off sticks and mud flew a hundred feet in
the air and coming down all around the pond. "There,
that takes care of one."

Rachel had no idea of the force of even one
stick of dynamite. She was glad Kirby had carried the
bucket with the dynamite. The second dam was longer
and wider, so he used six sticks. He made the fuses
longer, so they could run further away for cover. When

the dynamite went off Kirby and Rachel had not gone far enough away. They were covered with mud and laughing at themselves.

"I guess that'll take care of that problem."

Rachel said, "And we have almost $200 worth of beaver hides."

When they left the river they were carrying the hides over their shoulders and Rachel had taken some of the meat back with her. They were fortunate that they didn't have far to hike. They left the traps in the barn and Ronki-Tonk said he would take care of them.

*   *   *   *

It was late so they stored the beaver hides in the root cellar. The next day after breakfast they put the hides on boards to dry and then went off to the side of the shed and cut an ash tree. "The bark would peel off easier in the spring, but we need the pack baskets now," Rachel said.

They cut the trunk into six foot lengths and then removed the bark, which was a difficult task. Then Rachel took the axe and started beating the ash stick which loosened the white fiber wood into thin strips. While Kirby did that, Rachel started weaving the strips into a pack basket. She only had finished one that day and the next she completed the second.

During the day Rachel moved the hides into the sun. "The warm sun light will help to dry these. Then we can take them to Douglas' Store instead of leaving them here for the mice to chew on."

They made a list of things they would need to take for a longer trip this time. "We will be gone for two months," they told Jim and Ruth. "And when we get back, we'll start working on those tall pine trees."

Ruth had asked them to stay for supper and George and Mary were there also. "This winter, George is more or less going to run things. I'm slowing down and Ruth has hired another woman to take her place and one of the neighbor boys to keep the wood boxes full and do other errands."

On the way home Rachel said, "You were going to teach me to shoot the rifle."

The next day Kirby set up a target and showed Rachel how to line the front and rear sight up and to put the target on top of the front sight. "Now hold the rifle tight against your shoulder. Inhale and then let it out and hold it. Now squeeze the trigger."

The rifle roared and Rachel was knocked on her butt. But she hit the target, just below the bull's eye. "Not bad for your first shot."

"I wasn't expecting to get hit so hard. Let me try it again," she said.

She steadied herself this time and squeezed the trigger again. This shot was almost dead center. "One more time. Just to make sure it wasn't a mistake," Kirby said.

Rachel kind of bristled a bit. She loaded the rifle, inhaled and let it out and squeezed the trigger. The bullet hit right beside the second shot. "I don't see any sense in wasting any more bullets teaching you how to shoot. You sure you have never done this before?" "Positive."

They saw young Joe Chapman walking up the driveway. "Heard some shooting. Thought maybe you got a moose. Come to help," Joe said.

"No moose, only showing Rachel how to shoot."

"Joe, you want to earn some more money?"

"Yes sir!" He was excited.

"We're leaving next week to go up north for two months. I'd like it if you would come here once each week and walk around the house, make sure doors and windows are closed and the root cellar door is closed. I'll give you a nickel for each week."

Kirby gave him four nickels and said, "This is for the first month. I'll pay you for the second month when we get back."

"Gee thanks, Mr. Morgan."

Joe left and Kirby followed Rachel up to her favorite spot up the falls. 'Rachel's Perch.'

"Next spring we'll have to make a screened in porch on the front of the house. Or the spring insects will eat us alive if we try to sit outside in the woods like this."

"I'll plant some tansey plants here next spring. I saw a lot of them growing around the river by the farm."

"What does tansey do?" Kirby asked.

"It is a natural bug repellant. You rub the leaves on your skin and the bugs stay away. Let's go look for mushrooms. Wouldn't mushrooms and scrambled eggs sound good for breakfast?"

They walked towards the north where the ground was more moist and more dead falls on the ground. Kirby found some and asked, "Are these any good?"

"Their edible but not good tasting." She found some pale orange ones and then a small bear's head tooth and another orange one.

"How do you know which is poisonous and which are good?" Kirby asked.

"You got to be an Indian to know these things," and they both laughed and went home.

*　　*　　*　　*

They had all of their gear and supplies packed
and a list of things to get at Douglas's store. Kirby
packed all the beaver hides they had. He wanted to sell
these to Warren Douglas and put most of the money on
account with him. After a good breakfast and strong
coffee, Kirby harnessed Jake while Rachel cleaned up
the kitchen. When she had finished she put her
wolverine fur over her shoulders and closed the
windows and door.

As they rode by Chapman's house, Joe was on
the front lawn waving goodbye. All the way across
Grafton flats, people were outside waving goodbye.
Ruth and Jim were drinking coffee while sitting on the
porch.

"You be careful way up there and be careful on
the river," Ruth was sorry to see them go.

We'll only be gone for two months," Rachel
said.

"We'll be back probably before Thanksgiving.
Sooner if the lakes start to freeze."

They all said goodbye and Kirby and Rachel
headed for Douglas' store. There, they picked up the
traps Kirby had requested, the rifles and ammunition
and Rachel was busy filling her list. She picked up two
more heavy winter coats, two cans of tobacco this year
and more coffee, salt, sugar and enough felt hats for all
those who didn't have one yet.

Kirby picked up another can of coffee for them
as well as salt. He also picked up two boxes of wooden
kitchen matches. One he would give to Falling Bear.
Rachel picked up two more blankets. "We have enough
room for two more don't we?"

"I think we can manage." They settled accounts with Warren.

"Rachel there is still $50 on your People's account and Kirby after paying for everything else you have $140. Hope you have a good season. Bring back plenty of beaver. And otter too if there are any up where you're going," he added jokingly.

They loaded everything into the wagon and headed for Captain Wilson's landing on the Magalloway River.

* * * *

They had two months supplies with them on this trip, plus the gear for Falling Bear and their traps. The canoe was loaded heavy and their headway against the current was slow. They had to make camp an extra night this time before reaching Aziscohos Falls.

"Loaded down for bear this trip aren't you," Fred Cyr said as he met them at his dock below the falls."

This early in the morning, the deadwater behind the dam was calm, there was no wind yet. But as they neared the mouth of Parmachenee Lake a light wind was coming out of the northeast. So they stayed next to the eastern shoreline and out of most of the wind.

By the time they had reached Rachel's Point, as Kirby was now calling her campsite, they were both exhausted. After a hearty supper and a bath in cold pond water they both were ready for sleep. Kirby was on his back and Rachel was laying up next to him with her head resting on his chest. His arm was around her and he asked, "Are you horny tonight?"

"No."

"Good."

Chapter 6

The next morning before the sun was up the loon was out front calling. Welcoming them home. Kirby nudged Rachel and said, "He's back."

"Who's back?" half asleep still.

"The loon. Can't you hear him? He's right out front."

"Well.....it'll be a good day then," and she fell back to sleep.

Kirby laid on his back listening to the loon and the other forest sounds. This would be their home for two months. As he laid there, he was enjoying the idea that this would be home for two months and the more he thought about it the more he was enjoying the idea. And he was too excited to lay there any longer. He got out of bed, trying not to waken Rachel again. He dressed and went outside and started a fire. There was nothing like the smell of clean wood smoke. He went out behind the wikitup and found some more dry wood, in the dawning sunlight.

Rachel heard the wood snapping in the fire and got up. Kirby was sitting on the shore watching the loon out front and the rising sun when he turned to look at her. She saw the happiness that was all around him. It was like a halo that encompassed his being. "You're enjoying yourself aren't you my husband."

"Yes. My life has certainly changed since I came to Grafton and met you."

Rachel made some tea and warmed up some food while Kirby shaved and then reloaded the canoe with the supplies for The People. After they had eaten, they put everything else inside the wikitup for now.

Before they left, Kirby made sure the fire was out. They weren't long before they saw activity up ahead. Children were playing with the ball Rachel had given them on their last visit.

Falling Bear, Wonnocka and Pollinoke were there to greet them as Kirby swung the bow of the canoe towards shore.

They were both welcomed as if this was the first time they had been back. These were truly warm and friendly people, Kirby thought. And as much as he didn't want to think about it, there would be a time in their future when they would lose all of this. Either by integrating and blending with the whites or through modernization. Their present and future, he was afraid, had already been written. And although Falling Bear never spoke of it, Kirby knew in his heart, that Falling Bear was also aware of this.

Kirby handed the new rifles to Wonnocka and he was as excited as a little kid being given a present at Christmas. The winter coats were given to Pollinoke and the tobacco to Falling Bear. Rachel had brought just enough felt hats so everyone in the village now had one. Kirby handed Falling Bear a box of wooden matches and Falling Bear said, "Already have fire sticks. You keep."

Rachel walked over to speak to her friend Wiona and gave her a red bandanna and showed her how to tie it around her hair. The blankets were given to Falling Bear to give to those most needing them.

Falling Bear said, "Come, smoke pipe with me and Wonnocka. He will soon be leader. Rachel you come too."

They all followed Falling Bear to his lodge. They waited patiently while he opened the can of tobacco and filled the pipe. He gave it to Wonnocka to light. Before anyone said anything the pipe was passed to each. Rachel enjoyed the honor of being included, but she could not inhale the smoke and it was beginning to burn her eyes.

Falling Bear took a second deep puff and let it exhale slowly. "My son Wonnocka will soon be leader of Our People. My time is close. It is good you are here," and he looked at Rachel. "I would not want to go on to the land of my father without seeing you one more time. Your mother, father were not of our people. You Rachel are. Your father was great man, Dekanawida, the Great Peacemaker. You are of same spirit Rachel. You travel all over country, everybody see you are great too. When you first come to live with The People, we were a young tribe. You always helped me with The People. You taught everyone to speak your tongue and understand the English. You taught some to read. You will always be one of us."

Wonnocka had tears in his eyes, listening to his father. Falling Bear took another long puff and exhaled slowly. "Kirby Morgan you one of The People now too. Not because of Rachel, but because what is here," and he put the palm of his hand to his heart. "You have goodness of spirit and you care for The People. You saved Wonnocka's two sons, you almost lost yours trying to save the boys. You put The People before you."

He took another puff and passed the pipe around to everyone before speaking again. "My son Wonnocka, you will be leader in my place before the moon in the sky tonight. The rock that sits on me is getting heavier. You have heard my words here. You will always treat Rachel and Kirby as your brother and sister. Always.

"I think the Great Creator had chosen me to follow your father and bring news of his travels and what he told to all the tribes, back to you. I have always felt honored that it was me who traveled and watched your father 'Carajou'."

"Now, go. I must rest."

Once outside Rachel looked at Kirby, "We stay. I wouldn't think of leaving now."

Rachel hugged him and said, "Thank you."

*   *   *   *

Later that afternoon Kirby and Rachel were playing with the children with the ball and Wonnocka came to see them. "Falling Bear has left. It is a good thing you both came when you did. I know he is at ease now; making the journey to his fathers."

"Come, I need your help." Kirby and Rachel followed Wonnocka to Falling Bear's lodge. There they dressed him in his finest robes and propped him into a sitting position. "Tomorrow morning at first light, we must put my father in his canoe and I am to take him where he told me. I must go alone and tell no one where he lies. Now we must prepare him. So he can join his father. Come." They followed Wonnocka outside.

"Wonnocka," Kirby said, "I must talk with you. I know Falling Bear said I am one of The People now and I can use this land as my brother, you Wonnocka. Rachel and I want to trap beaver and other animals. We will stay from here to Parmachenee and not take beaver where you hunt and trap."

Wonnocka looked surprised, "You are my brother. You can go anywhere."

"I know, I just didn't want to crowd you. I won't do anything without telling you first."

"This is good. You have my word and my father's word stands."

"Thank you my brother," Kirby said.

As they laid awake in each others embrace they talked for a long time about Rachel's life with The People. "When Wonnocka leaves with Falling Bear in the morning, we can leave also.

*   *   *   *

Kirby helped Wonnocka carry Falling Bear to the canoe and positioned him in the bow. The body had gone rigid during the night, like Wonnocka knew it would and this is the traditional way to take the last canoe ride. Sitting up.

"Wonnocka, we leave also and go to Rachel's Point. We will come here often while we are here."

"This will be good." He climbed in his canoe without talking more and began Falling Bear's last canoe ride.

Kirby and Rachel said goodbye to Pollinoke and Wiona and left.

"Do you know what Wonnocka will do with the body?"

"He will go where Falling Bear told him. Only Wonnocka knows the location. It will be a nice place. There Wonnocka will leave him sitting and facing to the morning sun. Then Wonnocka will leave.

"By now Falling Bear's spirit will be gone and the bear and wolf will come to eat the flesh.

"I know this is not how Christians honor their dead. But this is The People's way."

"It makes a lot more sense to me than burying someone in the ground. Take them to a nice place where they will be at peace."

"Sometimes you think like an Indian," they laughed and the sadness and tension was gone.

Once they had returned to Rachel's Point, they sorted through their supplies and the traps were hung in a tree. While Rachel stored their food stuffs, Kirby took his axe and went after firewood. Inside the wikitup they would need dry wood that wouldn't smoke much. The outside fire could burn either. Green wood would last longer.

They worked all day setting up camp for a long stay and Kirby had brought in about a cord of dry fire wood. Rachel gathered dry pine needles and made a thick bedding under the bear hide. She brought cedar and fir boughs to make the wikitup smell good.

She shouldered a pack basket and said, Come on husband, let's go find some edible mushrooms. It is the season." They had to hike quite a distance before they were in hardwood, where edible mushrooms would be more likely to grow. They found bear's head tooth mushrooms, the pale orange ones, inky-caps, fawn mushrooms and a mushroom that looked like coral. When they had finished, the pack basket was full. "We can dry these in the sun and they'll stay good for a long time. While I clean these and set them out to dry, you can catch us some trout for supper."

*   *   *   *

The next day after breakfast Kirby and Rachel put the traps and gear in the canoe and went scouting for beaver. There were many streams emptying into the Magalloway River and methodically Kirby started with the first one to the west and would follow that to the end setting for beaver. When they had taken the large ones from that stream, they would move on to the next, staying to the west until coming close to the village. Then they would switch to the east side of the river and do the same.

After that first day Kirby decided they would be a long time on the first tributary alone. From that there were many other tributaries, all with beaver colonies.

They carried the rifle with them everywhere they went. They had heard a wolf howl way off in the distance. There were bear around and Kirby wasn't sure if there would be mountain lions or not. The beaver were skun and fleshed there in the woods and most of the time the carcass was left, which would attract all meat eaters. They ate a lot of beaver meat, but they didn't want a constant diet of it. So each day they shot rabbit, partridge or duck. Kirby let Rachel do most of the shooting. She was as good with a rifle as he was. "Shoot the head so not to waste the meat." Some of the beaver meat they took to the village where the women would dry it or smoke it for winter storage.

One day while they were tending traps at the very west end of a tributary, Kirby was skinning and fleshing the last beaver and Rachel had just rolled up the last hide and was putting it in the pack basket with the others, when Kirby looked up and saw a very large wolf lunge towards Rachel. Kirby hollered, "Rachel!" he said as loud as he could.

Rachel looked up just as the wolf started to lunge. All she had time to do was to cross her arms in front of her. Kirby reacted instinctively without giving it a split moment of thought. He stood up and jumped at the wolf and kicked it in the ass as hard as he could. Hoping to break the pelvis or spine. Instead of clamping its jaws onto Rachel's arm, the wolf let out a screeching, yelping howl of pain.

The wolf lost its focus on Rachel and turned. Kirby saw the wolf's hind legs were not responding normally, but the wolf made a snarling, growling lunge at Kirby's throat. Again, Kirby reacted instinctively and jammed his right hand into the wolf's mouth and down its throat. He wrapped his hand around the wolf's tongue and windpipe in a vise like grip. The wolf's momentum knocked Kirby over and he fell to the ground while wrestling with the wolf. He still held onto the wolf's tongue and windpipe, and the wolf could not close its jaw to bite. But he fought Kirby with every ounce of his strength.

As soon as Kirby and the wolf were on the ground, Rachel saw what he had done and she too, reacting instinctively picked up the axe, which was laying on the ground beside her; the rifle was leaning against a spruce tree eight feet away.

With all of her strength she swung the axe at the wolf's ribcage, cutting hide and ribs and blood spurting into the air. The wolf collapsed to the ground and Kirby removed his hand. Steam from the gapping wound was rising in the cold air. The wolf blinkned and rolled its eyes and then tried to stand. Rachel swung the axe again and hit the wolf on top of the head. Now he lay dead. The fight gone.

Kirby and Rachel looked at each other: first with concern and then they started laughing. They were relieving the tension of the close situation. Then they sat down holding each other.

"Are you alright Rachel?"

"Yes, I'm okay. But what about you? Let me see that hand." His hand had scratches from the wolf's teeth, only scratches though and they were not deep.

"What made you decide to kick him in the ass? I'm glad you did, but what were you thinking?"

"I guess I wasn't thinking. I just reacted naturally. It seemed like a pretty good idea while I was doing it. Anything to get it off you."

Rachel started laughing again and finally she was able to say, "I bet you are the only man in history who has ever kicked an attacking wolf in the ass."

"Why did you grab the axe and not the rifle?"

"The axe was right beside me and the rifle is over there. Besides, in all the excitement I might have shot you in the hand."

"You know, if we told this story to others, they would never believe us."

"You know, maybe there is too much beaver scent on this side of the big river, since we have been leaving most of the carcasses here. Let's try the east side tomorrow."

"Skin the wolf before we leave. I'll make a vest for you. Dog animals don't have as much fat, so the hide will cure fast. I think I can finish it before we leave to go home."

As they lay together in each other's warm embrace Rachel said, "Matelok lost a son killed by wolves. Keoka, Matelok's first woman had their son with her while she was picking berries. The wolf attacked and killed the son. Matelok was so grieved he swore a vengeance against all wolves, and he killed every wolf he saw.

*   *   *   *

Later that afternoon as Rachel was tending to the wolf hide, Kirby was stretching the beaver they had caught that morning. So far they had a total of fourteen extra large beaver. Next year they should be able to trap in the same colonies and get more extra large beaver as long as they only took the large beaver. Kirby figured in his head that those fourteen beaver hides represented a half year's work.

They found as many beaver colonies on the east side as there were on the west. That first day out they trapped three beaver and one large otter. That was a total surprise to them both. That evening it started to drizzle so they tied up the piece of canvas Kirby had brought along, over their outside cooking area. They pulled all the drying hides under the canvas.

That night as they lay awake talking, the rain had a melodious sound as it beat against the side of the wikitup. The rhythmic music soon put them both to sleep. When they awoke the next morning it was still raining, so they stayed in camp that day. Rachel rubbed hemlock bar on the flesh side of the wolf hide until it was soft and shined with an oil sheen.

She made sewing thread by washing out beaver intestines and stripping them to fine threads. She worked all day, cutting, sewing and hemming the edges. She had made three buttons from pieces of wood, so Kirby could button it. When she had finished the vest was a beautiful garment.

Kirby was speechless, "I don't know what to say. I thought it would take you a lot longer than this to make it. It's beautiful."

"Maybe that will protect you from other wolves."

*   *   *   *

It rained for two days before stopping. On the morning of the third day they decided to visit Wonnocka and The People. They all marveled at the wolf hide Kirby was wearing. When they told them the whole story, The People, Wonnocka included, thought the two of them were aberrations from a story. But when Kirby showed them the scratches on his hand, they slowly began to believe.

Wonnocka was pleased with their visit. Since Falling Bear's translation to his fathers world, he had not had much time for relaxing. Cold weather was coming and it was up to him now to delegate hunters to go out and bring back winter food. And others to get firewood. There was always something to do.

He was sad when Kirby and Rachel had to leave to return to Rachel's Point. "My brother is always welcome here."

That night the weather turned unusually cold and there was a layer of white frost on the ground. It was only early October, so Kirby wasn't too concerned. In spite of the cold, they went out and before the end of the day they had caught four otter out of the same colony and no beaver. In the next colony they had two beaver. "How many do you want to trap this year?" Rachel asked.

"Thirty if we have the time. We should be able to carry that many in the canoe. I figured we might leave some of our gear here, instead of hauling it back and forth every trip. If my count is correct we should have twenty beaver now."

Each day they moved on to new colonies; always taking only the largest beaver there and any otter that were caught by happenstance. Otter were bringing as much money as beaver and less work to take care of the hides.

The east side of the Magalloway River was more productive than the west and they had not seen any wolf or bear signs. Two weeks after switching to the east they now had thirty beaver and Kirby said, "We have our thirty beaver. Let's stop trapping beaver. I'd like to try the mink and otter. We'll stay away from beaver dams, so we don't get one accidentally. I don't want to be greedy and thirty beaver will represent a years pay for us both." Rachel was pleased when Kirby said no more beaver. To leave some for seed for next year was good Indian logic.

*   *   *   *

They set out a few mink and otter traps and then fished for trout. As Kirby fished, Rachel would clean the trout and then hang them over the rack to smoke and cure. Loaded heavy with beaver hides the trip back would be a little slower and they would need more food supplies.

As a boy growing up on the farm, Kirby had trapped for mink and each year he would get a few. The mink were more difficult to trap than either the beaver or otter. But up here, it seemed as though no matter where they set traps mink would find them and get caught. They now had twelve mink, six otter and thirty beaver. "That's enough trapping this year."

Rachel just smiled and was pleased. "When all the hides are dried let's go visit The People and stay a couple of days before we head for home."

Neither of them knew the date. Just that this must be October. The foliage had peaked two weeks ago and most of the leaves had already dropped. But there had been no sign of ice yet.

That night the temperature dropped sharply and there was a thin film of ice on the pond. During the night as the air got colder and colder, they could hear the trees freeze and then snap as the wood would crack from the expanding moisture in the fiber. There was a layer of heavy frost covering everything when they got up.

They left for the village after eating and everything was taken care of and cleaned up. They broke through the thin film of ice with ease. But there was a lot of noise as the ice broke against the canoe.

There was no ice in the main river. The current was too swift, but they had not canoed very far when they came to an ice covered cove, sitting back off the north side of the river. Just as they were canoeing by the cove, Kirby noticed something strange and swung the bow around towards the cove. "What is it Kirby? Why did you do that?"

"Look," and he nodded his head towards the icey cove.

Rachel turned to look. "What is it? I don't see anything. What are you looking at?"

"There, on the ice." There were six softball size rocks sitting on top of the ice; all in scattered directions. "How did those rocks get out on the ice? They certainly didn't get there by themselves. Somebody had to put them there. But why? And the ice isn't strong enough to hold even a small child."

"Oh, I see what you're looking at now," Rachel said and she began to laugh. "Moskuos, the rat that swims."

"Muskrat?"

"Yes, that's it."

"Buy why?" Kirby asked.

"In winter on frozen swamps and shallow water, you must have seen the grassy mounds on the ice? Breathing holes for muskrat."

"Yes, I know what you are saying."

"When water freezes, muskrat can't gnaw through the ice to make the breathing holes, so as soon as ice makes, the muskrat digs rocks out of the bank and pushes them over the ice. The sun will eventually warm the rocks and it melts through the ice and makes a hole for the muskrat to make the grassy mounds on top of the ice. Grass and plants he gets from the bottom. Look, there goes one now," and Rachel pointed with her paddle towards a muskrat out in the middle pushing a rock across the ice.

"Well I'll be damned," Kirby said. "I would never have guessed."

Rachel turned to look at Kirby and playfully said, "You can learn a lot from an Indian."

They laughed and continued on towards the village.

*   *   *   *

Life for The People in the village continued on, after Falling Bear's passing, pretty much as it had before. Wonnocka was trying to live up to his father's honor and other young men were helping.

Rachel spent a lot of time with her good friend Wiona. Telling her about the life she had found in a village called Grafton, about Ruth and Jim Brown and about the day Kirby had arrived at the Brown's farm with their son's body.

Kirby spent a lot of his time with Wonnocka. Wonnocka wanted to learn more about the white man's ways. "Do you my brother, think that the white man will come into this land?"

"There are fishing camps already on Parmachenee Lake. People from big cities outside, pay a lot of money to come to the camps to fish for brook trout."

"All this land from Parmachenee to St. Francis in Canada belong to Indians, to the Cooshuake People. We have paper that says this," Wonnocka said.

"I know. You and I Wonnocka may not live to see the white man come into this land. But they will come eventually."

Wonnocka was quiet then, and Kirby knew he was worrying about his People. "If I see any white man come into this land of Wonnocka's People, I will stop them."

To change the subject, Kirby asked, "Where is Noison? I have not seen him."

"He go to St. Francis People, look for wife to bring back soon."

"Why did he have to go to St. Francis? Did he know someone there?"

"Wonnocka's People all family. If young brave wants wife, he goes to St. Francis." The only way Wonnocka could explain was to say, "New blood," and he nodded his head towards Kirby. Kirby understood.

"Young braves from St. Francis come here for wife." This was making sense now.

"How did Noison go to St. Francis, walk?"

"Walk trail by Slologan to Arnold Pond in Canada. Not long walk. Take canoe down river to St. Francis." Now Kirby understood where the path went that he had wanted to follow beyond the marsh.

* * * *

After two days both Kirby and Rachel were glad to be leaving. They would spend one more night at Rachel's Point and then at first light they would start the trip back home.

Before going to bed that night they packed all their gear and what few supplies were left, all except for what would be left behind in the wikitup.

As they sat around the fire cooking supper, Kirby asked, "Are you sorry we'll be leaving in the morning?"

"No, I want to get home and start making our new house into a home. I love it when we come here, but its time to go home."

They would be taking back a lot of the smoked trout and beaver meat. There was very little corn meal left, enough to make enough dough to wrap on a stick and roast over a fire. Rachel had some dried berries and mushrooms. It was just as well they didn't have many supplies left to take back, as they would be loaded heavy with hides.

As they lay wrapped in each other's arms Rachel said, "I have wanted to give you a son, but I don't come pregnant. You must think me terrible woman."

"No, not at all. There are some couples who can't have babies. I don't understand it, but it happens."

"Are you disappointed my husband?"

He thought for a moment before answering. He didn't want to offend or upset her. "You know love, maybe this is the Great Creator's way. The lifestyle you and I live, would be difficult for raising a family. I would not leave you behind to go off and trap and leave you to raise sons and daughters. I think there is a purpose why you do not get pregnant."

She snuggled closer and hugged him tight and said, "You make me happy."

They were awakened at first light by old Mr. Loon. He had come to say goodbye that morning and to see them off. While Rachel prepared food, Kirby loaded the canoe with everything that was going back. Then he covered the load with the piece of canvas.

They ate all they could, because they probably wouldn't stop to eat again until they made camp for the night. Then they put the cover back on top of the wikitup and tied the front flap closed. "Let's go." But first Rachel walked over and stood in front of Kirby, looking into his eyes. He put his arms around her and kissed her passionately and whispered in her ear, "I love you sweetheart."

Kirby climbed into the stern of the canoe and then Rachel pushed away from shore and jumped in and sat down. The water was calm like a mirror and the loon was following behind them.

Neither one spoke as they paddled along noiselessly. In next to shore in places there was a thin layer of ice. The sun was just coming up over the tree tops and a gentle breeze was blowing at their backs. They were out in the open lake now and the water was still calm. They made good time canoeing the length of Parmachenee and they reached the narrow outlet and the loon that had followed from Rachel's Point, now ran across the surface flapping its wings and calling.

When he finally was airborne he circled once over their head and called out one final goodbye and then he headed south. Probably for the winter.

*   *   *   *

Between Parmachenee and Aziscohos deadwater, beaver had built a dam across the river since they went up river about two months ago. It was solid and holding water. Rachel climbed out and stood on the dam and then Kirby and then they lowered the canoe over the top and into the water. It was only a minor hold up.

The wind had changed direction and was now coming from the south, directly at them. The water was rough, but not too bad. Loaded heavy as the canoe was they rode the rough water in fine shape. But the headway was a lot slower. It was more than twelve miles down the length of the deadwater to the dam, following the shoreline, as they had to and they were all that day getting to the lower end.

Fred Cyr was at the dock when they pulled up. "Well, hello folks. I thought you'd be coming back any day now. You wanting to go through now, or wait 'til morning?"

"Right now would be good Mr. Cyr."

"Okay, let's get it loaded up. This is a big cache of beaver. No wonder you were sitting lower in the water."

Fred was obliging and didn't complain that his supper was getting cold. Kirby gave him $2 this time and said, "For the extra weight. Thanks Fred. See you in the spring."

There was a half hour of daylight left and they wanted to make it to their usual stopping point. They pushed on and pulled ashore in the dark. As soon as a fire was burning, everything was alright again. And they were feeling warm and comfortable.

They were both hungry and ate all of the cornmeal stick bread and filled up with smoked trout. They would have the beaver in the morning, as that would give them more energy than the trout.

Before going to sleep, they gave each other a massage. The wind blew all night, but in their shelter they were not aware of it. When they awoke the next morning the wind was still blowing. But that would not affect them much on the river. They ate all they could of the smoked beaver and then cleaned up and were on their way. There were ice crystals hanging from the branches that were close to the water. "It must have gotten real cold last night. Look at the ice crystals," Kirby said.

"Maybe we left just at the right time."

Even with the current today, the progress was slower than usual. They were sitting that low in the water.

Instead of pushing to late into the night that day, they held up on the same island as they had in the spring. This would be their last night out in the cold and sleeping on the ground. They were excited with the thought of reaching home tomorrow and with the combination of the beaver meat, which contained a lot of protein and nutrients, they found it difficult to sleep. They were too hyped, too excited.

They laid awake way into the night, talking excitedly about how successful this trip had been and also excited that it was over and they would soon be home and excited they had each other. Some time after midnight, they both finally drifted off to sleep.

But by first light they were awakened again by a loon calling from the river. "Do you suppose that is the same loon?" Kirby asked.

"I don't know. Let's go out and see if it swims off when it sees us. If it does then we'll know it is a different one."

They crawled out from their blankets and shelter and there was the loon, and he wasn't moving. "What do you make of that? What do you suppose he wants?"

"Maybe he's simply lonely."

"I hope he knows how to fly south. Cause after today we'll be home and there's no water there for him."

"Maybe this is only as far as he got yesterday and he's telling us he is surprised to see us."

"Maybe." They laughed and went about getting ready. "Any more beaver meat?"

"Yes. The smoked trout I'd like to save for the Thanksgiving celebration," Rachel said.

Once they were back on the river, it didn't take long to reach Wilson's Landing. Rachel helped to harness ole Jake and load the wagon. Captain Wilson heard the noise outside and came out. Kirby paid him what he owed and they were on their way. "Do you want to stop at the hotel for breakfast?" he asked.

"That goes without saying."

Kirby tied Jake to a hitching rail and the two walked inside. There were a few hunters and they all stopped when they saw Kirby and Rachel. Particularly how they were dressed. He wearing a wolf vest and Rachel a wolverine and topped off with green felt hats. After a moment, Enoch Abbott recognized them and led them to a table against the far wall. He then went into the kitchen and brought out a coffee pot and three mugs. He poured the coffee and sat down to join them.

He wanted to know all about their excursion. And in particular about the wolf vest Kirby was wearing.

A young woman from the kitchen came out and took their orders. Kirby and Rachel both had pancakes and a thick slice of bacon. Enoch had another cup of coffee.

When they had finished they said goodbye to Enoch and continued on to Warren Douglas' store. "Hello folks. That's some fine looking beaver. Let's get them inside and take a look at 'em."

Kirby had to make a second trip for the otter.

Warren was sorting the hides. "All extra large, that'll make it easy. Thirty beaver, that's $650." He looked at the otter next, and ran his hand through the fur. "Nice," he said. "Ten otter, $300. Six mink, $60. You're going to break the bank with this catch. I owe you $1,010."

"We'll take that, cash or check and we need to stock up with supplies. We'll use up what we have on account here for those items." When Rachel had finished, they had most of a wagon load, and still $20 left on their account.

"Thank you Mr. Douglas."

On their way to see the Browns now Rachel said, "We still need to make a trip to Bethel before it snows."

It was the middle of the afternoon when they arrived at the Browns. Jim was just walking across the bridge from the mill. "Hello, I wasn't expecting you back quite this early."

"Ah.....what is the date? We lost all track of time."

"It's November 15th, Wednesday." Jim laughed. How could anyone not know the day of the week or the

date? Then he thought about their lifestyle for the last
two months and laughed

"That's an awful pretty vest, Kirby. Rachel
make that for you?"

"She did, and there's quite a story that goes with
it."

"Come in and have some coffee, probably Ruth
would like to hear the story also. This way you'll only
have to tell it once."

The coffee pot was already on the stove and hot.
Ruth poured cups for everyone. Kirby started the story
off and then Rachel would chime in, then back to
Kirby, to Rachel and finally the story was told.

Jim finished his coffee and Ruth poured him
another cup. "Back in 1850 Charles Bean did that to a
bear. He and young Henry Dunn were out berrying and
a bear attacked Charles. He didn't have a gun and all
he could do was ram his hand into the bear's mouth and
grab a hold of its tongue. Charles was squealing like a
pig at Henry. Telling him to reach into his pants pocket
and get his pocket knife. Young Henry didn't like that
bear none and didn't want to get any closer than he had
to. But Charles kept hollering at him. Finally Henry
got up enough nerve to get the knife. Then Charles
said, 'Open it.' Henry did and handed to Charles. He
slashed at that bear's neck several times while hanging
onto his tongue. He finally killed it and took his hand
out of the bear's mouth. His hand was pretty mangled
but his mother patched him up pretty well."

"Can you stay for supper?" Ruth asked.

"We really shouldn't. We have a wagon load of
supplies we picked up at Douglas'. And to be honest
with you, I'm a little anxious to get home."

"Jim," Kirby said, "we have to go into Bethel
tomorrow for more winter supplies, when we get back,

we'll start cutting those pine behind the house and haul the saw logs up here. And if it wouldn't be too inconvenient, could we have our wages that you have been holding?"

"Sure thing. I'll be right back." He disappeared into another room. When Jim returned he gave a ledger to Rachel and one to Kirby and said, "Here is all of your wages up to date."

"Thank you. When we have all the saw logs hauled up here and the two mast logs to Bethel, if you need extra help this winter, we can help out."

"I know Ruth and Mary can use Rachel here and you can work the yard and or mill."

"That'll be fine," Kirby said.

Ruth had given Rachel a short list of things she would need. Kirby folded his money and gave it to Rachel. This surprised both Jim and Ruth.

When they had gone Jim said, "Have you noticed Ruth that whenever either one of them is talking, it's always we, we are going to do something, we thought, always we? Never I or me. And they are always together. What was on your list Ruth, that you gave to Rachel?"

"Oh not much. Some new patterns for a dress and a shirt for you. Sewing things and some under garments for me. Why?"

"I'll bet you dollars to donuts that when Rachel goes to fill your list, Kirby will be right there with her. Most men wouldn't bother, they'd say that's women's stuff. He's different Ruth. They both are different, like one is the right hand and the other is the left. Neither one of them would ever consider taking a trip to Bethel alone or back to her people alone."

"Yes Jim I have noticed also. And it makes me happy to see two people who need each other as much as they do."

Chapter 7

There were so many townspeople at the Thanksgiving celebration, the Tavern was full, so Ruth had to open her house also. Everybody brought food and Rachel brought four of the huge trout she had smoked. Even Ronki-Tonk donated. He had made an excellent batch of apple cider. Of course he had twenty gallons hidden in the barn that was getting some age on it.

Rachel helped Ruth and Mary in the kitchen getting all the food set out in bowls on tables so people could serve themselves.

After the feasting was over Kirby and Rachel headed home. "Tomorrow we start cutting those pine and see if ole Jake here can twitch the logs down to the road, where I built a loading ramp. I'll be glad when we have Jim paid back for all of the lumber."

After breakfast the next morning Kirby went out back to find an easy route off the ridges to the loading ramp beside the road. He finally decided the best way would be to use the path he cleared earlier for the tall pine. This way, by dragging the pine logs down this path the logs would carve a groove in the ground and then with water and snow he could more easily make his flume.

"Rachel, I'm going up to start notching the first tree, when you're ready, bring the big saw and sledge hammer with you. We might have to wedge the tree over."

Kirby went up and walked around and around the first pine tree looking for the best angle to drop it. He finally settled on where he wanted it to land and began cutting a notch with his new axe. It was sharp and he was sinking the bit deep into the wood.

Rachel arrived before he had the tree all notched and she watched him swing the axe, blow after blow without stopping or tiring.

"There, that should do it. I hope it falls where it is supposed to."

They each grabbed an end of the two man crosscut saw and began sawing back and forth.

It was hard work and they both were sweating. When they were about half way through, they stopped and Kirby started a wedge in the saw groove to help the tree fall in the right direction.

"When this starts to go over Rachel, get away from the butt end. Sometimes it'll bolt back and could hit you, if you're standing too close."

Every inch they gained with the saw, they would stop and Kirby would drive the wedge in further with the sledge hammer. There was only about three inches to go. "Okay, I'll man the saw alone Rachel, while you drive the wedge in."

"Okay," and she picked up the sledge hammer and began driving the wedge in. It was going easy and then the tree started to lean and Kirby said, "Okay clear away from it."

They stood back and in slow motion it seemed, they watched the huge tree crash to the ground.

"Now the hard work begins. Sawing this brute into sixteen foot logs. You ready?"

It took longer to saw out one log than it did to fall the big tree. But by noon they had managed to saw out all the logs. They had four sixteen foot logs and two twelves.

That afternoon they had two of the logs down the hillside to the loading ramp. That was enough for one day. "I didn't know work could be this hard. Every muscle in my body aches. How about you?" Kirby asked.

Rachel already had her clothes off and filling the tub for a bath.

Ole Jake was tired too. Kirby gave him a good rub down and a ration of oats. Jake was doing good, considering he wasn't a draft horse.

The next day they twitched the rest of the logs down and fell another pine tree and had the logs sawn out by dark. Two days later they had a third tree all logged out and piled up at the loading ramp. The next day Kirby and Rachel went to see Jim.

"Good morning Jim. Would you have a spare team and a heavy wagon we could borrow to haul the pine logs up here with. Jake was able to drag 'em down hill to a loading ramp I built, but he can't haul 'em up here."

"Sure. Take the spotted brown pair and have Ronki-Tonk show you where the heavy haul wagon is. How many have you to haul?"

"Three trees total. It'll take a couple of days to get everything up here."

While Kirby and Ronki-Tonk were getting the team and wagon ready, Rachel went inside to visit with Ruth and Mary.

Ruth asked, "Who does Kirby have helping him log?"

"Just me," Rachel replied.

Ruth was thinking, she should have known better than to ask. Of course she would help.

"Ronki-Tonk, is there an extra kent-dog laying around?"

"Yes, I have a couple in the barn. Behind the oats bin. Did you break yours?"

"No, Rachel needs one. I guess I should have bought two when I picked up the saws and stuff."

Jake was put out in the pasture and the wagon parked out of the way. Kirby and Rachel drove home and went right to work rolling logs onto the wagon. This was all new to Rachel, and in spite of her petite frame, she was a lot of help to Kirby. They only had enough time to make one load to the mill that day.

At the end of each day after the team had been put away, watered, fed, and rubbed down, then Kirby and Rachel bathed and ate supper. "If it was warmer we'd bathe in the brook under the falls," Rachel said.

They could only make two trips a day to the mill and they hauled logs for four days before everything was sitting in the mill yard. Jim walked over to see the wood, and said, "There's more than enough lumber in these logs Kirby to replace what you used. Why don't you scale them and the extra, I'll pay you for them."

"I'll gladly scale them for you Jim, but you don't have to pay me anything."

"When we get ready to fell those two mast pine I'd like to hire this team and the sled runners for the long logs."

"Sure thing. I made a special set of runners for the rear set. They sit two feet higher than the front, so the tree won't hang up going over the notch. When are you figuring to do it?"

"Just as soon as we have enough snow to build a flume."

"A what?" Jim asked.

Kirby told Jim all about his idea of making an ice flume to slide the tall mast pine down off the ridge to the road. "It sounds good, but I never heard it being done before. Good luck."

Another week passed before it snowed. During the day Kirby kept snowshoeing up and down the path where he was going to make the flume. Jake dragging the logs along this path had worn a shallow ditch along it and now Kirby was trying to pack snow along this. Then he would improve the design by scooping out a trough in his snowshoe trail and then freezing that down with water and smoothing out any rough spots. He was deciding it was more work making the flume than anything else. The day finally came when he was satisfied with the flume. He and Rachel had made over a hundred trips from the brook with water buckets. They were exhausted so they took a day to rest.

The following day after a hardy breakfast, it was time to bring those trees to the ground. They loaded up with axe, saw, sledge hammer and wedge. Kirby had already scouted out many times which direction he wanted the tree to go. He had decided that the tree would slide down the flume the easiest, top first. So he started to make the notch with the axe. His axe was sharp and the notch was cut in short order.

Rachel looked at him as if to say, "Are you sure?" without saying a word she handed one end of the big saw to Kirby and they started to saw through the butt. Half way through they stopped and Kirby started the wedge. After a while Kirby said, "Now," and Rachel let Kirby have the saw alone while she drove the wedge in with the sledge hammer. Kirby could see the saw groove widening. Widening until the tree started to fall all on its own. "Okay Rachel, that's good," and they stood clear of the butt as the tree fell through the other tree tops to the ground. It was down and laying about two feet away from the flume. Kirby limbed the top and then measured it where the top was a foot across. "One hundred and ten feet."

They cut the top off there and hauled all the branches out of the way. "Now, how do we move it over to the flume?" Rachel asked.

Kirby held up one kent-dog and handed it to Rachel and said, "We roll it with these."

He showed her how to set the dog and lift on the handle. "Working together we should be able to roll it enough to get it to the flume." He hoped.

Rachel went down about half way and Kirby planted his kent-dog in the heavy butt end. When Rachel had hers set, they began to roll the tree. Kirby was actually surprised how easy it rolled. It was on the flume and Rachel began to shout excitedly, "It's moving! Kirby it's moving!"

Sure enough. Inch by inch the tree was sliding down hill. With each inch that it slid, it would gain momentum. Finally something let go and the long tree began sliding down the flume and picking up speed.

"Wow! Does that ever work good."

"Yeah, I just hope it doesn't jump across the road."

They hiked down behind it. It was already out of sight. The top end was jutting two feet into the road.

"This is good. We'll leave this end and roll the butt end out of the way for the next tree."

They walked up the driveway and then through the woods to the second tree. This one was about twenty feet up the ridge from the first one. Again he notched it and they began to saw through and set the wedge. This one came down with a thundering whoosh through the tree tops.

When Kirby topped this one off it was 112 feet. As before, they used the kent-dogs to position the tree on the flume and like the first one, it began to slide on its own. They followed it down the flume and this one was laying right beside the first tree.

There was just enough daylight left to chain the sled runners onto both ends and Kirby with the team pulled the first tree out onto the road and then left it there and unhooked the team and walked back to the house. "We'll start for town tomorrow. Maybe we'll make it before dark."

*   *   *   *

The temperature had dropped during the night and after harnessing the team and a large breakfast they were ready for the trek to town. Kirby was surprised how easy the tree on the runners was to haul on the ice-snow road. The team was not even working very hard. "This isn't as bad as I thought it would be."

"Yeah, but you know, all the time we have spent with these two trees, and by the time they're both in Bethel, we could have trapped more beaver that would be worth a lot more. And, we wouldn't be so tired."

"I hear you. After this is done, we'll take a long hard look to see if we cut any more lumber."

The team was wanting to step up the pace across the flats; they were not that far above the notch, but Kirby held them back. It was a long trip to Bethel. They were coming up to the notch now, and the water through Screw Auger Falls was loud and sending a mist into the air. They went over the notch and had two inches to spare under the tree. Jim's extension on the rear runners sure worked.

Down on Newry Flats the wind was blowing snow across the road. They met the stage out of Bethel. Probably they had stayed at Kilgore's Station during the night. They met other people going to work and they met a freight wagon heading for Upton. "Last trip this year," the driver hollered as they passed each other.

It was now noon and they pulled to a stop at the T House at Newry Corner. The team needed a break and some oats. Kirby and Rachel had lunch and some hot coffee.

People inside looked strangely at them at first. They were wearing the wolverine and wolf hides. Mr. Henderson recognized them and asked them to come in and sit down. When the others saw Mr. Henderson talking with them, they stopped staring.

They had hot beef stew and coffee and went on their way again. The team was acting frisky again. A good thing too, because they now had an incline to climb. Then a long flat.

"When we come back, I want to stop at the T House. I saw something I'd like to get for the Browns for a Christmas gift," Rachel said.

"What? You going to tell me? What did you see back there?"

"Two wicker rocking chairs."

"Yeah, I think they would like that."

They reached the depot and the team still had stamina left. Good, because they still had to reach Kilgore's for the night.

The yard man at the depot was glad to see Kirby with the mast tree. "How long?"

"One hundred and ten."

"I'll have to measure also, you understand."

"Not a problem."

The agent ran out his cloth tape measure and said, "One hundred ten. You were right. That's $210. Cash or on account?"

"On account for now. We have one more to bring in."

They left then. And would have to hurry to be at Kilgore's by dark, and stop at the T House again. The team still wanted to run, so Kirby let them for a short ways. They had a makeshift seat on the forward runner and the other one trailing behind. They made a quick stop at the T House and tied on the two wicker rocking chairs.

"We'll have to hurry now."

"Is there anything saying we can't arrive after dark?" Rachel asked.

"No. This is just a time table I have set in my mind."

*   *   *   *

After a hot meal, they were feeling better and went upstairs to their room. The next morning Kirby went out to the barn to feed the team and hook them to the harness before breakfast.

"People keep staring at us. Maybe we need new traveling clothes?"

"I'd sooner think people are questioning in their own minds about these furs we wear. They'll get used to it."

They were home earlier than Kirby's schedule that he had in his mind and had plenty of time to hook up the sled runners to the next tree and pull it along roadside for the morning. Rachel set the two rocking chairs in the living room for now.

The temperature dropped sharply during the night and the road surface was frozen solid, making it more slick, and easier for the team to pull their load. But when they came to the first sharp decline, the load started sliding on its own and Kirby had to make the team go faster to take up the slack. "That was a close one. Before we get to the next hill, I'll have to get off and throw the chains under the rear runners. If we need more braking I'll throw the front ones, too."

Hauling over frozen roads the sled could slide faster than the team and run into their hind legs injuring them. Jim had fashioned short lengths of chain to both sides of the runners so they could be looped over the top of the runners and drag underneath on the road surface, slowing the sled down.

At the head of the next hill Rachel jumped off and when the rear runners came by she looped the chains under the runners. This slowed the sliding enough so the team had to pull. But before they got to the bottom, the sled started free sliding again over a patch of ice and Kirby had to throw the chains under the front runners. This helped but there was still too much slack in the harness between the team and the load. Kirby had to have the team almost running to stay ahead of the sled.

They found the road extremely icy and slick all the way to the T House. By then, the sun had warmed the road surface enough to soften the ice some. They arrived at the depot at about the same time as before and this tree measured another one hundred and twelve feet, $212. "This is the last of these, we'll take our money for both trees today."

Before leaving Bethel they stopped at the bank and deposited that money in their account. "How much do we have now in the bank?" Rachel asked.

"$2,215.79."

"Is that a lot of money?" Rachel asked.

"Yes, and to anyone, it's a lot of money and since we own our home and don't owe any money against it, that makes this worth even more to us. Remember, I still have my government check each month, being deposited. We should be able to live off what we make this winter, at the Brown's and the mill.

"If you're going to return the team tonight, I'll get off at the driveway and walk up and get the house warm and start supper."

"Okay." Kirby let the team have the reins going across Grafton Flats. They still had a lot of energy and they were kicking up the snow with their hooves.

Ronki-Tonk helped to rub the team down and take care of the harness and sled runners, and then to harness Ole Jake to the wagon. Kirby went inside to say hello to Jim and Ruth, and paid him for the use of the team and sled runners.

"Any problems going over the notch?" Jim asked.

"Not at all. We had two inches to spare. That extension you put on the rear runners really helped."

"Actually, it was Ronki-Tonk's idea. I just built it."

Before leaving, Kirby went back to the barn and handed Ronki-Tonk $2.00. "For all of your help Ronki-Tonk."

"Ronki-Tonk, do you have any hard cider left?"

"You wanting some is that it?"

"Yeah, a couple of gallons if you can spare that much. I'll give you a $1.00 for the two gallons."

Ronki-Tonk gave him two jugs and took the dollar. "I'll be wanting those jugs back too. Maybe I should go into the liquor making business." He laughed then and added, "Nah, if I did and Captain Jim found out, he would kick me in the ass and probably kick me out of here. No, I get it pretty good as it is. Have a good ride back Mr. Morgan."

After supper and in the glow of the kerosene lantern, Kirby poured a glass of hard cider for each of them. Kirby pulled his big chair closer to the woodstove and Rachel sat in his lap. The cider had a bite to it and Rachel's face was feeling flushed; she was giggly and said, "My this is good. I have never had it before. Leastwise how it bites your throat going down."

Kirby poured more in each glass. They were quiet as they sipped the cider. Rachel was feeling warm and snuggly, Kirby was relaxed and enjoying his wife's happiness and poise.

"We did good; you and I," she said.

The wind was howling through the trees overhead and the temperature had dropped to 0°F. But inside their house they were oblivious to everything, except each other. She whispered in his ear, "I'm horny."

*   *   *   *

Christmas arrived and many of the townsfolk met at the Poplar Tavern for the usual dinner festival. Again this year too much food was brought and no one walked away hungry. While Jim and Ruth were busy talking with others at the party, Kirby and Rachel unwrapped the rocking chairs in the wagon and took them inside beside the dining room fireplace. There was a fireplace in every room except the kitchen and closets.

When the celebration was over and everybody had left, but Kirby and Rachel, "Come on inside and we'll have another cup of coffee before you leave," Jim said.

When Ruth stepped into the dining room and saw the two rockers she burst into tears hugging both Rachel and Kirby. "You didn't have to do this."

"We know," Rachel said, "but you two have done so much for us, we wanted to do something extra for you."

"Well thank you. These will go good on the porch come summer."

It was already twilight outside, but they continued talking and sipping coffee. "Our daughter Mary is starting up a library here. She has received some donations to start buying books. The Bethel Library has sent her some money and a few books," Ruth said.

"I don't have any money with me, do you have any Kirby? We should make a donation also."

Kirby pulled $10 from his shirt pocket and gave it to Ruth.

It was dark and no moon tonight. Kirby went into the barn, "Hey Ronki-Tonk, I need a pole about twelve feet long. Do you have anything like that?"

"I have a twelve foot river pick pole. Will that do?"

"Yes and I'll need some small rope too. And a kerosene lantern."

Ronki-Tonk knew what he was going to do then.

Kirby thanked him and then tied the pole to the harness on Jake and extended the pole out in front of him as far as it would go and then hung the lantern on the end and secured it. They had to go slow to keep the lantern from swinging too much. But they weren't in any hurry.

On their way home that night Rachel said, "We both could use some new traveling clothes. That will take five deer hides."

"I'll see what I can do about that. I know the crew camps shoot a few dear each winter to feed the men. I'll speak to George."

*   *   *   *

That winter before the mill was running everyday and there was plenty of room in the yard, Kirby went into the woods to shoot deer and moose for the crew camps scattered throughout the valley. He shot all in the head or neck, not wanting holes in the garments Rachel was going to make into clothes. And he took particular care of the hides, fleshing as he skun each one.

They didn't work every day at the Brown's or the mill. It was too far to travel both ways each day in the winter. That was okay also. When they were at home Rachel spent her time turning the hides into soft material for their clothes and Kirby built a table, kitchen counter and floor cabinets and then wall cabinets also. They turned out better than he had figured. Their house was slowly turning into a home. And it was certainly nice having the water piped inside and the hot water tank on the cook stove. Kirby didn't know or care how people in the cities were living. But both he and Rachel were comfortable and considered themselves fortunate.

Young Joe Chapman would come by on snowy days when there was no school and Kirby would give him a dime to help shovel snow around the yard and the length of the driveway when the snow got to deep for Jake.

Chapter 8

The years passed and anyone who knew Kirby and Rachel, knew they were inseparable. People had become accustomed to the two showing up at a tavern or hotel somewhere wearing fur of wolverine and wolf. No one stared any longer. The stories had circulated and everyone had accepted them.

One day an elderly gentleman traveling on the Bethel stage to Upton during the spring happened to see Rachel at the Brown farm while she was wearing her wolverine fur. She and Kirby were on their way to Wonnocka's village. Percy Lelling had been an aspiring newspaper reporter from New York City and had heard stories and myths about the man the Indian tribes were calling Carajou. That he was actually the Great Peacemaker, Dekanawida. He had searched in vain for any physical or corroborating evidence that such a man existed or was Carajou only a myth. All he was ever able to discover was stories told by different tribes.

So when Mr. Lelling saw Rachel wearing the wolverine fur, his first impression was that this was Carajou. But after taking a second look, he realized that she was a woman instead. Kirby noticed the attention this stranger seemed to have with his wife and this upset him. He kept a close watch over Rachel.

Lelling could no longer resist, he had to speak to this person. He walked over to her and Kirby stepped in beside Rachel. "Excuse me. I've been noticing this fur you wear Madame. May I ask from what animal?"

Rachel turned to look at who was addressing her and said, "It is wolverine."

"I thought so," Lelling said, "Carajou."

Kirby bristled up in defense of his wife, but Rachel replied, "No sir, that was my father Emile LaMontagne," she turned then to Kirby and the two started to walk away.

"Ma'am, I used to work for the largest newspaper in the country, in New York, and I once devoted a lot of time and energy researching the legend of Carajou. And now I find you here, wearing his fur piece. I will pay you well for your story."

Rachel bit her lip, literally, thinking how to respond. Then she replied, "I'm sorry Mr. Lelling, that was my father not me." Rachel turned to leave.

Lelling tried to follow. He had more questions, but Kirby blocked his way. "Do not disturb my wife any further Mr. Lelling."

George Otis had been watching and came over. "Mr. Lelling, your stage is about to leave. Maybe you should be on board and not stay over here."

Everyone around heard about the legend of Carajou and his daughter Rachel. And no one seemed to care. She and Kirby had been accepted into the family there in Grafton and whether she was the daughter of Carajou or not, really didn't matter.

Before school buildings were built in Grafton, school was usually held in farm houses. Shifting locations so the same children didn't always have the longest distance to walk. The Grafton school decided that they would like Rachel to talk with the children in the three different schools to tell them about Dekanawida, the Great Peachmaker and Carajou her father and about Indian life. All the children, as well as the teachers, enjoyed her classes very much and many of the students wrote reports about what they had learned.

Rachel was so enthusiastic about teaching the children about life in an Indian village and her father carrying information of the white settlers to the western Indians, one night as she laid in Kirby's arms she began to cry with joy. She was so happy to be teaching the children about this.

"See sweetheart, in a different way you are continuing your father's work. He was teaching the different tribes about the white settlers and now you are teaching the white settler children about Indian tribal life.

"When your father died, the reign of Carajou was handed to Falling Bear, to see that you were safe and teach you his People's ways. Now you are teaching that knowledge to the children. Your father's, Carajou's, legend continues through you. Everything in life has a purpose."

"I can see that now. Alvin Brown had to die, so that you would bring his body back to Grafton and we could meet. I knew from the first moment I saw you, that you had come to Grafton for a special reason. If Alvin had lived we would never have met. He died and we met and now because of you, I am teaching these children about The People's way of life. You are part of this legend too, my husband."

No one ever again questioned why Rachel wore the wolverine fur.

*   *   *   *

George and Mary had taken over totally for Jim and Ruth. Neither one of them could do the work any longer. They were tired and deserved to rest in the summer warm sunshine. They would spend a lot of their time on the porch rocking in their wicker rocking chairs.

Ronki-Tonk was slowing down also and George had hired a teenager to help out around the barn.

Visitors from Bethel and beyond were coming in every week by stage. They had heard of the tremendous brook trout fishing in the Cambridge River. The Poplar Tavern was busy and some of the local men got jobs guiding those well-to-do fishermen. Upton was even busier with tourists and fishermen.

There was news of steamers being built and used to transport fishermen and tourists from Rangley and down the Richardson Lakes to sporting camps that were popping up along the shores of Richardson, Mooselookmeguntic and Capsuptic Lakes. Yes times were changing and some of the local people from Grafton would make the excursion to Middle Dam to see for themselves.

Landlocked salmon had been introduced in Parmachenee Lake in 1875 by Henry Well. This brought more fishermen to the Caribou fishing camp on Treats Island. And this worried both Kirby and Rachel. They could see these white sportsmen with a lot of money, pushing their way closer and closer to Wonnocka's village. Kirby decided not to tell Wonnocka about this, hoping that the fishermen would stay on the lake where fishing was better. But he and Rachel both could see the end, of a way of life, coming for The People.

Warren Douglas sold his store to Enoch Abbott. Kirby was sorry to see Warren leave. He had enjoyed his occasional visits there when he and Rachel bought goods and sold their fur. He liked Enoch also, but seeing the change was upsetting.

There was talk of bringing a railroad in from the paper mill in Berlin, New Hampshire to the Maine border near Success Pond. So far there was only talk. Most of the good wood that was within easy access had already been harvested, and the Brown Paper Company needed pulp for its mill.

All these changes brought new and more people into the area and Kirby and Rachel could feel the pressure. But Kirby and Rachel's biggest concern was the growing interest at Parmachenee Lake. And what made matters worse was the Farrar's Illustrated Guide Book. Farrar told how good the fishing and hunting was and how easy it was now to make the trip to Parmachenee Lake; in one day now from Portland. But this was providing guiding jobs for some of the men. They could make more money guiding one day, than five days in the woods. But come cold weather and snow, they all regretfully returned to their secure jobs at the lumber camps.

One day Kirby and Rachel stopped to visit with the Browns and have some coffee. Jim was having a difficult time getting in and out of chairs. "My knees have gone bad on me Kirby. Ain't got no strength in them anymore." Ruth wasn't fairing must better.

"Go sit on the porch with the men Ruth, I'll make the coffee," Rachel said.

"Read last week in the newspaper where legislature is forming a new commission to protect the wildlife. This commission is going to deputize men and give them the same authority as sheriffs to patrol the woods. It seems, and it'll be soon, that we'll have to have a license to hunt deer and moose. Then there's talk about maybe having to have a license to fish too. Damned waste of time if you ask me. The article said that lumber camps could continue to feed deer and moose meat, only if the animal was legally taken. They want a yearly limit of three deer per season per man and one moose.

"That's not going to stop the camps from hiring maybe three or four hunters. I don't ever see it happening myself."

"Did it say anything about trapping or new laws?" Kirby asked.

"Not a word. It explained that there are now sixty fish wardens who would be empowered as game wardens, if this passes legislature, they expect to have to hire even more men if all of the back country is going to be enforced."

"Well, times are changing fast Jim. Rachel and I were talking about that yesterday."

"Speaking about changes. George has a crew cutting a new right of way right to the New Hampshire border near Success Pond. It seems the Brown Paper Mill, who owns most of the woodland around, has talked the owners of the railroad there in Berlin to extend a spur to the state line. Then all the wood we harvest out that way and around Silver Stream will be loaded onto railcars for the mill. George says the

Brown Company is extending his contract, almost doubling it."

"That's good news," Kirby said.

"Yeah, I suppose, but what happens to the local people when the Brown Company has all the wood cut off here. People will have to move away to find work."

They talked for a long time about all the changes they had seen and the growth of the town.

"Rachel, all the school children have said how much they enjoy learning about Indian life. It has been a real educational opportunity for them," Ruth said.

*   *   *   *

Before going home they stopped at the post office and Rachel went inside. She came out with a package she had ordered a month earlier and an official looking envelope for Kirby. "Well, are you going to open it, or just stare at it?"

He was afraid he might be called back into active duty. But it was from the State of Maine and not Washington.

He opened and extracted a single sheet of very official looking paper. "It's from State Representative Crockett in Bethel. He is coming to Grafton on September 5th and wants to meet with me at the Poplar Tavern."

"Does it say why?"

"No, and it'll be ten days of worrying." And they would be leaving soon for Rachel's Point and trapping. They tried not to think about the letter and went ahead with their plans for the upcoming trip.

Unlike the first year of trapping and building a new house, now before their September trip, they were all prepared for winter. They had more than enough wood in the shed, plus four cord split and piled under a huge hemlock three. The root cellar was full of food and they had extra provisions set aside for the trip. Their bank account had grown considerably through the years and they had a nice nest egg, just in case they had an off trapping year. But they still were only taking thirty beaver and what otter and mink they could. The price on fur had all gone up, especially for beaver and otter. An extra large beaver was now worth $35 and a large otter $40.

*　　*　　*　　*

September 5th came and Kirby had the horse and wagon all set to go, early. "You seem anxious this morning," Rachel mused.

"I am." That's all he could say. And he never said another word during the ride up. Even when Joe Chapman came down to the road to say good morning, Kirby only nodded his head. He did notice though that Joe was dragging a bag of salt behind him.

When they arrived at the tavern, there didn't seem to be much activity there. He asked Ronki-Tonk, "Would you unharness old Jake for me Ronki-Tonk and give him some oats?"

"Sure thing Kirby."

Kirby opened the door of the tavern and let Rachel enter first and not until he had closed it did he see two strangers talking with Jim.

Jim pulled himself up standing. It was s hard and painful job. "Kirby, I'd like you to meet Representative Crockett from Bethel and this is Commissioner Henry Stanley from Dixfield."

"Hello gentlemen. This is my wife Rachel."

They all sat down. There was already a coffee pot on the table. "I'll come right to the point Mr. Morgan."

"Please do."

"After January 1st of next year (1880) legislature is expecting to enact a bill that will create a division of men to enforce game laws. They will be called game wardens. We now have sixty fish wardens scattered along the coast and their title will be changed to game warden to enforce both the fishing laws as well as new laws which will be forth coming. These fish wardens have all said that they are not interested in traveling deep into the back country for undefined periods of time. So this legislature, if enacted will give me the power to hire men for this position."

Kirby sat motionless, as did Rachel with full attention of what Commissioner Stanley was saying.

"The State of Maine is fast losing a valuable natural resource. You probably aren't so aware of it happening around here, but all along the Canadian Border, wagon loads of moose and deer are being taken across the border illegally. And rail cars of illegal deer are going south. If we don't stop this commercial hunting (slaughter), we'll lose our moose and deer herds.

"Along the coast, in swampy areas deer are being driven with dogs to men waiting to slaughter them. It's wholesale murder. And lumber camps can not continue hiring meat hunters to feed the crew." Now he was looking at Jim. Jim only grunted.

"The hunting interest and popularity is fastly increasing. A big percent of non-residents we have learned are buying or paying their guides to kill them a large buck.

"We need capable men that want to be Maine's first Game Wardens."

"Why me?"

Representative Crockett said, "I put out feelers in Grafton and Upton and settled on two possibilities. You're my first choice. The other lives in Upton. You're a decorated Civil War hero, you commanded hundreds of men. And you come highly recommended by Jim here, and George Ortis. You obviously aren't afraid of confrontation and you know and understand the woods and wildlife."

"I have some questions. What's the pay?"

"Right now starting as soon as legislature has enacted the bill, $1,500 a year. I know that isn't much, but there are other bills for the legislature to consider next year. This will deal with funding the new department."

"You're right. We can make that much trapping in two months. If I were to take it, it would be because of the enjoyment of the lifestyle. I'm 41, you don't think that's too old?"

"Under these circumstances and your abilities.....not at all."

Kirby was quiet, thinking. "I have a question," Rachel said. Jim looked up at her with a smile on his face. This didn't surprise him at all.

"What about the Indians? I came to live with Falling Bear and his People of the Cooashuakas Tribe near the Big Magalloway River north of Parmachenee Lake, when I was six. I was raised by these people. What about their rights to feed themselves?"

Representative Crockett answered, "Mrs. Morgan, we have talked about this to great lengths in Augusta. There will be no change with Indians hunting

for sustenance on their own land." This pleased
Rachel.

"Before I can answer you, I need to go for a
walk with my wife and talk about this."

They walked across the mill yard to the field
road that would take them through the wheat and oats
out to the woods. "What do you think about this?"
Kirby asked.

"It isn't so much what I think. What do you
think? Do you want to do this?"

"In a way yes. There would be no more farm or
mill work. I was only doing that to help out the
Browns. The pay isn't much now, but Commissioner
Stanley seemed to think it'll get better soon."

They walked to the end of the fields talking,
then sat down on the grassy bank. "If we had a family,
I'd say no. We could still be together. I don't see any
reason why you couldn't go along with me."

The sparkle in Rachel's eyes returned. This is
what she was wanting to hear. That she would be
included and not left behind. "Let's do it," she said.

"Are you sure?"

"Yes. Are you?"

"Yes, I am too. If we don't like it, I can always
quit."

They walked back hand in hand back to the
tavern.

"We've talked it over and.....yes I'll do it. With
one provision. That if I don't like it, I can quit."

"I can accept that," Commissioner Stanley said.

Representative Crockett said, "Legislature will
convene first of the year and as soon as the bill is
enacted Commissioner Stanley will come up here to
swear you in."

"Who will I be answering to?"

"Until we can establish a chain of command, you'll answer to me. When this is approved, I'll come back with a lot of paperwork for you to go over. In the mean time, I'd suggest you get a revolver to carry with you. You'll be issued a badge and a winter wool jacket and that's it."

They talked excitedly about the idea of being a Maine Game Warden, on their way home. Joe Chapman was dragging a deer across the road. A deer he had just shot from his salt lick. "Once you're sworn in, you know you'd have to charge him."

"Yeah, I know."

They agreed not to tell anyone just yet that he had agreed to take the job. There wouldn't be any confirmation anyhow until legislature had enacted the bill. They stopped to see Joe Chapman before going home to tell him they would be leaving in the morning for Parmachenee and asked him to check the house every week. Instead of a nickel, it was now $2 a week.

*   *   *   *

There was a light mist in the air when they pulled the canoe ashore at Rachel's Point. "We'll have to dry everything now inside the wikitup."

Later as they were laying naked on the bear rug Rachel asked, "You have been very quiet on the trip. What are you thinking?"

"About Commissioner Stanley's offer to become a game warden. On one hand I like the idea. Maybe I could do some good. Then on the other, I know lumber contractors depend on deer and moose to feed the crews."

"But didn't he also say the bigger problems were commercial hunters. Maybe you should just forget about it while we are here to trap the beaver and visit The People."

Kirby tried to put the idea out of his mind and concentrate on trapping, but every once in a while something would trigger the idea of becoming a game warden and the thought was soon at the forefront of his thinking.

There were plenty of beaver this year. Like in the past, they were catching more mink than otter. They had decided to stop trapping beaver when they had thirty. By the end of the third week they had 32, so they concentrated on mink and otter.

Kirby laid awake all night one night after they had stopped going after the beaver. He couldn't shut out of his head what Commissioner Stanley wanted of him. Then just before daylight when the loon called to awaken them, he decided that if he was a game warden, then perhaps he could help Wonnocka and His People.

When Rachel awoke she found Kirby in a different mood than when they had gone to sleep. He was happy, chatty and he wanted to play. Rachel giggled and teased him for a few minutes and then she gladly submitted.

Kirby told Wonnocka that he was going to be a game warden after the first of the year. "What's this? Game Warden."

"In French it's Garde-chasse."

"I will be protecting wild animals from too much hunting."

"You stop my people from killing moose and caribou! This not good my brother."

"No, not you Wonnocka. There are men south of here and north along the Canadian border who are killing hundreds of moose and deer and selling them. And this must stop."

"Then this is a good thing you do. You become game warden."

"Yes, it will be a good thing and I will have more authority now to keep hunters and trappers off Wonnocka's land."

Wonnocka understood this and the expression on his face showed. "Come, you also Rachel, we smoke pipe. Tobacco fresh."

They followed Wonnocka to his lodge and spent several hours smoking and talking. Wonnocka wanted to know more about the white settlers.

"Wonnocka, I have a lot to tell you. And I tell you as my brother." Rachel looked questioningly at Kirby wondering what he was going to say.

"Wonnocka. The white settlers are many times more than your people. Of the People of all the tribes. The white people have machines to help them work. Horses that pull carriages that people ride in. There are boats that go up and down the lakes by steam. No one paddles. There is a machine that makes the boats go. There are trains that travel all over the land on iron rails. There is so much you have never seen, that is outside your land. If you and your people don't change, your way of life will be lost forever.

"In two days Rachel and I will be going back. We invite you and your oldest son to come with us. So you can see for yourself what I tell you. You stay with us in our house for two days and then you come back here before ice covers the lake."

Wonnocka was silent. He was deep in thought about everything Kirby had said. Rachel elbowed Kirby in the side and said, "When were you going to let me in on this?"

"Sorry, I just thought of it, and I didn't think it would be polite in front of Wonnocka if we left to discuss this."

"I think it is a great idea."

Wonnocka broke the silence, "We go with you."

"Good. In two days meet us at Parmachenee Lake when the sun reaches the tree tops. Bring some food; enough for two days and blankets."

The next day Kirby and Rachel pulled all their remaining mink and otter traps. They had 32 beaver, 12 mink and 8 otter. Later they packed everything in the canoe except for what food they would eat in the morning.

*   *   *   *

As the sun was beginning to peak over the tree tops, Kirby and Rachel met Wonnocka and his eldest son Moskuos. "It is good to see you. We thought maybe you changed your mind," Rachel said. "Moskuos it is good to see you."

Wonnocka held up his double ended paddle to show he had made one like Kirby and Rachel's. Moskuos was using a one bladed paddle. But they kept up with Kirby and Rachel, stroke for stroke.

The last time Wonnocka had canoed down Parmachenee Lake there not been a fishing camp on the island in the narrows. He was curious, but he didn't want to stop. He was amazed that anyone could build a dam like he saw at the outlet at Aziscohos.

"Why?"

"In the spring when there is a lot of water men float logs down the river to sawmills." Kirby knew this didn't mean much to him now, but later things would come together for him.

Fred Cyr met them and loaded both canoes and their gear in the wagon, but the men had to walk. There was no room. When Kirby paid him, he gave Fred enough for when Wonnocka would come back through. "Everything alright Fred? Wonnocka and his son will be back through in a few days."

They made camp below the falls and the four talked long into the night. Both Wonnocka and Moskuos had seen things today that they could never before have imagined. They had seen horses pulling wagons at St. Francis but had never been close to one. But more wonders awaited them the next day.

They were full of excitement the next morning and eager to be on their way. They ate sparingly and left before the sun was up. Moskuos was eager to see more. They canoed by farms and fields in Wilson Mills, but didn't stop.

People were out and working when they pulled ashore at Wilson's landing. Kirby explained that Wonnocka would be leaving his canoe also and he paid Captain Wilson in advance. "Captain, this is Wonnocka and his son Moskuos. Wonnocka is chief of his people the Cooashuakas, a band of the Abenaki, and Rachel's people. They are traveling with Rachel and me and we are showing them things in the white settlements."

They loaded all of their gear into the wagon, while Kirby harnessed Jake and hooked him to the wagon. Before going up to (now) Enoch's store to sell their fur, they rode out the Carry Road to Middle Dam. When they arrived, the Diamond Steamer was just getting ready to leave. Wonnocka pointed to the thick dark smoke.

"Fire heats water and turns it into steam. You know you have seen steam when the women are cooking?" Wonnocka nodded. "The steam is powerful and makes the big paddle wheel on the side move. It's like many people paddling together." He wasn't sure if Wonnocka was understanding or not. It would have been so much easier, if they could have gone aboard, so Wonnocka could see things work.

The steamer started to move and then faster and faster. Wonnocka and his son were impressed.

"What name this water. I have never been here before. Never traveled below Parmachenee."

"This is Lower Richardson Lake." Wonnocka looked all around. He had never heard of such things as he was now seeing.

They all got back into the wagon and they drove back to Wilson's Landing, crossed the bridge and rode out the Magalloway Trail to Upton. Kirby stopped the wagon when they were close to Tyler Cove and they walked through the trees for a short distance and Rachel pointed to an island. "You see that island Wonnocka? That's called Metallak Island. That's where Matelok lived when he was in this country."

"He had many friends here in Upton, and he helped a lot of people."

"Is that where his body rest?" Wonnocka wanted to know.

"No, he was very old when he left here. He went to Stewart's Town, in New Hampshire. He wanted to be buried there where he could face the morning sun, on North Hill."

They walked back to the wagon and rode out to Upton and stopped at the Lake House for a late morning breakfast. This would be quite an experience for Wonnocka and Moskuos. Kirby ordered bacon and eggs and a pot of hot coffee for everyone. Rachel showed them how to hold and use silverware. There were other people, and they had become so accustomed to seeing Rachel and Kirby in their deerskin clothes (traveling clothes) and wearing the wolverine and wolf furs, they actually paid little attention to Wonnocka and his son.

After twenty minutes a young waitress brought their breakfast out. Wonnocka and Moskuos watched Kirby and Rachel eat with the fork and spoon. After several attempts they had mastered the spoon, but not the fork. Coffee served in delicate cups was totally foreign to them. They put extra sugar in and drank until the cup was empty. All in all, things were going quite well.

Wonnocka watched as Kirby paid for their breakfast. He had little experience with money. They left and rode up the hill to Enoch's Store. Enoch was there this morning and Rachel introduced him to her friends. "How much money do you have on my account Mr. Abbott? The furs I trade with you are Wonnocka's People."

"There is $215.45 on account now. Are you going to sell these today?"

"Yes," and everyone, including Wonnocka and his son helped to carry the hides inside while Kirby was dickering with Enoch over the price. Rachel walked around the store with Wonnocka and Moskuos.

"For the beaver $1,120, $180 mink and $320 for the otter. That's $1620. You two are going to break the bank some day," Kirby laughed.

"Cash please."

Wonnocka saw a pair of boots and asked Rachel, "I like those. Do I just take? I have nothing to trade."

Rachel explained that the beaver hides she brings out in the spring, she trades for the blankets and such. And sometimes there is money left that goes on account and now he had $215.45 left on that account. And he could have the boots."

"Moskuos, you want these for your feet too?"

They found the right size and tried them on. He saw a new axe and a nice hunting knife. Then he picked out two blankets that he knew his woman would like. All tolled, it came to $65.18. "You still have $150.27 left on your account Wonnocka."

Wonnocka nodded his head that he understood.

"Can you believe this Rachel? We got more for three weeks trapping than I'll make all year as a game warden."

"Are you having doubts my husband?"

"No, just an observation."

They said their goodbyes and headed down the road for Grafton. "All those buildings.....families live?"

Rachel said, "Yes there is a family in each house. Each farm raises animals to eat and plants vegetables too. Instead of looking for food in the forest, they grow crops, and animals. Have you ever seen a cow, or watched as one is milked?"

Wonnocka shook his head, he had not.

"All paths of white settlers like this," and he pointed to the gravel road they were on.

"These are roads that horse and wagons travel on."

Just before reaching the Brown farm in Grafton, they met the morning stage out of Kilgore Station. Two men rode up top and four inside. Kirby saw the puzzled look on Wonnocka's face. "That's a stage coach. It carries people and not cargo."

"All white settlers ride. No one walks," Wonnocka observed.

Kirby understood this. In his culture, you either walked or traveled by canoe. Rachel must have been tuning in to his thoughts. "The Abenaki People would travel great distances using rivers. It would take several days sometimes to reach their destination. That's why Wonnocka finds it difficult to understand why so many whites depend on horses. His People have never owned a horse. Never had any use for one."

Ronki-Tonk was in the farm yard when they arrived.

"Back early this year." Then he saw Wonnocka and his son. "Brought visitors with you I see."

Kirby introduced them. "Ronki-Tonk. That's strange name," Wonnocka said. "Strange for white man. Good Indian name." And then he smiled and so did everyone.

Jim and Ruth had not come out to greet them yet. So Rachel led the way inside. Mary was making some tea and said, "Their both in the living room. Dad hasn't been feeling so well. Says he's just tired that's all. Mother is sitting in a chair beside him. Go on in." She didn't know what to think about the two visitors they had with them.

Jim was lying on the couch and Ruth was sitting beside him in a chair. As soon as Ruth and then Jim saw Kirby and Rachel, their facial expressions changed and their eyes seemed to come alive. "Well son, you're back early this time. Trapping must have been good." He took another breath and asked, "Who are your two friends?"

Rachel guided Wonnocka and his son over next to Jim. "Ruth, Jim, I'd like you to meet Wonnocka and his son Moskuos. Wonnocka is the leader of his people. His father was Falling Bear who raised me."

Jim sat up and extended his hand to shake Wonnocka's. Wonnocka wasn't sure what Jim wanted and when he turned to look at Rachel, she nodded her head towards Jim. Wonnocka took Jim's hand in his, and shook hands. "I am pleased to meet you Wonnocka." Then he shook hands with Moskuos.

"Help me out off this couch Ruth. I want to sit in my chair and talk with our visitors."

"What's the matter with you Jim?" Kirby asked straight out.

"Oh, nothing really. Just tired. Ruth keeps reminding me that I'm a lot older than she is and I'm too old to be trying to do a day's work."

"He needs to eat stew of beaver and drink some our tea. Not English tea," Wonnocka said.

"What's this beaver stew and tea he is talking about?"

"Beaver meat will give you energy like wolf or bear. The tea is made from roasted beechnuts and teaberry leaves," Rachel said.

"Maybe I should try some. Kirby, there's beaver not far below the dam," Jim said.

And Ruth added, "I always pick beechnuts across the river at the end of the field road on the hillside, and there is teaberry plants growing there also."

Kirby explained to Jim and Ruth why Wonnocka and his son had come to Grafton to visit. All the while they were talking, Jim kept getting stronger and stronger. Ruth was smiling and when she looked at Rachel, she stood up and said, "Let's go to the kitchen and let the men talk."

"That's all Jim needed was someone to talk to. You and Kirby are good medicine for him. What about this tea?"

"Before we leave, we'll get the beaver and I'll take it home and cook up a large stew and bring up tomorrow. After we get the beaver we'll go out back for the beechnuts and teaberry."

While Kirby and Wonnocka went downstream to get the beaver Moskuos went out back to gather nuts and teaberry leaves with Rachel. "You want me, Moskuos, who will be leader when my father is gone, to gather nuts and teaberry? Nunksqua's (woman) work."

"There is something I want to show you Moskuos. If you don't want to help gather nuts and teaberry, you won't have to."

They crossed the mill yard and followed the road out back. Moskuos stopped to look at the wheat and oats growing in a large field. Rachel explained that some is raised to feed the horses and farm animals and some is made into people food. She stripped the pearls out of a wheat bran and gave them to Moskuos, "Eat, they're good." And she chewed a few to show him it was okay.

Kirby found the beaver and broke out troughs and then the two stepped back to wait. Wonnocka was going to shoot it with his bow and arrow. Kirby pointed to a ripple on the water surface and he elbowed Wonnocka and said, "Get ready."

As the beaver swam into the trough to investigate, Wonnocka pulled the bow string back and released an arrow. It struck the beaver behind the head and it died there without struggling. "Good shot Wonnocka."

It was a big beaver and would make a large stew. Rachel and Moskuos met Kirby and Wonnocka on the bridge. "That was quick."

The beaver was loaded into the wagon and they drove home.

"Everybody live away from everyone else?" Wonnocka asked.

"Yes, every family has their own farm, and crops to tend to. In your village, Wonnocka, everyone helps everyone else. Here, it is different. People are more independent," Kirby said.

"Our way better for my people."

"There are times Wonnocka when I would agree with you."

"You live long ways from friends."

Joe Chapman was working by the roadside when they rode by. "Welcome back Mr. and Mrs. Morgan. Home early this year ain't you? Are these your people Rachel?"

"Wonnocka is now leader of his people in the village where I was raised."

Kirby gave him a few dollars for looking after his house. "Why you give him money?"

"When Rachel and I leave to travel to your village, Joe looks after our house while we're gone."

Wonnocka thought about this for a minute before answering. "You must pay him to do this for you? My people would ask nothing to do it. I also see you pay money to other people for doing something for you. Is this how you live? Always having to pay someone for help?"

Kirby thought now before answering. "In our culture, Wonnocka, we can't live without money. We need money to buy clothes, food, shelter and everything in our lives we need money for. So most of the time we have to pay someone to help us."

"I don't understand all this," Wonnocka said. "I no want to live like that."

At the house Wonnocka asked, "Only you two live here?"

"Yes," Rachel replied.

"You have no animals, no fields with crops. How do you eat?"

"By selling the beaver we trap for money which we use to buy what we need. In the winter we work some at the Brown farm and mill also."

Wonnocka was seeing so much on this trip. He couldn't fully understand why the white settlers chose to live like this. And he had seen so much in the way of how the white man had used his ability to make life easier. Even still, with all of this machinery and horse drawn wagons, the white man's life still seemed to be tougher than his.

As they were eating supper, Rachel had a brilliant idea. "Tomorrow Kirby, before we take the stew and tea up to the Browns, I'd like to stop at the school and introduce Wonnocka and Moskuos. Wonnocka would you talk to the school children tomorrow and tell them about your ways and your people?"

"This would be a good thing. Will teacher let me talk?"

"She would be happy to have you talk to the children."

*   *   *   *

Wonnocka and his son slept on the floor in the living room on bear rugs. It had been an exhausting day for them and they slept well.

The beechnuts that Rachel had roasted the night before in the oven had cooled and now she ground them into a fine powder and then ground the teaberry leaves and added that. She put the tea and the stew kettle in the wagon. While she explained the running water and the hot water tank, Kirby harnessed Jake and hooked him to the wagon. "Are you ready for school?" he asked jokingly.

The children were just going inside when they arrived. At first Mrs. Tenney didn't know what to think. Then she recognized Rachel and she relaxed. She was delighted to have Wonnocka and his son talk to her students about their way of life. At first Wonnocka was shy and slow about speaking the English words in front of so many people, but eventually he seemed to enjoy being the center of attention.

"Who will be the leader after you Mr. Wonnocka?" the little Otis girl asked.

"Moskuos, my oldest son. He will be a better leader than I, 'cause he is here seeing how our white brothers live. This will make him better leader."

"You speak English Mr. Wonnocka, did you go to school?" the Davis boy asked.

"Rachel, when she came to live with our People, she taught the children to speak her words. Some of our People can read and write, too. I can see some words I know, but can't read or write."

This proved to be the most exciting day ever for the school children. Like everyone, they had preconceived ideas about Indians and how they lived. When class finally stopped for lunch Mrs. Tenney said, "I can't thank you enough for talking to the children. Maybe you could come again next year and talk some?"

Wonnocka looked at Rachel and she nodded her head.

"That, Wonnocka can do. Give me and Moskuos more time to understand your ways."

Goodbyes were said and they rode up across Grafton Flats to the Browns. Jim was in the kitchen and about to have lunch. Wonnocka was carrying the kettle of stew and said, "No eat that. Heat up kettle and eat beaver and drink tea."

Mary took the kettle and put it on the hot stove and Rachel poured tea in a cup and gave it to Jim. "It is good cold too."

Jim drank the cup full without stopping and exclaimed, "My God, it is good."

When the stew was hot Mary dished out bowls for everyone. "I never thought I'd ever eat beaver," Mary said, "but this is delicious. Really delicious."

Everyone agreed and Kirby and Rachel smiled to themselves. Wonnocka and Moskuos asked for more. Then everyone had a second bowl.

"How is the tea hot?" Jim asked.

"Good," Wonnocka said. Everyone laughed and Mary poured a cup for everyone and the tea was gone.

"Now that we know how to make this, we'll drink it more often," Ruth said.

When lunch was over Kirby said, "Jim, I'd like to show Wonnocka how the mill works. Is it running today?"

"By-gorry it better be," he said jokingly. "Come, I'll walk over with you."

"Now Jim, do you think you should. You get awful tired you know, when you go over," Ruth was concerned.

"I'll be okay. If I get tired, these strong boys will carry me back."

As they crossed the bridge, Wonnocka was studying the dam construction. It certainly looked simple enough. But one would have to have the tools to work with.

Kirby showed them the paddle wheel, where the saw got its power and how the circular motion was transferred to up and down motion for the vertical saw blade. Then the sawyer started the carriage through, to show them how the up and down motion cut through the log.

This interested Wonnocka and he understood how the paddle wheel motion ran the saw. But he shook his head and said, "Too much work just to build place to live. Wikitup much easier to build and comfortable."

Kirby took them next to the barn where Ronki-Tonk showed them how to milk a cow. He only filled the pail part way, as he had already milked once. "What you do with milk?"

"We drink, make butter, cheese or thick cream."

Jim took them to the root cellar and gave them a taste of butter and cream and a slice of cheese. They particularly liked the cheese. "This," and Wonnocka held up a piece of cheese, "good. Better than milk or cream."

Jim was delighted. He really enjoyed Wonnocka's company. He wrapped up the rest of that round of cheese and gave it to Wonnocka and said, "You take this back to your people."

Wonnocka took the cheese gladly, "But I do not have anything to give you."

"That is okay Wonnocka. The cheese is a gift." Wonnocka didn't understand and he looked at Kirby. Kirby nodded his head that everything was okay.

Ruth was on the porch when the men walked across the yard. "Jim, you better come sit down before you get too tired."

Jim hadn't noticed it until now, but he was feeling better, more alive than he had been in a long time. "I don't know if it was the tea and stew or just your company, but I feel great. I haven't felt this good in a long time."

"Well we'll just have to eat beaver stew more often," Ruth said. "There should be enough beaver around here, so's I can make you a stew every week."

*   *   *   *

After supper that evening Kirby, Rachel, Wonnocka and Moskuos went out back and picked a good mess of beechnuts and teaberry leaves. She roasted the nuts that evening and made up some tea for Wonnocka to take on the trip back. She also put together some dried meat and cornbread.

The next morning Kirby and Rachel took Wonnocka and his son back to Wilson's Landing on the Magalloway River. When the canoe was loaded Kirby asked, "Are you sure you know how to get back?" Then he shook his head. "Of course you know." He'd forgotten for a moment who he was talking to.

"Much thanks for bringing Moskuos and Wonnocka here. We see and learned plenty. You have good people here you call friends. I feel good now."

With that said they got into their canoe and started for home.

Chapter 9

Kirby and Rachel made another trip to Bethel with a load of freshly sawn pine boards and they deposited most of the trapping money and Rachel picked up a few more household items.

At the T House, Kirby traded his .44 Winchester towards a new .38-55 Winchester. The bullet would reach out to longer distances. He also bought a .45 Colt revolver for himself and a smaller .38 Special for Rachel. His new position as game warden, when it would come through, would require him to carry a side arm. And he didn't want Rachel facing any unsuspecting dangers without the protection of a gun either. Since she would be traveling with him always.

He bought extra ammunition so Rachel could practice and get used to shooting a revolver. He also needed to hone his own skills. Christmas was nearing and Kirby wanted to buy something special for Rachel.

While she was looking at household items, Kirby bought a full length mahogany framed mirror.

He asked the sales person to wrap it and loaded it into the wagon while he kept Rachel's attention in the store.

On the way home Rachel asked why they were going so slow. Kirby just said, "No particular reason. Just enjoying the ride."

They stayed over at Kilgore's and had a hardy breakfast the next morning before leaving.

*   *   *   *

During that winter, Rachel, when she wasn't helping Mrs. Tenney at the school, she was helping Mary feeding the crews. Kirby stayed busy in the mill yard except on days when it was storming or the snow was too deep for travel.

In February Kirby received another official letter from Representative Crockett in Bethel, saying that the legislature had enacted the bill as written and he would be out to see Kirby on April 1st.

"It still isn't too late to change your mind."

"I'm sure this is what I want to do. I think I can do some good."

"You already have, my husband, and I am proud of you," and she kissed him.

"How do you mean?"

"By suggesting that Wonnocka and his son make the trip out here to see for themselves the white settlements. The Canadian border protects them from the French settlements to the north. Now maybe Wonnocka can be a better leader for The People and encourage them to adapt some of our ways."

The next day while Rachel was working with Mrs. Tenney at the school, she overheard some of the older children talking about how little food the

Chapman family had. "Do we have enough supplies so we can give some to the Chapman's?" Rachel asked.

"I think we can spare some. Tomorrow we can ride out to one of the harvesting areas and shoot a deer. Then we can load the other supplies and take everything in one trip."

The next day Kirby grabbed his new rifle and he and Rachel headed out towards the west side of Hemenway Ridge. Crews were cutting spruce there near a cedar thicket and there was sure to be deer. On the ride out Rachel said, "Just remember, next week you'll be a game warden and you won't be able to do this."

"I hear ya."

Rachel spotted a lone deer on top of the small knoll in an old harvest area. She elbowed Kirby and pointed. He brought Jake to a stop and brought his rifle to his shoulder and squeezed the trigger. The deer dropped. "That would have been a maybe shot for the other rifle. It was a little farther than I would have liked it. But this new rifle reaches damned good."

They dressed the deer and dragged it back to the wagon and returned home and loaded the rest of the supplies they could part with.

Abby Chapman met them at the door. They had really been up against the wall trying to pay off some bank notes and had not had enough left to buy food supplies for the winter. Abby was certainly appreciative. "As soon as Joe comes home from work, I'll have him take care of the deer. Thank you both so much."

The word spread throughout Grafton that the Chapmans were down on their luck and everybody was glad to help a neighbor. That's the way life was in Grafton.

The wood crews were all done for another winter and many went home to their families. A woods cruiser snowshoed along the river making sure there were no obstacles when the river drive started. About one half mile below Poplar Dam he found a really large beaver dam that had to be removed. He hiked back to the mill and told George, who employed Kirby to dynamite the dam. Since he alone had any experience with dynamite. Rachel and the cruiser went with him. Two carried dynamite and the third, the fuses. "This is going to take a lot of dynamite to clear this. And we have to clear it all with one shot."

They set four charges with three sticks to each charge. When it went off, mud and sticks flew a hundred feet in the air and it was a half hour before the smoke cleared.

*   *   *   *

The days passed and finally April 1st arrived and there was a knock on the Morgan's front door. When Rachel opened it Representative Crockett was standing there with a box in his arms. "Come in Mr. Crockett."

"Good morning Mrs. Morgan. Kirby, what have you decided?"

"We have decided to take the job."

"Good. I know Commissioner Stanley was counting on you. The first thing we need to do is to swear you in. The Commissioner has authorized me to do this.

"If you'd stand and raise your right hand." Rachel stood also and was standing beside him.

When Kirby said I do, Representative Crockett gave Kirby his badge and shook his hand. "Congratulations, Kirby."

"Now down to business." Crockett emptied the box and handed Kirby a new black and green wool jacket. "This and the badge is all you get at the moment. As more funding becomes available you will be issued more equipment. Do you have a handgun?"

"Yes, I do."

"Here is a government check, a stipend of $30 to help cover the expense of equipment you'll have to provide yourself. How would you like to receive your monthly wages?"

"Can they be forwarded to our bank account in Bethel?"

"Certainly." Crockett gave Kirby a form to fill out. While he was doing that Rachel asked, "Would you like some coffee Mr. Crockett?"

"Yes, please. Black."

"The laws have been enacted by legislature banning the practice of commercial hunting and the sale of deer and moose. There is now a season established, beginning September 1st. In the near future hunters will have to obtain a yearly hunting license and the cost of that hasn't been worked out yet. The proceeds of the license will be used to fund the new Warden Service. You will be informed when to start enforcing the license laws.

"I have a stack of the recent laws enacted and you are to see that each lumber camp in your region has one and it is displayed in the camps where everyone will see it. This will be your first priority; in each hotel, town office and sporting camp. As big as your region is this will probably take until fall to complete."

"Just how big is my region?" Kirby asked.

"From the Newry-Grafton town line in a straight line west to the state line. Umbagog Lake area all the way up along the Richardson Lakes, but not beyond

Upper Dam on Mooselookmeguntic Lake. Aziscohos and Parmachenee Lake north to the Canadian border and all along the Magalloway River Valley."

"Does this seem enough for you?"

"It'll keep me busy I guess."

"After you have notified all the crew camps and sporting lodges, etc., later in the fall if you find an obvious violation, then summons the person to the Rumford Court. The court will handle game warden complaints the first Wednesday of every month. If they do not appear, the court will issue a warrant of arrest and then you'll have to bring the person to jail in Rumford. Some time in the future the country may establish a magistrate in Upton. But until then, all violations and violators will be in Rumford.

"If you apprehend someone, who you believe will not appear in court, then you have the authority to arrest that person and take him to jail in Rumford.

"Remember, you can only arrest if you witnessed the violations. Sometime in the future there will have to be some service training, but for now you're on your own. So use good judgment.

"If while on your travels, if you have to stay at a tavern or hotel, keep all receipts for lodging and for meals. You probably will want to use the steamers on the Richardson Lakes, so keep all receipts.

"Any questions?"

"In the spring Rachel and I travel north of Parmachenee to visit an Indian village there. This is where she was raised. Then in the fall we go back and trap beaver. Will I still be allowed to take the time?"

"Trapping? Probably not as this would be at your busy time of the year. As far as visiting the village, you still can. You'll have to use your own judgment about trapping. Just remember that your position takes precedence.

"There will be very little communication with Augusta. So you'll be pretty much on your own. Once the warden service has more funding from license sales, supervisors will be appointed by the Commissioner.

"Just remember, we are mainly concerned about stopping the commercial slaughter of deer that go out of state, and the selling of deer by guides to their sport hunters, and eventually stopping the use of dogs to hunt deer.

"I'll leave you the Commissioner's address in Augusta. Send in all receipts with a brief explanation and once a month he expects a written report of your activities or as soon as you get back from the woods."

"So far, all you have addressed is hunting. What about fishing?"

"No changes yet, but in the future as more pressure is put on fishing, licenses will have to be bought and limits enforced."

"So as I understand it, I am now a game warden and my duties start immediately."

"Yes you're correct."

"So if I find someone with a deer before September 1st, I am to summons that person."

"You would be all in the right to do so. But I must stress that the Commissioner is mainly concerned with wholesale killing and marketing of deer and moose. The Commissioner would prefer, for now, that you spread the word about the new changes. Give it some time before enforcing it to the letter."

"Do you have any written authorization for me that I am an agent of the Commissioner. Other than just a badge?" Kirby asked.

"Good question. But yes. I almost forgot. I have it here inside my coat pocket." He removed it and handed it to Kirby. "You'll probably want to keep this document with you until people get used to you and the new laws."

"Before the Commissioner and I approached you about the possibility of becoming one of Maine's first game wardens, he had me do a background investigation on you. I sent a letter off to General Chamberlain and he said he was sorry you didn't take the full Colonel's promotion. He also said, if you had, there's no doubt in his mind that you would have been promoted to General by now. He had the utmost to say about you. We also talked with Jim Brown. He couldn't think of a better man for the position.

"This new warden service department needs men that they can send into the fields and woods alone and know the job will be done and will be a credit to the new department.

"I realize the wages are lower compared to your usual trapping income, for only a few months, but if you stay with it, in a short few years, the pay and benefits will get better.

"Now, if you don't have any more questions, I would ask that you give me a ride to Poplar Tavern where I shall wait for the afternoon stage to Newry and the T House.

*   *   *   *

The next day Joe Chapman was sitting out on his front steps reading the newspaper. He read with particular interest the article about the legislature enacting new laws governing hunting and the hiring of new game wardens. And when he read Kirby Morgan's name....."What in hell has he gone and done!" he exclaimed. "And me living right beside him! He'll starve me right to death he will. Damn!" He crumbled the paper up into a ball and threw it.

Joe was so agitated, he got up and started walking around the house. Cursing with every step. He looked out at Speck Mountain and all was a blur. The air was cool, but he had worked himself up until his face was red and he was sweating profusely. He looked across the road and he couldn't believe his eyes. There was a nice slender buck; antlers just showing above the ears. He was almost crying. He thought his whole world had come crashing down around him.

He just stood there watching that deer. "If this had been yesterday, you'd be in my barn by now." He bent down and picked up two rocks about the size of a baseball and he threw them at the deer. The deer heard the rock hit the ground, between it and the road, he perked its ears up and stood there looking back at Joe.

Joe threw the other rock, harder this time and hollered, "Go on get! Get the hell out of here!" Tears filled his eyes.

He lit up a cigarette and sat on the step, chain smoking and looking out across at Speck Mountain without really seeing anything at all.

Kirby and Rachel had gone up by right after daylight. Because they had not asked him to watch their house, this meant they would be back that same day.

Kirby and Rachel had headed out towards Silver Stream along the new right of way the crews had cut that winter. The workers were all gone, but the woods boss and camp cookee would still be there. Kirby pulled Jake to a stop out front of the cook camp and they went inside to talk with Jason Rydout the woods boss and Alfons Tipple.

Jason and Alfons were closing the camp and filling out the last of the season's log reports.

"What brings you two way out here today?"

Kirby gave Jason one of the notices of the recently enacted law changes and the information about game wardens. He gave Mr. Tipple a notice also. "This is to be posted in the dining room by orders of George Otis."

There was very little conversation after that. Next, they went over to Red Ridge and Cedar Brook. There too the woods boss and camp cookee were securing everything for the summer. Their attitudes about the new changes were about the same.

Late that afternoon as they rode by Chapman's farm, Joe was out front and he was acting rather peculiar towards them. "What do you suppose is his problem?" Rachel asked.

"Oh, he probably has heard by now that I am a game warden, and since he shoots a deer or moose whenever he needs meat, he probably thinks of me now, like a threat to him."

"Would you charge him if you found out he was still doing it?"

"Right now, no. Remember what Crockett said, about being more concerned about the commercial rings. But when the time comes, well. I'd have to, wouldn't I?"

The rest of Brown's outlying lumber camps were already closed for the summer, so Kirby and Rachel decided to go around the crew camps at Upton if they had not been closed up for the summer. They met Enoch at the mill yard and told him all about the new changes and asked him to post the notice in his mill, the store, hotel and town office.

They returned home later, figuring to take a couple of days to put their gear together and make preparations to make an extended trip around Umbagog Lake, the Magalloway River and Wilson Mills area, to Aziscohos and to the Parmachenee Fishing Club camp on the island. And lastly to visit with Wonnocka.

In case they ran into foul weather that lingered for days, Kirby packed extra canvas, to make a good water tight shelter. Their fishing gear, some line and hooks. Rachel packed cooking utensils and food stuffs that would last. She packed two quarts of canned venison to make a stew with, wild edibles and this time they brought along two kerosene lanterns. Kirby made up packets of matches wrapped in paper and sealed with wax to keep the water out. They would need extra clothes this trip. And he almost forgot; they would need some rope. When they had finished, they had almost too much for the canoe. Even as large as it was.

While Rachel was getting supper ready, Kirby saddled Jake and rode out to see Joe. "Rachel and I will be leaving in the morning and I'm not sure how long we'll be gone. A month maybe."

"I heard you're one of those new game wardens now," Joe said flatly.

"Yeah, that's right. You still going to look after the house for me?"

"Sure, why not."

"Here's $2 in advance. Joe, you understand that if you shoot a deer or moose out of season, I'll have to do my job and charge you. I just don't want any misunderstandings between us."

"I heard ya. I may not like this new law, but I do respect you Kirby."

*　　*　　*　　*

Before leaving the next morning Rachel pulled
her wolverine fur over her shoulders and Kirby pulled
on his wolf vest, and Rachel wore her green stone that
Kirby had given her years ago. And they each were
wearing new deerskin traveling clothes and wearing
green felt hats. They actually looked like a matched
pair.

When they rode by the Chapman farm, Joe was
outside. He waved goodbye and said, "Looking how
you two are dressed, nobody in their right mind would
want to cross either one of them," he said it low enough
so they could not hear him.

*　　*　　*　　*

They stopped first at Enoch's store and posted a
notice and bought two compasses. Their was no more
room in the canoe for blankets for Wonnocka's
Poeople. They stopped at the Lake House, Town
Office, Abbott's office and mill.

When they crossed Rapid River below Pond in
the River they turned right on the Carry Road and
stopped at the Pondy Wangan and talked with Mr.
Tibbets about the new laws and posted another notice.
They stopped at the Cameron Farm and posted a notice
and at all the farms and woods camps along the
Magalloway Trail to Wilson's Landing. He posted
notices there and at the Magalloway Town Office. And
it was almost dark by the time they reached their
campsite below Aziscohos Falls.

Everywhere they went and everybody they
talked to had similar feelings about the new laws. No

one that he had talked with, had known anything about the commercial hunting of deer and moose and many were disturbed when Kirby told them. Nobody wanted their moose and deer going out of state or to Canada. And then nobody wanted to lose the opportunity to shoot a deer or moose anytime of the year, if food supplies were getting low. Even though since 1873 there had actually been seasons established by and enacted by legislature. There had not been anyone to enforce those laws. Now that there was a new Warden Service Department, everybody kind of grunted at the idea of controlled seasons and laws. They wanted the commercialization stopped, but they wanted to be able to shoot a deer or moose anytime of the year for food.

Sometimes Kirby was very quiet on this trip as they paddled. He was beginning to understand how Falling Bear and now his son Wonnocka felt about the encroaching white settlements. It wasn't the white settlers that had Kirby concerned, but the influence money would eventually have from influential people from the outside.

He hated the idea of the sport fishing club buildings in the narrows at the head of the lake. They catered to the affluent city people who probably were the only ones who could afford the long and hard trip up into this country. He had seen the difference in cultures, from the pioneer country side, as compared to city and flatland dwellers. And frankly he wished there was a law keeping all outsiders out of Maine. "They'll some day ruin this country."

"Did you say something Kirby?" Rachel asked.

"Oh, I was just thinking out loud. I can understand how Falling Bear must have felt about all of the white settlements; coming closer to his land each year." He told Rachel how he was feeling.

At the falls they had to ring the bell several times before Fred Cyr answered back. Then it was another half hour before he showed up. During the ride up Kirby explained to Fred about the new warden service department and the changes in the laws and said, "I'd like you to post this notice where people will see it Fred."

"Sure, sure thing," he said as Kirby handed him one of the notices.

"You know young fella," Kirby was 42 but Fred would be mid-sixties, "when those rich dudes come here to fish in the fall, sometimes they go back with huge buck heads and antlers. No meat. Just the head and antlers, probably to have mounted. And then there's a bunch who go out about a week before you usually do, they all have huge head and racks. And again, no meat."

"Okay, thanks for the information."

"What information, I didn't tell you anything sonny."

There was no way of paddling through the narrows without having someone at the camps see them. But he had to post notices here also. He wished they could simply canoe by the camps and not stop, but he knew they had to, to post a notice and advise Mr. Danforth of the new laws and changes.

They pulled up to the wharf and climbed out and walked towards the main lodge. They were met part way by one of the owners, "Can I help you? I'm Pete Danforth. One of the owners."

Kirby advised Mr. Danforth about the creation of the warden service department and he was the game warden. He explained the changes in the laws and why. He had the same reaction as everyone else had had. He grunted and said, "You have an awful big country to patrol." That was all and Kirby read between the lines and understood what wasn't being said.

*   *   *   *

They set up camp at Rachel's Point and the smell of fresh fur boughs inside the wikitup was refreshing. He kindled a fire outside so they would have coals to cook on and then the two went for a walk out back looking for dinner. Rachel found some rotting hardwood trees on the ground and she broke them apart looking for edible mushrooms that had survived the winter. "I don't know how these are called, but you can only find them in the spring after the snow and ice has gone. They will soon die off in summer heat," Rachel said.

They picked all they could find, "These will dry well and remain edible for a long time," she added.

They found fiddleheads growing near an older slologan and a pair of nesting black ducks flew off. "Oh! Look Kirby, these eggs are fresh. We can have eggs in the morning." There were six eggs in each of the two nests and Rachel took four from each.

When they returned to their campsite, Rachel opened the canned venison and put the kettle over the coals. She made up something like dumplings with the corn meal and put the mushrooms and fiddleheads on to boil.

Later as they sat up and talked inside the wikitup, they decided to save the kerosene in the lanterns for when they had to make shelter along the Richardson Lakes. Here inside the wikitup there was plenty of light from the soft glowing fire. The temperature outside was dropping, but inside the wikitup they were warm and content. "You have adapted well to living like an Indian," Rachel said.

"Yeah, maybe a little too well."

"Oh, do I detect something wrong?"

"No, not wrong. I just don't like seeing this beautiful country being turned into a sporting club for the rich. People with their money will soon over run this country and in order for us to survive, we must change. And quite frankly, I hate the idea of becoming what I see in these influential outsiders."

"You even sound Indian now my husband."

"I don't know. All I do know is that I hate to see an influx of people coming into this country; and they're called sports. This country here around Parmachenee will see more of these changes, than we will at our home in Grafton.

"I really don't see Grafton growing any larger. There isn't enough work to support more people and farming has such a short growing season nestled in the mountains like we are, that farmers will never be able to depend on crops for an income. I think you and I Rachel will even see the day when Grafton will start to shrink."

Rachel understood Kirby's concerns and fears and there was absolutely nothing either one of them could do about it. She smoothed out the bear rug and spread out their bedding and took her clothes off in the soft glow of the fire. "Maybe I can take your mind off your worries," as she laid down and watched as Kirby took his clothes off.

* * * *

The next day they canoed up river to Wonnocka's village and planned to stay two nights there. While Rachel visited with her friend Wiona, Kirby would go for walks with Wonnocka. The second day he and Kirby followed the path, that Kirby had wanted to know about, to Canada and Arnold Bog. There hidden in a cedar thicket were many canoes. "From here we go to St. Francis. Two days time from village.

"This summer I go to St. Francis and talk with mission there and put my son and others in mission school. My people must learn the ways of the White Settlers if we are not to die."

"I think that is a wise decision Wonnocka."

Later that afternoon while Wonnocka, Kirby and Rachel were smoking, Rachel said, "Wonnocka, we will no longer be able to take your furs with us to trade. With Kirby's new job we have to carry many supplies for long stays away from home."

"This is okay as I will be going to St. Francis soon. I trade there. You still come to visit, no?"

"Yes, we will still come to visit."

They left Wonnocka and his village and returned to Rachel's Point and packed what they would be taking with them in the morning. They would leave one kerosene lantern there. The next morning before daylight, the loon had returned and he was calling them to get up. They ate the last of the eggs with some of the venison stew that was left, with two cups of black coffee. They closed up the wikitup and doused both fires and climbed into the canoe. The old loon followed them to the lower end of Parmachenee.

As they entered the flood waters of Magalloway River behind the dam, they met two canoe loads of sport fishermen heading to the Danforth camps.

The current in the river was swift and they were making good time. "I wonder if Fred has opened a gate for the log drive in the Androscoggin?" Kirby asked. "Maybe. There does seem to be a strong current here this morning."

Fred was still on the dam when they arrived and he loaded their gear and headed below the falls. When Fred said goodbye they reloaded the canoe and pushed off. If things worked on schedule they'd stay that night at the Middle Dam Camps, (Angler's Retreat).

"We have heard you would be traveling here. How may I help you?" Mr. Godwin asked.

"We would like a room and meals for the night."

"Certainly, breakfast comes with the room, $1.75 each and with supper that's $2.75 each."

"That'll be fine Mr. Godwin. I'll need a receipt also."

People here, around the Richardson Lakes were not as accustomed to seeing Rachel with her wolverine fur and Kirby with his wolf vest and both being dressed in deerskin clothes. People naturally stared with curiosity. They certainly carried themselves with demeanor.

Kirby asked Mr. Godwin to step over where it was quiet and he explained to him about the new creation of a warden service and the changes in laws. And that the new department's chief concern was the wholesale killing of deer and shipping them outside. "I can certainly understand that, Mr. Morgan, but I'm not in favor of the license requirement or the seasons."

"Well, Mr. Godwin, there has to be some way to fund the new warden service and the Commissioner and the legislature are anticipating that license sales will do that."

Mr. Godwin was satisfied with that. "So what is your destination from here?"

"We would like to take one of the steamers up to the head of the lake with our canoe and gear. Then we'll work our way back talking to other outfitters and lumbering concerns."

"The Welokennebacook leaves at 0800 hours tomorrow. It'll reach the Upper Dam about 0930 hours. The Helen is a small steamer and you might not be able to get your canoe and gear on board. The captain will probably let you debark anywhere along the way, seeing how you have your canoe."

"Thank you for the information. And our room?"

"Top of the stairs, second door on your left. Supper will be served at 1800."

*   *   *   *

Kirby and Rachel enjoyed relaxing in a hot bath. Then they put on clean clothes and Rachel as always was wearing the green stone Kirby had given her years ago. They left the wolverine and wolf furs in their room. They were just in time for the last table. Still, people stared, because none of the guests knew anything about them. And their clothes were not archetypical. But they all noticed that they carried themselves with dignity and poise. And their demeanor required respect.

The word was passed along fast and soon everyone knew that Kirby was the newly appointed game warden. All through supper, people kept looking and glancing at or towards them, not wanting to stare and make them uncomfortable. But the same question was on everyone's mind, "Who is she?" Not caring any longer about Kirby; for everyone knew him as the new game warden. But all were intrigued and captivated with her beauty and poise. Although she looked Indian there was just something there that said no.

When supper was over and before people had started to leave the dining room, Mr. Godwin stood and said, "May I have your attention please?" He was now looking at Kirby and Rachel. "I have noticed this evening that everyone here is interested in you two. Since you have never been on the Lakes before, maybe you'll tell us a little about yourselves. You certainly are conversational, and no one wants to demean you, but you both are new to this area."

Kirby stood and said, "I am Kirby Morgan and," Rachel stood up beside him, "this is my wife Rachel. I am the new game warden in this region." Then he told them all about the new warden service department the Commissioner had formed and legislature had enacted. He explained why the warden service had been created and how it would be funded in the future.

They were interested with what Kirby had to say, but everyone wanted to know more about Rachel.

She told them about the drunken white men who had raped and killed her mother where they lived near Cincinnati and how Falling Bear had rescued her and had raised her and how she had come to meet Kirby in Grafton. She had left out about the wolverine fur or that her father had been Carajou. "I travel with my husband."

After everyone else had left, Mr. Godwin joined Kirby and Rachel for a last cup of coffee, he wanted to talk with them some more. He, like a lot of people were curious about them and he had heard stories of a woman who wore the fur of a wolverine. And he could remember reading an article in a newspaper when he

was in school, about a man that the Indians called
Carajou who wore a wolverine fur. "He was my father.
And the Indian tribes, all the way to the Black Hills said
he was Dekanawida the Great Peacemaker."

*   *   *   *

They slept well that night, on a soft mattress and
unlike the rest of the guests, they were up at first light
and outside watching the sun rise. "It'll rain sometime
today, look how red the horizon is."
The Welokennebacook steamer was tied up to
the dock. "I have never seen one of those until you
showed Wonnocka one. Will we be safe out there on
it?"
"We'll be okay."
After breakfast they unloaded the canoe and
brought everything on board. "Put everything forward
on the bow," Captain Hanley said. They chose to ride
up front also and enjoy the morning air and not inside
the canopy like the rest of the passengers. Even loaded
as heavy as it was the steamer plowed through the water
with little effort. Rachel was so surprised.
When they reached Upper Dam and the Upper
Dam House, Kirby jumped off the deck to the dock
with a rope to tie up the boat. He waited for all of the
passengers to disembark before he and Rachel unloaded
their canoe and gear.
Kirby explained here also, about the changes in
the law and why and how the new warden service
would be funded and posted the notice and then he and
Rachel boarded their canoe and left. The sky was
covered with dark clouds and the breeze had stopped.
"We'd better find a place to set up camp soon."
"I agree. Let's hurry," Rachel added.

They had had enough of the public stares and their lordly ways. They wanted to be alone. Once back out on the lake they crossed to the west shore and canoed behind the big point near Big Beaver Island. There they found a nice quiet sheltered spot and made a lean-to frame and secured a canvas over it and then tied off the second piece of canvas over the area in front of the lean-to so they could have a cook fire, a make shift table and so they could store all their gear out of the rain. They cut fir and cedar boughs for a bed and to lean up against the lean-to and for a door in front at night to keep out the wind.

"This isn't as nice as the wikitup, but it'll have to do until the rain stops." Kirby held his hand out, palm up. It was misting now. He turned the canoe over and then kindled a fire. Rachel had read his mind and she was starting to make coffee.

"I never drank coffee until I met you. Now, I like it as much as you do."

While the coffee was making, Kirby threw out a fish line and anchored it to a branch. So when a trout took the bait, he would see the branch moving, and know he had a fish.

The rain drizzled all day and no wind. Kirby had caught two trout and Rachel had found an abundance of crayfish. Some were six inches in length, but most were three or four. They ate well and sat back and enjoyed each other's company.

During the night the wind started to blow and then the rain came down in torrents. Then lightning. Rachel had never liked the loud thunder and she snuggled close to Kirby and buried her face in his chest under the blankets.

It rained all the next day and cleared up during the night. Everything they had was a little damp;

mainly from the wet air. So they stayed there an extra day drying things out. They took the canopy canvas down to let the breeze blow through and the sunshine in. They had plenty of food, but if they ran low, they could buy what they needed at any of the lake cottages.

The sun was out bright and the air warm. Rachel laid a blanket on the ground and they removed their clothes and laid in the warm sun.

They packed up and left the next day, heading for the south arm end of the lake, to Lakeview Cottage, which was owned by the Richardson-Rangley Lakes Transportation Company, who also had almost exclusive transportation rights on the lake. On the way down the lake, Kirby marked on his map where he located lumber camps, lumber operations and saw mills. Those he would have to visit during the winter.

It was mid afternoon before they reached the South Arm and the Lakeview Cottage. There were more people here, because of an access road from Andover. People here, like other places along the way, stopped to stare at the two dressed in deerskins and wearing wolverine and wolf fur. By the attitudes of many of these people, Kirby decided that they had more wealth and fewer manners. They were openly snubbed.

A well dressed man came over to inquire what these two ruffians wanted. "I'm the manager of the Cottages. We don't allow pan-handling, lollygagging and I would prefer if you'd stay away from the guests."

"We have no intentions of bothering your guests. My business, I guess, is with you." Kirby stood a good head taller and broader shoulders too. Rachel wasn't smiling.

"I didn't get your name by the way."

"It's Smith, Eugene Smith."

"Okay, Mr. Smith, I'm Kirby Morgan and this is my wife Rachel. I am the new game warden in this region. And in the future, if I have business with any of your guests, I certainly intend to do so, without worrying about you. I am here to advise you of the new laws enacted by the legislature and to post this notice in the lobby of the main building." Kirby went on to explain why the new department was created and how in the near future it would be funded.

"Now Mr. Smith, thank you for your hospitality and I think we'll leave now."

Back in their canoe heading for the Angler's Retreat at Middle Dam, Rachel said, "You were a little rough with him, weren't you?"

"Yeah, maybe. He just came across wrong. Like we weren't good enough to talk with his guests.

Chapter 10

During winters when Joe had been trying to pay off some bank loans and not able to buy enough food for the winter, Kirby had come to his rescue with some fresh deer meat. And then when the rest of the Grafton folks learned of his demise they had all pitched in and helped him through the cold winter. Now he was out of meat again and low on funds. He had just bought garden seed and a new draft horse.

There was no bacon or ham to be had with his eggs at breakfast and he was tired of eating only vegetables. There was a nice young buck at the salt lick across the road. He opened the kitchen door and stepped back so the muzzle of the rifle would be inside of the house. He was afraid someone up the road might tell Kirby on him. He took one more step back and pulled the trigger. The deer dropped right in sight of the road. "Oh my God, look at that. If the stage should be on time, the driver will see that deer, as sure as hell." He set the rifle behind the door and grabbed his knife and ran down across the yard and across the road. The deer was kicking and trying to get up. And worse than that, he could hear the stage coming. It was getting close. He threw himself on top of the deer trying to hold it still against the ground so he could stick its throat.

The deer got its right hind leg free and kicked out and caught Joe behind the head. It felt like someone had hit him with a piece of wood. He finally stuck the deer and it went limp. The stage was coming closer. Covered in blood now, he dragged the deer behind the nearest little fir tree and laid down. The stage was just going by. Joe dared a peak and he could see the driver. He was looking towards Joe's house.

He eventually got the deer back across the road and taken care of. He was sweating and covered with blood and dirt. "I hope to God no one heard that shot or someone from the stage see me down there with that deer. Sure wouldn't want to rile Kirby none, but what's a man supposed to do when he has no meat?"

*   *   *   *

Kirby and Rachel arrived back home two weeks after Joe's episode with the deer. They had been gone for six weeks. Before leaving the Richardson Lakes he wanted to canoe completely around them and have a look see at the lumber crew camps and saw mills. He wanted a clearer picture in his mind of the goings-on here on the lakes since this was his first time here. They had run into more rain and had to hold up a few days more and they had to make one trip to Middle Dam for more food supplies.

"That was a fun trip," Rachel said, "but I'm glad to be home."

"Yeah, me too. Now I have a report to write up for the Commissioner and submit these receipts for food, lodging and ferry fees."

The next few days they stayed at home. Working around the house, working on next year's fire wood and kindling and spending a lot of time up above the house next to the falls, where Rachel called her special place. They went for walks in the evenings and early mornings as the sun was peaking over the mountains. They visited with the Browns and they wanted to know all about the goings on at Richardson Lakes.

Jim could see that Kirby and Rachel were intoxicated with excitement with being a Maine Game Warden. "Just think Kirby, you have this whole region to explore now and play in. I envy you. I really do. And I can't think of anyone better suited for the job. Unless of course it was Rachel." Everyone laughed.

"Kirby, we need some chickens here. So we can have our own eggs and a chicken to roast once in a while."

"Okay, when we get back from our next trip we'll see if we can buy some from the Browns. If not, we can go to Bethel and get some."

By early July, they were getting bored with staying at home. So they packed up their gear for a few days trip around Umbagog Lake, and the Magalloway River down to Errol. "How long you planning to be gone this time?" Joe asked.

"Probably no more than a week at most. Not sure really." Then he added simply to rile Joe he said,

"And Joe, this wouldn't be a good time to shoot something." And they drove off leaving Joe shaking in his boots.

"He knew damn it! He knew. How? How in hell did he find out?"

After they were up the road away from Joe's house, Rachel asked, "What makes you think Joe has been shooting anything?"

"Did you notice all the ravens perched in the trees behind his house? Dead give away that they're feeding on something dead out back."

"Then why did you say anything to him at all, if you're not going to charge him?"

"Oh just to have a little fun with him. Get him thinking."

They stopped at Abbott's Store before going downhill to the village. They would need a few more supplies. "Hello Kirby. Wish you had been here about two hours ago. Some fishermen came in and were complaining about some young fellas going around the north end near Sunday Cove, shooting at anything they saw."

"They at Sunday Cove?"

"I only know they came in from Middle Dam. They must have set up camp somewhere close to Sunday Cove."

"Thanks. See what we can do."

They picked up their supplies and were on the road again for Upton Village. "What are you thinking?" Rachel asked.

"How best to catch these fellas. Maybe we'll continue out to Sunday Cove with the wagon and stop before we get to the turn off and go in on foot and see what we can see."

Once they were at the bottom of the hill Kirby had Jake pick up the pace a little. He was on a mission now and no time for lollygagging. They rode through the village without stopping. They weren't long before they had crossed the bridge at the Pond in River and then turned left towards Sunday Cove. Kirby pulled back on the reins to slow Jake a bit. Then they both heard it. A gun shot echoing across the lake. It was impossible to say how close or which side of the lake. There was a turn out beside the road in amongst some fir trees which would afford Jake some shade. Then they made their way through the woods to the shore down below from where the steamer, Helen, would tie up by the camp.

They couldn't see anything in the cove, so they made their way to the point on the lake. They still couldn't see anything, but it was a pretty big body of water. Kirby didn't know whether to continue waiting or go on to Wilson's Landing and come down by canoe to the lake. After a few minutes he said, "Let's get to Wilson's Landing and come in from the outlet of the lake and work our way up along the other shore. Maybe we'll stumble onto their campsite."

They hurried back to the wagon and untied Jake and continued on to Wilson's Landing. Kirby made Jake earn his keep. He made him run all the way. Jake didn't seem to care, he needed the work out.

Rachel loaded the canoe while Kirby unharnessed Jake and the wagon and paid Captain Wilson. "Haven't time to chat today Captain. We're in a rush."

They pushed off in the canoe, paddling in unison and stirring up a wake that was breaking on shore.

Even though they were making good time in the canoe they still had more than twelve miles (river miles) to reach the outlet of Umbagog Lake. He wanted to find their campsite before dark. They had eaten a good breakfast and now there wasn't time for lunch. It seemed to take forever to canoe through the oxbows below Magalloway Village. But after they were through, the river straightened its course a little.

It was mid afternoon by the time they reached the lake. They hid in some tall reed grass along the shore and waited. Nothing. They couldn't see anything on the lake and the only noise were loons calling back and forth. They waited there for an hour before moving slowly up along the west shoreline. Staying as close to shore as they could. They were still in New Hampshire and neither of them knew where to find the boundary line.

They had only gone a short distance when Rachel said softly, "I smell something awful."

"I do too."

Then she saw it. The bloated bell of a moose riding the water surface. As they came closer, they could see the rest of the animal under water. It was all there and at least two or three days old. Kirby tried to hug the shoreline closer. And at the same time looking for any sign of the three young fellas. He was glad for Rachel's help.

Rachel pointed with her paddle to something else in the water. There was no smell to this. "A deer," she whispered. Kirby nodded his head. A little ways beyond that was a little dead fawn. The first carcass was probably the doe. He and Rachel both were getting angry. And they were still in New Hampshire and he had no authority in that state.

They continued on, following the marshy shoreline north. All the way they kept finding dead animals. Eventually they came to a red painted post on the shore and decided this must be the state line. "We make camp here where we can watch Sunday Cove and this end of the lake."

They pulled the canoe on shore and out of sight. While Rachel was busy setting up camp and gathering fire wood and rocks for a fire pit, Kirby kept watch on the lake. She made a lean-to facing the lake so one of them could always be watching. She hung a canvas up vertically so to shield the flame and light. As Kirby sat and watched for the three fellas, he kept thinking how in-tune he and Rachel were together. He never had to say anything how to set up the lean-to and fire. She knew instinctively what to do.

When the canvas was up, Rachel cut short fir trees to stand up around the front of the lean-to to mask it from being seen if anyone should pass by in a canoe or boat.

They saw no one on the lake and there had been no more shooting. When it was finally too dark to see out on the lake, Kirby kindled a small cooking fire. Now the smoke could rise through the tree tops and no one would see it. "What do we do now my husband?"

"Well, I doubt if they do any shooting until after day light. We stay here and watch and listen.

"From what we have seen today, it appears they are doing most of the killing from a boat or canoe when deer and moose are feeding along the shore. Since deer and moose feed generally in early morning and early evening, I'd say our best chance of seeing anything will be in the morning. When we arrived at the lake, they probably had canoed back to their campsite, wherever that is, and started drinking. But I'd sure like to know where they are camping."

"What are you going to do when we finally catch up with them?"

"Can't charge them with anything they do in New Hampshire. We'll have to see them do something on this side of the state line or find something in their camp.

"I would really like to look at their campsite before we approach them."

When they had finished eating, Rachel heated some of her wild tea and they sat beside the fire sipping tea. There was no noise on or about the lake. Kirby had hoped he might hear them. Every once in a while Kirby would go out to the shore and scan the opposite shore looking for a light. Around 10 p.m. he gave up and said, "We might as well get some sleep, we'll be up early."

*　*　*　*

In the dawn's early light just before the sun comes up when you can see through twilight and see shadowy figures, Kirby and Rachel were awakened by a high powered rifle shot. Kirby jumped out of bed and ran for the shore. He couldn't see the opposite shore, but he waited for another shot. And then it came and echoed up and down the lake. Just one more shot. Probably the kill shot. "If I'm not mistaken I think that last shot came from behind us and to the east. There must be another cove in that direction. We'd better forget breakfast and start through the woods and see if we can spot them."

They got dressed and Kirby strapped on his gun belt. Rachel saw what he was doing and she did also.

Kirby took the lead as they started up towards Sturtevant Cove. He wasn't positive that that's where the shot had come from. The sun wasn't out yet and they couldn't hurry, fearing sticking a tree branch in their eyes.

They'd been hiking for about forty minutes when they finally reached the point at the mouth of the cove. It was daylight now and Kirby spotted a column of smoke rising through the tree tops. They had set up camp on the opposite shore almost at the end of the cove. They had another mile or so of hiking. "I don't want them to know anyone is around, so we'll hike around, instead of going in by canoe."

They kept well back from the shore, so they wouldn't be seen from across the cove. They could now see a canoe. "I wonder what they killed this morning, if they're still in camp?"

"Whatever it was, had to be close for them to see it in the dawn light. I'm thinking a moose."

When they reached the end of the cove, they stopped and listened and Kirby looked to see if the canoe was still there. "They haven't moved yet. I only hope it is this group responsible for the shooting and we haven't wasted our time."

They continued on. They couldn't see the smoke any longer, and they set back even more from the shoreline. Kirby wanted to come in behind the campsite. Since they were sneaking through fir and spruce trees the ground was quiet, not crunchy as if they been walked on dried leaves.

Kirby put out his right hand and stopped. Then he turned to face Rachel and touched his ear and pointed ahead and towards the lake. Then she heard it also. Conversation in the distance. They inched slowly ahead. Only enough so they could make out what was being said. They were just finishing breakfast and talking about the kill, one of them made that morning. "Sniff the air," Rachel whispered.

Kirby did and said, "They were frying deer meat this morning. It sounds like they are getting ready to leave and do some more killing."

"What will we do then?"

"We stay here and watch and listen. They'll have to return here before night, or when they get hungry."

Kirby laid on his stomach and motioned for Rachel too, also. Then he started crawling forward until he could look down on their campsite. There was a four man tent blocking their view of the three young fellas. Kirby pointed towards two canoes. They had fashioned a crude table from small logs tied together. There was garbage everywhere.

"Come on Ben, will you hurry up," one of them said.

"Frank, where'd you put my jacket?" Vince wanted to know.

They finally boarded the canoe and the one in the center was carrying a nice looking rifle. It looked new. "Did you bring any bullets, Frank?"

Frank just scowled. "There were three deer at the end of this cove only a few minutes ago," Ben said.

"That's good, 'cause we need some fresh meat. What we have is beginning to smell," Vince said.

"This is a lot more fun than fishing," Ben said.

Kirby and Rachel waited until they were out of sight before standing. They still could not see them, so they started down towards the tent when a shot rang out. It jumped both Kirby and Rachel. They still could not see them. They were around the bend. They stood behind the tent and waited.

They could hear them talking, but not what was being said. They came in view eventually and instead of coming back to their camp, they were canoeing around the cove and probably headed back where they had seen so many dead animals yesterday on the New Hampshire side.

They sat down to wait. "Have you figured out yet, what you're going to do with them?" Rachel asked.

"I know what I'd like to do. I'm still thinking on it. I would like to haul all three to the Rumford jail, but from here do you realize what that would involve?"

"At least a two day trip. And we'd have to feed 'em."

Eventually the three canoed out of sight of their campsite, so Kirby and Rachel started to look around. From the shore they looked to the right and saw a dead moose floating in the water. "This morning's shot."

Off to the north side of the campsite Rachel found where one of them had dug out a hole in a spring run off stream and rocked it up and covered it with fir boughs to keep the heat and sun out. She removed the boughs and found what was left of a deer hind quarter sitting on rocks above the cold water. "A nice ice box," Kirby said. "Better leave it just as you found it. For now. Until we decide what we're going to do." She put the boughs back over the spring.

Next to the second canoe, Kirby found empty 8mm shells. He showed the shells to Rachel and said, "I think more animals have died in this cove besides that one moose."

They checked out the tent next. Kirby opened the flaps and went in. There were three cots and two handguns lying on two of the cots. Kirby checked them and unloaded both .45 Colts, like he was carrying. He put the handguns back on the cots and put the bullets in his pocket. There were dirty clothes lying all over the floor; even if it was a dirt floor, they could have picked up after themselves. He was looking for something that would tell him where they were from. But nothing.

He left the tent and closed the flaps like before. "Did you find anything more out here?"

"Nothing," she replied.

"Let's walk out this way, maybe we can see them around the point."

Rachel was following Kirby and they had only walked maybe a hundred yards away from the campsite when they heard another gunshot. Just one this time. Probably another deer. They climbed up on a knoll and sat down where they had a better view of the canoe across the lake. "I'm getting hungry, how about you?" Kirby asked.

"I'm surprised they can't hear my stomach growling."

"The last year of the war, I was issued a new telescope. Sure wish I had one now."

"What is a telescope?" Rachel asked.

"It's a device you hold up to your eye and look through and objects at a great distance will look much closer."

"Look," Rachel said and pointed. "The canoe has turned around and pointing towards here. I hope they are coming back, so we can go eat."

"Yeah, me too."

As they watched the canoe, it was obvious they were coming back. Instead of following the shoreline as they had earlier, they were now coming across the lake. "Come, let's get up behind the tent on the knoll. I don't want to approach them until they have what they killed earlier, on the ground."

"I have to pee," Rachel said.

"Me too, do it here. We can't afford any moving around."

The three young men were close enough now to hear them talking. They were paddling straight towards their campsite. The one in the middle had the rifle cradled in his arms. It was probably still loaded. The one in the bow was saying how hungry he was and it was Ben's turn to cook. They sure weren't being very cautious. Talking so loud. But if it didn't bother them in shooting so many animals in broad daylight, then why should their talking be any different.

The canoe ground to a stop on the sandy bottom and Frank jumped out and pulled the canoe in and held it while his two friends climbed out. Vince handed the rifle to Frank and then picked up two hind quarters of a lamb deer and stepped out into the water and then came ashore. When Ben was out, he pulled the canoe out of the water, up and onto dry ground.

Frank put the rifle in the tent and then he started to rekindle the fire, while Ben put the kettle of beans on the coals and Vince was skinning the hind quarters.

Kirby whispered in Rachel's ear, "Now would be a good time. Go slow and easy and above all keep anyone from going into the tent."

Kirby started through the trees very slowly with Rachel right behind him. Their deerskin clothes blended well with the surroundings. Kirby was surprised how close he was coming to them and yet no one knew they had company. When he was directly behind Vince he said, "That's an awful small deer."

Vince jumped straight forward and let go of the deer and said, "Holy shit! Who the hell are you?"

Rachel had stepped over in front of the tent in Frank's way. She just shook her head no. Frank stopped and turned to look at Kirby. Ben was so shell shocked, he stood there by the fire speechless.

"Boys, I want you all to come over here and sit on the ground," Kirby said.

"Just who in the hell are you?" Vince said again.

Kirby looked squarely at Vince and said, "I'm Kirby Morgan and this is my wife Rachel. And I am a game warden for the State of Maine."

"What the hell do you want with us mister?" Frank asked.

"First off, I want the three of you sitting on the ground over here." No one moved. "I can sit you down, if you prefer." One by one they sat down where Kirby had said.

Kirby explained to them about the newly enacted laws creating a warden service department. "And I am charging each of you with killing both moose and deer in closed season. I know there are a lot of dead animals on the other side, in New Hampshire, but there's nothing I can do about that. But I am going to do something about the animals you have killed in Maine."

"Rachel secure the rifle in the tent and unload it, and see if you can find some paper to write on."

"What are you going to do with us Warden?"

"I haven't decided yet."

"We didn't know nothing about no damned season on dear and moose," Ben finally spoke up.

"Well, it isn't a new law actually. It's been in effect since 1873, except there hasn't been anyone to enforce it. Now there is.

"Where are you boys from?"

"Boston."

"What do you do for work in Boston?"

"Frank and I work for Vince and his old man," Ben said.

"What kind of work are you and your father doing in Boston, Vince?"

"My old man owns an overseas shipping company."

"Then that 8mm Mauser rifle is probably yours Vince." Not a question.

"So what?"

"Well, it's a fine German made rifle and probably only someone with money could afford one."

Rachel came out of the tent and handed the paper to Kirby. She laid the two handguns on the makeshift table and was admiring the new rifle. Kirby handed the paper and a pencil to Ben and said, "Write down all three of your names, addresses and age."

"Frank, how many deer and moose have you three killed here?"

"In all or just on this side of the lake?"

"In all."

He looked at Vince and hesitated. "Come on Frank, how cooperative you are depends a lot on what I decide to do with you."

"Three moose."

"How many deer?"

"Seven in all."

"What do you think I should do with you Vince?"

"Let us go man."

"Ah, can't do that. I have two choices. One, I could summons each of you for court in September. But you'd probably never appear. Two, I could arrest you and take you to jail in Rumford, which is at least two days travel from here."

"When my old man learns about this mister, you're dead meat."

"Well Vinny, you just made up my mind for me. All three of you are under arrest for closed seasons violations and if there is a 'wanton-waste' law, I'll charge you with that also."

"How you going to get us out of here?" Vince asked.

Ben handed the paper with their names and addresses to Kirby. Ben Johnson, Frank Sirois, and Vince Howard. He folded the paper and put it in his pocket.

Rachel put all of the firearms and deer quarters in one canoe and two paddles. "Okay, boys get in your canoe." They did without question. Then Kirby and Rachel pushed off in the other one.

"If you have any idea about trying to tip us over or run away, I'll shoot you."

"We'll go back to our site and pick up our canoe and gear first," he said to Rachel.

"You just couldn't shut your mouth could you Vince. Now look where we're going," Ben said. "Why couldn't you just shut your mouth for once?"

*   *   *   *

"Now, you boys sit right here in your canoe. We'll only be a few minutes packing up. Oh, yeah, in case you think about leaving…..don't…..'cause I'll let Rachel shoot a hole big enough, in the side of your canoe, to sink you. She's a good shot. Better'n me."

They folded up the canvas tarps and packed away their supplies and pulled on their wolverine and wolf furs. "Now we're ready. We'll take our own canoe and tie yours to ours and tow it. Now we head for Upton at the south end. Let's go."

As soon as they had pulled on the fur Vince's face went white with shock. He couldn't speak. Not until they were well down the lake. "Do you two know who these two are?" he asked softly.

"No. Who?"

"There was an article in the newspaper last summer about these two. She is Carajou's daughter. He killed that wolverine with his hands. And the game warden? The wolf vest he wears? The wolf had attacked them and he shoved his hand in the wolf's mouth and down his throat and hung on while she killed the wolf with an axe."

All three turned to look at Kirby and Rachel, and turned white. "Take it easy boys. We're almost there," Kirby said.

As they canoed closer to the boat landing at the Lake House, Kirby could see someone standing on the wharf. As they came closer, he recognized Enoch Abbott Sr. He was waving.

Kirby pulled their canoe along side and Rachel got out, carrying the rifle and the two handguns. She stood guard and Kirby helped the other three out and secured the three canoes.

"What's going on here Kirby?" Enoch asked.

"I've arrested these three for killing moose and deer in closed season and now we have to take them to Rumford."

"How you going to do that?"

"I'll have to wait for the stage."

"Well, today's Friday and normally there wouldn't be another stage due here until Monday afternoon. I can lend you a team and wagon," Enoch offered.

"Thank you. I guess we'll have to. We need to eat first. Rachel and I haven't eaten today. If we could eat at the Lake House, I'll send a voucher to the Commissioner so you'll get paid."

"While you're eating I'll get a team harnessed."

Kirby and Rachel took the three inside and they all sat at a corner table. Beef stew, biscuits and coffee. Everyone was watching.

When they were back outside, Enoch took Kirby aside to speak with him. "Kirby, there's no way you can expect to reach Kilgore's tonight. What are you going to do?"

"I might have to put them up at the Poplar Tavern in Grafton. They won't be as busy as you."

*   *   *   *

Before they had even left town, the word about the new game warden taking three prisoners to jail spread faster than a wildfire. But they had also found a new respect for the law and the one enforcing it. They knew now that Augusta meant what it said this time.

By the time they arrived at the Poplar Tavern there was only a little daylight left. Kirby explained to George the problem he had and asked if they could stay the night in the Tavern. "Put all three in one room and I'll lock their door."

As tired as Kirby and Rachel were, someone would have to stay up and watch over the three prisoners all night. Kirby took the first watch and then Rachel would relieve him about 2 a.m. Ronki-Tonk unharnessed the team and fed and watered them and promised to have them all ready again at first light.

When they left town the next morning, the sun was coming over the mountains. Word was spreading throughout Grafton also about the three prisoners who had been killing moose and deer out of season. Rachel wore her wolverine fur and Kirby his wolf vest as they left town. Joe Chapman was out front when they rode by. He knew something terrible was afoot, he just didn't know what.

The team was young and strong and once below the notch, Kirby gave them some reign and let them run for a while. They went by Kilgore's in a cloud of dust, before mid-morning.

The only time they stopped was to rest the team and stretch their own legs. They made it to Rumford in one day. And all were exhausted.

"What are you charging them with Mr. Morgan?" Sheriff Atwood asked.

"I'm charging each one of them with killing moose in closed season and two counts each of killing deer in closed season and if Maine had a wanton-waste law, I'd charge them with that also."

"How much bail do you want set on each?"

"There's no doubt in my mind that none of them will appear for court, so how does $100 each sound?"

"We don't have that much money," Vince said.

"Then you can send a wire to your father and get it. Either way, you don't leave here until you do."

Sheriff Atwood locked them in a cell and Kirby wrote out summons for each and a detailed report for the District Attorney.

*   *   *   *

Kirby never heard another gunshot for the rest of that summer. People now understood the law, and the new warden service had a bite to it. Fishermen were beginning to leave their firearms at home when they went on a fishing trip.

In the middle of September Kirby received a letter from Commissioner Stanley praising him for a good job. All three defendants failed to appear and a bench had been issued for each. The $300 bail money was turned over to the Warden Service Department and Kirby and Rachel's bills for lodging and food came to $95. But the point was, the Commissioner understood it also, that people were realizing that the Game Wardens were here to stay and would do their job.

Jim Brown's health was failing and now instead of looking after things around the farm and mill, he was spending most of his time inside. He had lost weight and he was pale. Ruth was fifteen years younger and she was still strong and active, but all the years of hard work and long days were showing.

Joe was unusually subdued and quiet around Kirby and Rachel. He still thought the world of them both, but he also figured it was his right to go out and shoot a deer when he needed food. Without having to have a license and not just during the season. He wasn't about to stop and then at the same time he was awful afraid of offending them. "I'll just have to be more careful." So he made another salt lick behind his house between two apple trees.

Kirby and Rachel left for another trip to Parmachenee to visit Wonnocka. As they were leaving Parmachenee Lake, starting up the narrows of Big Magalloway River, they spotted a canoe hidden in a blind, over looking a slologan. There were two people in the canoe and they saw Kirby and Rachel swing their canoe towards them.

As they approached, Kirby realized they were wearing hunting attire and not fishing. Then he noticed the rifles. "Good morning. See anything?"

"We did earlier. We're hoping he'll step out into the marsh again. Biggest damn buck I ever saw."

"Gentlemen my name is Kirby Morgan and this is my wife Rachel. I'm the game warden and I'm going to insist that you not hunt beyond the lake, where the river begins."

"And why not?"

"Because this land from the lake all the way to St. Francis in Canada belongs to the Indians. And white men are not allowed to hunt here."

"Do you represent the Indians?"

"Yes, I do. My wife grew up in a village not far from here and I also belong to this same tribe."

"Okay, mister we don't want any trouble." They unloaded their rifles and laid them in the bottom of the canoe. He looked first at Rachel and the wolverine fur and then again at Kirby and his wolf vest. "We're terribly sorry Mr. Morgan."

"When I first saw you, I thought there was something about you that seemed familiar. You are the 'Carajou Woman' and you're the 'Wolf Man'. There are stories in all the newspapers in the northeast about you two. I don't think you'll be having many problems from the sporting camps in your region. I mean everyone knows or has read about you two."

"When you get back to the Caribou Camp would you tell Mr. Danforth about this being Indian land north of the lake?"

"Yes. I'd be glad to do so." He pulled his canoe closer to Kirby's and wanted to shake his hand. "My name is Rodney Thurston and this is my son Daniel. "We're awful pleased to meet you."

Rodney pulled against Kirby's canoe until he was now close to Rachel and he shook hands with her also. "Pleased to meet you Mrs. Morgan."

"Thank you," Kirby said, "and have a nice day."

Chapter 11

Kirby and Rachel returned home in time for Thanksgiving celebration at the Poplar Tavern. They had been gone for two and a half months. And they did a little trapping. As Rodney Thurston had said, word had indeed spread and Kirby had no more problems that year. People were even asking where they could buy a license the following year.

They were glad to be home amongst friends. Jim and Ruth were particularly glad to see Kirby and Rachel. Jim said, "You know, you two have made quite a name for yourselves. Every newspaper in the state has printed articles about the both of you. A reporter from the newspaper in Portland was here, two weeks before you got back, looking for you. He wanted to do both your life's story. He was as interested with your story Rachel as he was with Kirby's." There were tears in Jim's eyes, but he managed to say, "You two are the best thing that has ever happened in Grafton."

"Your exaggerating a little there Jim. If it hadn't been for you, there never would have been a Grafton."

"You're a pioneer Jim." Ruth was standing behind him and she put her arms around him and hugged him.

Kirby and Rachel wandered off talking with other people and Joe joined in with conversation. "Joe," Kirby said, "I don't know why it is, but every time when we come home there always seems to be a large flock of ravens in the trees behind your house. Do they have nests there or are you feeding them?"

Joe's face went red, but he was quick to respond, "Oh, that's probably because my farm dump isn't too far behind the house."

Joe sidled off to one side and thinking to himself, "He knows damn it. No matter how careful I am he always knows."

                    *   *   *   *

Kirby and Rachel spent a lot of the winter going around to the lumber camps in the region. They didn't visit them all, as they had to snowshoe when the snow was too deep for the horse. Jake was too old and he was put out to pasture and Kirby bought another Morgan horse.

Late one afternoon Ronki-Tonk rode down to see the Morgans. "Hello Ronki-Tonk, what brings you out here?"

"It's Captain Jim, Mr. Morgan.....he ain't doing so well. Ruth thinks he's dying. Ruth ask me to come tell you."

Rachel already had their jackets. "We'll be right up as soon as I can harness up."

It was a fast trip and they caught up with Ronki-Tonk at the cemetery and passed him. "Go on in

Rachel. I'll take care of the horse. We'll be here all night."

When Kirby walked into the house everyone had gathered in the kitchen. "How is he Ruth?" The obvious question.

"Not good Kirby. I'm afraid it's his heart. He wants to see you and Rachel."

They talked for a long time and Jim was getting tired. They each had said what they had wanted to. There was nothing more anyone could do, but let him rest. They went back to the kitchen with the others and Ruth joined her husband and sat with him all night. Then the next morning, April 8th, 1881, at the age of 82, Jim Brown, the Grafton Pioneer, breathed his last and went to sleep forever.

Every Grafton resident was at the funeral; even the young children. Everybody was family and they had all lost one of their own. Kirby offered to help Ronki-Tonk fill in the grave. He was getting on in years also. "No thanks, Mr. Morgan. This is something I have do. Just me and the Captain."

Kirby and Rachel waited for Ronki-Tonk in the wagon, to take him home.

When Jim Brown died, a little of Grafton died along with him. Everybody felt the loss. George Otis was a good man in the woods and he was easy to work for; but he still wasn't his father-in-law Jim Brown.

Ronki-Tonk missed his friend so much, he wasn't doing all his work around the farm. He wasn't eating, but he found solace with drinking. So he drank everyday. And three months after Jim Brown's death, Ronki-Tonk died.

Kirby still had a job to do and he and Rachel were spending as much time in the woods as they wanted. They were having fun. This was a great way to live. But they too were getting older and slowing down. Particularly during the winter months. They would often sleep out in the snow; Rachel had shown Kirby how to make a warm shelter of fir boughs and banked with snow. But the long snowshoe treks were over. Sometimes they would harness the horse to a sleigh and go out on the hard packed snow cover on the lakes.

*   *   *   *

Fourteen years had passed since Jim Brown's death and there had been a lot of changes. Timber was getting hard to find in Grafton and any harvesting at all was near the state line near Success Pond. All the pine, spruce and fir had been harvested.

There wasn't enough work for all of the men in town, so families had to leave to find work. Some men found jobs guiding fishermen and hunters and the women found jobs in the hotels and sporting camps. But the winter months were the worst. With the snow and cold and no work. Some men went to work over at Bemis, clearing the right of way for the train out of Rumford to Oquossoc, following pretty much the eastern shore of Mooselookmeguntic Lake.

Finally at the age of fifty seven Kirby said one night to Rachel, "Hey Rachel, would you be disappointed if we didn't make these forays in the woods chasing poachers?"

"What do you mean Kirby?"

"I mean, I think it's time to say we have had enough. It's a young man's job now. We have been doing this for the last fifteen years. I think it's time we stopped. What do you think? You have as much to say about this as I do. I want your opinion."

"I'm three years older than you and frankly I don't look forward to these winter trips any longer. Can we survive on what money we have in the bank?"

"We own everything we have and we now have over $12,000 in the bank. I think we'll be okay."

That night Kirby wrote a letter of resignation to Commissioner Stanley in Augusta.

Kirby and Rachel began making only one trip a year to visit Wonnocka's village. They would leave in late summer and stay long enough to do some early trapping. Beaver and otter prices had increased and now they didn't need as many fur pieces as before. They were hobby trappers. They would spend a lot of that time with Wonnocka and his people. The young boys who Wonnocka had sent off to school in St. Francis had now come back with many new ideas for their people.

When Kirby and Rachel were back in Grafton, Rachel would help out at the schools and Kirby at the mill. The chickens they had gotten long before Kirby resigned were now producing enough eggs, so she was selling them to the farm and Poplar Tavern. Once a month Rachel would roast a chicken for Sunday dinner. Usually an old rooster or a hen that wasn't laying.

When they were away on their trips, Joe would look after the chickens daily and he kept the egg money. Which wasn't enough for an income but it did buy groceries. Plus he was being paid to look after their house.

They would spend a lot of time, especially on hot summer days, on the shelf by the falls that overlooked Speck Mountain and the Notch. Kirby had fashioned steps from wood and had to replace the old rope he had put up when they first started living there.

Chapter 12

After the winter of 1900, work was terribly difficult to find at Grafton, so some of the families sold out to the Brown Paper Company in Berlin, New Hampshire and they moved to other towns where there was work. Brown Company came in and burned and bulldozed the buildings and then planted spruce trees in the fertile fields.

If Jim Brown had still been alive this would have broken his heart. Ruth was still alive and now living with her daughter Mary and her husband George Otis. She would live another year before joining her husband. She hated to see her lifetime friends leave and their homes burned, but people must have jobs. It was simply the changing of the times.

Joe's faithful dog Whippy died. He was eleven years old and this almost broke Joe's heart and spirit. He bought a slab of marble and chiseled Whippy's name and age and buried him under a fir tree on a little knoll beside the road where he could look at Speck Mountain, and he stood the stone up in front of the tree.

Rachel was now sixty five and Kirby sixty two. They had spent most of the hot July day on the shelf beside the falls underneath the huge cedar tree. Although they were in their early sixties, neither of them looked a day over forty. This can be accredited to their lifestyle and all the natural foods Rachel knew how to gather and prepare. They never seemed to ever stop talking. Most of this day they reminisced about being on patrol and catching poachers. And how life in Grafton was so completely different than in other towns. They had been very fortunate to have found Grafton and each other. Perhaps Alvin Brown had subconsciously been aware that his death would bring these two together. At least he did not die in vain.

When the hot temperatures made them too uncomfortable they would take their clothes off and sit in the cool pool. The water was so cold they couldn't stay long. Just long enough to feel refreshed.

"Are you hungry Kirby? I am."

"A little bit, yes."

"Well, it's time we climbed back down to the house and start supper."

Kirby let her go ahead of him. The hill was so steep they had to hold onto the rope to keep from sliding. Rachel was almost at the bottom when one of the rotting wooden steps gave way and she fell on her back and hit her head on one of the wooden steps.

Kirby rushed down to her. She wasn't moving but her chest was still rising and falling. Which meant she was alive and breathing. He cradled her in his arms calling out to her over and over, "Rachel, Rachel, Rachel!" She finally opened her eyes and saw Kirby kneeling beside her. "Oh my head hurts. That was a clumsy thing to do."

"The step broke apart under your feet."

"Oh, my head is still hurting."

"Don't move sweetheart, I'll rinse my handkerchief in the cold water, for a cold compress for your head."

He hurried and put the compress on the back of her head. There was swelling there, but no open wound.

"That feels better. I'd feel a lot better if I was lying on our bed instead of this steep side hill."

Kirby helped her to stand. She was a little dizzy, so he supported her all the way into the bedroom. He helped her to lie down and he straightened her legs and went for another cold compress.

When he returned he asked, "How are you feeling now?"

"Better. At least I'm not dizzy now, and my head is better also."

Kirby put the new compress on her head and she lay back against it. "You stay right here, I'll fix us something to eat. You sure you're feeling better?"

"Yes sweetheart, I am."

Kirby went out into the kitchen and started heating up leftovers. When Rachel screamed out to him, "Kirby! Kirby!" Kirby ran to her side, "What is it?"

He could see the pain in her eyes and her head seemed to have swelled. "My head," she could barely utter the words, ".....hurts so much."

Kirby started to remove the compress and she stopped him, "No. Don't move me.....hurts so bad." There was another burst of throbbing pain. Tears were streaming down her cheeks, the pain was so intense.

She reached up and cupped his face with her hand and whispered, "I have always loved you so much. Do not bury me here. Take me to our special place." She was gripped with another burst of pain. She opened her eyes and started to say, "I love you my husband," but she didn't finish. The pain was gone now and so too was her life.

Kirby cradled her in his arms, rocking back and forth crying like he had never cried before.

Darkness came and it was dark inside the house. And still he cradled her and cried. Midnight came and he stopped crying long enough to do what he knew he had to. He had watched Wonnocka prepare his father for his last canoe ride and now he must prepare Rachel. He managed to prop her up against the bed headboard in a sitting position with her legs crossed.

He waited, sitting beside her, holding her hands waiting for rigor mortis to set in, so she would be sitting up for her last canoe ride. He sat with Rachel all night holding her hands. Even after the warmth had left her body and her hands were cold. He talked to her almost continuously, when he was not crying.

*　　*　　*　　*

When daylight came, rigor mortis had set and now he would be able to sit her in the canoe. But first he had to hitch the horse and wagon. Then he had to shave. He never looked unkempt with Rachel by his side. Even on the forays into the wilderness, he shaved every day. He put on his traveling clothes and managed to slip the wolverine fur over Rachel's head and shoulders. He pulled on his wolf vest. The only thing he took with him was a razor to shave.

After he had her arranged in the wagon, he left and stopped at Joe Chapman's house. He was up and he came down to see what the matter was. "Rachel died last night Joe. I'm taking her body back to Rachel's Point, near her people's village. Look after the house okay?"

"Sure thing Mr. Morgan. I'm awful sorry." Joe wanted to say more, but he couldn't. His throat was tight and tears welled up in his eyes. He stood by the road and watched as Kirby rode out of sight.

Kirby rode by the Brown farm and never knew or realized he had done so. He rode through Upton without stopping. Friends shouted hello and waved, but he never heard or saw anything, except the smiling image of Rachel's face in his mind.

At Wilson's Landing, he loaded Rachel's body in to the bow of the canoe. He had to break out the front seat so he could set her on the bottom. He unharnessed the horse and wagon and turned the horse loose. He climbed into the canoe and began paddling. He paddled through the day without stopping, into the night. The moon was full and he didn't stop then either. Not until he reached the Azischohos Falls. Fred Cyr was there.

Fred thought something was wrong when he noticed Rachel sitting so low in the bow. "My God Kirby, what happened?"

"She fell and hit her head and died a short time after." That's all he would say.

He paid Fred. He reached into this pocket and brought out a fist full of money and gave it all to Fred, then he got back in his canoe and continued.

After leaving the driving dam on Azischohos behind, he started talking to Rachel. Carrying on a normal conversation. Telling her what he was seeing, how the water was, the weather, the loon that was following. Somehow this seemed to placate him and at times he would almost seem happy as he talked.

He was not aware of leaving the Magalloway River behind as he entered Parmachenee Lake. As spirit, he was with Rachel and not in his earthly body. He was only guiding that part of him to Rachel's special place. He canoed past the Caribou Camp and Peter Danforth stood on the wharf and waved. He knew he was getting close when he left the lake and for the first time recognized where he was. He shortly found the entrance stream to the pond and Rachel's Point. He breathed a sigh of relief as he pulled the canoe on shore. It was evening and shadows were darkening. He carried Rachel's body inside the wikitup and propped her up so her back was still straight. Then he unfolded the bear rug and laid it on the floor and laid on it and fell asleep. This was his first sleep since her death two nights before. He was exhausted and he slept until daylight the next morning.

When he rose, he removed his clothes and bathed in the pond water, then he shaved and redressed. He carried Rachel's body outside and set her in front of the great pine tree, with her back against the trunk. He removed the wolverine fur and he sat down and buried his face in his hands. He was talking with Rachel one last time.

When he had finished, he stood and with the wolverine fur he climbed into his canoe and paddled north towards Wonnocka's village. It was a perfectly beautiful morning and when Wonnocka, who was standing next to the river, saw only one person in the canoe, he knew something terrible had happened. He steadied the canoe while Kirby stepped out. He saw the grief in his eyes. He noticed also, that Kirby lovingly carried the wolverine fur. "She fell two nights ago and died a short time after. I brought her back to her special place and did like you did for your father, Falling Bear." He handed the wolverine fur to Wonnocka and said, "You and your people should have this." He handed the fur to Wonnocka.

Then he started to leave and Wonnocka said, "You are my brother. Stay here. We are your people now."

The terrible sadness was returning and Wonnocka knew Kirby would not stay. Kirby got back in his canoe and Wonnocka asked, "What you do now? Where you go now?"

Kirby looking at him with tears running down his face and he answered, "I don't know." He swung the bow around and started to paddle. Where? He didn't know.

Wonnocka stayed by the river until Kirby had disappeared. His throat was tight and he was crying. He had just lost two very dear friends. And he knew, he would never see Kirby again.

Epilogue

In 1910, Mary Brown Otis died. Her husband George Otis died two years before her in 1908. Mary stayed on at the farm in Grafton and traveled out to stay with a daughter in Lewiston during the winter and then in the spring back to her beloved town.

She was the first child born in Grafton to Ruth and Jim Brown and she was the last pioneer family still living in Grafton. The Brown Company had purchased the farm and buildings and for years used the buildings for storage.

In 1919 there were so few residents left in Grafton the town lost its charter and reverted back to a forest territory. One resident remained, Joe Chapman. He loved Grafton and had no where to move to.

*   *   *   *

Joe was quiet, thinking about what Leslie had said. Leslie was right of course, but Joe simply hated the idea of leaving and having to live with someone else. Even if Leslie was a close friend.

Joe started laughing and he was several minutes before he could compose himself. "Well," Leslie stammered, "you going to tell me what you find is so funny?"

"I was just thinking when the Morgans were gone on one of their trips up the Richardsons. They left right after ice-out that year and were gone for two and a half months. One day, I think it was in June, 'cause the damn black flies were out and really bad that year. I looked out the back window in the kitchen and there standing not more than fifty yards back was a fourteen point buck. I know because I had a chance to count the points later. You don't often get to see a buck with fully growed horns in June. They're usually in velvet. I've always figured he must have kept his all winter. Well, I couldn't pass on that. I ran to get my rifle and in all the excitement I shot plumb through the window." Joe began laughing again. "The bullet shattered that whole damn window and glass flew all around the kitchen. In food, dishes, towels, cracks in the floor, everywhere. I was years before I got it all cleaned up.

"The buck though, he was dead. Beautiful rack of horns it was. The rack is till in the living room. I use them for a gun rack. It took me all day to take care of that deer. And then to keep the ravens from gathering and telling Kirby I had shot something, I dug a hole and buried the remains. It was after dark before I had finished. I'd forgotten all about that blasted window and the inside of the house had filled up with blackflies. I fought them all summer before they finally died out. I had to board up the window. A new one cost $5 and I didn't have it. Stayed like that for two more years.

"One day Kirby and Rachel stopped and I invited them inside for coffee. I'd forgotten all about the window. When Kirby saw it, he asked what had happened. I couldn't tell him the truth so I said a chunk of ice fell off the roof during the winter and took out the window. I always believed he knew what I had done, but he never let on. I sure have missed him."

"Joe, you know you have to come with me," Leslie said.

No answer. "The Brown Company has already paid you, right?"

"Yeah, not what it's worth though."

"Did they give you a deadline when you had to be out?"

"Yeah, two days ago," and he laughed. "I put it over the Brown Company a few times. I hated the idea of them buying up all the farms, so during the summers I'd go out back with my draft horse, ole Babe and we go way off the farm to the nicest stand of hardwood on Brown Company's land. One day I'd just finished bucking the last of the wood when one of Brown Company's foresters stopped. He saw me with my bucksaw and asked where I got the wood. I said out back. He never checked. I was way out back about a half mile up on the side of Hedgehog."

"Well Brown Company won't have to worry about me no more," Joe said.

"Come on Joe, we'd better load your things in the wagon and go."

"Okay Leslie, but after we get things loaded, I have one more stop at the Morgans before we can leave."

Joe wasn't taking much. His clothes and personal items and his rifle. There wasn't much sense in trying to take much. His health had been failing lately and he knew there wouldn't be much time left.

"I guess that's everything," Joe said.

"You said earlier, there was one more thing you had to do before we leave," Leslie said.

"Yes, we'll have to drive down to the Morgan house."

Leslie didn't ask why. He'd wait and see what was so important when they got there.

Surprisingly the driveway had never washed out and the bushes on both sides looked like they had been cut back. There were no weeds or bushes in the yard, and in fact the house looked lived in. "Joe, how long have the Morgans been gone? The house and everything around here looks maintained."

"It is maintained. I have been doing it."

"Why?"

"Because when Kirby and Rachel would leave on one of their trips, I always took care of the house and the chickens."

"But.....Rachel died, when did you last see Kirby?"

Joe cleared his throat before answering. "It was July of 1900. It was the day after his wife Rachel died. He stopped and asked if I would take care of the place. Rachel was sitting behind the wagon seat in back, but she was dead. Kirby said he was taking her back to her people."

"Joe, that was 39 years ago. And you have been taking care of this all these years? Why?" Leslie asked.

"I always took care of the house when they were gone. I wanted things to be okay when Kirby came back."

"How old are you Joe?"

"Oh, eighty or so."

"Kirby was a Major in the Civil War, wasn't he?"

"That's right."

"Then he would be more than twenty years older than you Joe. What happened to him Joe?"

"No one knows. He was seen on his way to Parmachenee with his dead wife, but nobody ever saw him come back. No one knows."

"But why did you continue maintaining his house?"

"He was my friend Leslie and I thought, hoped, he'd come back some day. I miss him Leslie."

"What did you have to do here?"

"We'll have to hike up this steep hill behind the house beside the falls. I'll show you when we get there."

Leslie followed Joe out back to a roped path that went up along side the falls. The wooden steps having rotted out years ago. "Who put this rope up?"

"Kirby."

"What's up here that's so important," Leslie asked.

"You'll see." For a man eighty years old or so, he wasn't having any trouble climbing the steep path.

They finally got to the shelf and Joe said, "Look at that view Leslie. This was Rachel's favorite place. She and Kirby used to spend a lot of time here. I've been working on this headstone for years. I cut out a piece of granite from that ledge on the other side of the brook and it took me a long time to hand chisel a headstone. It's heavy and I need your help to stand it up. I chiseled a half moon piece for the base.

Leslie tipped the headstone up and Joe placed
the half moon piece so to hold the headstone in
position. Leslie read the hand chiseled inscription:

IN MEMORY OF THE MORGANS.

The end.

Author's Notes

In 2005 while exploring in the Grafton area I came upon a brook that doesn't exist on any map and the remains of an old log cabin at the base of a 1000 foot waterfalls. I followed the brook uphill to see from whence the brook started. About 200 feet above the cabin I found a natural shelf. There was a nice pool in the brook a giant cedar tree and a beautiful panoramic view of the mountains. A really nice spot.

I sat down to rest and seeing a peculiar square stone, I pulled back a 3 inch thick moss matting and found a hand chiseled headstone. I stood it up and then removed the moss at the base and found a half moon piece of rock, that had also been hand chiseled. When I stood the headstone up, the half moon piece fit snuggly as a base. There was an inscription chiseled into the back of the headstone, but I was never able to determine what it was saying.

I have talked with many people about this find, and no one seems to know anything about it.

So, to offer an explanation in this book, I created the characters Kirby and Rachel Morgan. Alvin Brown is also fictional and he was only a means of introducing Major Kirby Morgan to the Brown family and Grafton, where he was to meet Rachel.

Since Kirby and Rachel are fictional characters their experiences are also fictional. But I tried to include some of the actual history of the area in the book. The Maine Warden Service was created in 1880 and some of the laws and causations what created this new department are also true.

The Indian, Matelok, was real and I located his grave in the North Hill Cemetery in Stewartstown, New Hampshire. He was a remarkable individual with a great sense of love for all life and his land. His home was anywhere he chose to stop, in the Magalloway Country.

Before the Aziscohos Dam was built on the Magalloway River in 1909-1910, there had been an archaeological dig on the shore of the Magalloway River, where the Abenaki Indians once set up camp while they hunted caribou that followed a migration trail up along the river and then crossing to the north shore, on their way to Canada.

A section of the original road through the notch can still be seen just beyond Mother Walker Falls, on the right.

While researching the history of Grafton and then writing, I came to understand the uniqueness of the town and the residents. In 1834 Captain James Brown from Canton, Maine, found an area in what was then only known as Letter A Township, a valley with good farming soil and an abundance of tall pine and spruce trees. Later when he married Ruth Swan of Newry, they together pioneered a new town and in 1852, the town of Grafton was awarded a town charter from Augusta, making it official.

In the 80 years of its existence, the town had never had any form of law enforcement, no doctors and neighbors helped each other, building homes, barns and taking care of each other. They worked hard together and played and celebrated together. They were their own best medicine. The citizens of Grafton had forged and created a lifestyle that we today aspire to have. But unfortunately the timber ran out and the people had to go elsewhere to look for work. Although there were 1,000's of acres of cleared farmland, the town was situated in a cold valley, where frost in July and August was common. The farms grew mostly hay and grain and a few potatoes. What would substantiate their existence.

But the Brown Paper Company also knew that these cleared fields would grow nice spruce trees. So starting in the early 1900's the Brown Company started buying up these farms, one at a time and burning the buildings and planting spruce trees.

The current road, Route 26, now goes through what was once the Brown Farm. There are no remains left to indicate that there had ever been a beautiful set of buildings there, or the remarkable pioneer people who lived there. Nor the hotel, tavern, sawmill or gristmill. Everything is gone with only a wilderness now, where over a 100 years ago there had once been a nice family community.

Upton survived longer than Grafton because of its location on the south end of Umbagog Lake, where the people there had a flourishing sporting and tourism business, because of the lake.

About the Author

I was really intrigued with the writing of this book. As I wrote, the story seemed to take on its own direction. And certainly when I had finished, it was so different than what I had imagined at the start. The character Rachel, from 'COURIER DE BOIS' seemed to slip into place all on her own. Almost as if she was guiding the direction of the story.

I also discovered that Grafton and its residents were unique, and I think this lifestyle probably could be attributed to the lifestyles and genuine characters of James and Ruth Brown.

Other books by Randall Probert:

A FORGOTTEN LEGACY
AN ELEQUENT CAPER
COURIER DE BOIS
KATRINA'S VALLEY
MYSTERIES AT MATAGAMON LAKE
A WARDEN'S WORRY
A QUANDRY AT KNOWLES CORNER
PARADIGM
TRIAL AT NORWAY DAM

Visit my website at: www.randallprobertbooks.net

James + Ruth Brown
Alvin son died civil war

Poplar Tavern = Grafton Flats
   14 rooms   5 fireplaces
   Parents Hannah + Aaron
daughter   Mary / Mrs George Otis

Davis family
Chapman family